Phoenix Rising
DAY OF
JUDGMENT

Phoenix Rising
DAY OF
JUDGMENT

WILLIAM W. JOHNSTONE
with J. A. Johnstone

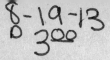

PINNACLE BOOKS
Kensington Publishing Corp.
www.kensingtonbooks.com

PINNACLE BOOKS are published by

Kensington Publishing Corp.
119 West 40th Street
New York, NY 10018

PUBLISHER'S NOTE
Following the death of William W. Johnstone, the Johnstone family is working with a carefully selected writer to organize and complete Mr. Johnstone's outlines and many unfinished manuscripts to create additional novels in all of his series like The Last Gunfighter, Mountain Man, and Eagles, among others. This novel was inspired by Mr. Johnstone's superb storytelling.

All Kensington titles, imprints, and distributed lines are available at special quantity discounts for bulk purchases for sales promotions, premiums, fundraising, educational, or institutional use. Special book excerpts or customized printings can also be created to fit specific needs. For details, write or phone the office of the Kensington special sales manager: Kensington Publishing Corp., 119 West 40th Street, New York, NY 10018, attn: Special Sales Department; phone 1-800-221-2647.

This book is a work of fiction. Names, characters, businesses, organizations, places, events, and incidents either are the product of the author's imagination or are used fictitiously. Any resemblance to actual persons, living or dead, events, or locales is entirely coincidental.

PINNACLE BOOKS and the Pinnacle logo are Reg. U.S. Pat. & TM Off.

ISBN-13: 978-0-7860-3061-3
ISBN-10: 0-7860-3061-5

First printing: June 2013

10 9 8 7 6 5 4 3 2 1

Printed in the United States of America

First electronic edition: June 2013

ISBN-13: 978-0-7860-3060-6
ISBN-10: 0-7860-3060-7

The End ...

When Mehdi Ohmshidi was elected President of the United States, he campaigned on the promise of "fundamentally transforming America," and that is exactly what he did, carrying out that promise in a way that few could imagine. The result was devastating; a complete breakdown of America's infrastructure, including a total rupture of the power grid, dissolution of the military and law enforcement, the destruction of all commerce, including distribution of food, clothing, and services, as well as the cessation of all newspaper, radio, television, telephone, and Internet access.

Paper money lost its value and hundreds of billions of dollars lay undisturbed in worthless trash piles. Taking advantage of the collapse, Islamic terrorists detonated three nuclear bombs, and the United States ceased to exist.

All across the nation millions of Americans died and their unburied, decaying, and putrefied bodies not only created a horrific landscape, but spread diseases that took millions of more lives. One third of the remaining population became homeless, while nearly as many turned to crime as their only chance for survival. Because of the actions of one self-absorbed, arrogant, and incompetent president who was elected, not on a basis of qualifications, but as an expression of open-mindedness and social experimentation, what had been the most powerful nation in the twenty-first-century world was thrust back into the eighteenth century.

That time before the collapse of the United States, before Ohmshidi became president, was now referred to as the "pre-O" time.

Here and there across the country, groups of Americans formed enclaves of mutual assistance and survival. One such team was headed by army veteran Jake Lantz, who took them to Fort Morgan. The fort is on the Alabama coast at Mobile Point, a little spit of land that separates Mobile Bay from the Gulf of Mexico.

When Jake and his team showed up at the fort there was nothing there but old casements and stone walls. Jake chose Fort Morgan for a number of reasons, number one being the most obvious. It was a fort, and Jake knew that when conditions deteriorated even further in the country, it would spawn armed bands of hooligans to prey on anyone and everyone they thought might have something they could use. As Jake and his group were going to be well off, relatively speaking, he knew they would be a prime target. He knew, also, that the fort would provide them with protection against such groups.

Inside the fort was a rather large area of arable land, probably the only place down on the beach that had real soil, rather than sand. Immediately after arrival, Jake and the team planted the seeds they had brought with them. There was also plenty of fish, and there was a considerable amount of game, from rabbits to possum to alligators.

Once the group reached Fort Morgan, they encountered families who were living in beach houses next to the fort. One was Bob Varney, a retired army Warrant Officer and former helicopter pilot who had done three tours in Vietnam. Bob was also a successful novelist, who, in the pre-O time, before the collapse of the nation and currency, had been doing quite well. Now, however, money was useless, and Bob welcomed the invitation from Jake to join his team.

After detonation of the nuclear bombs and the complete dissolution of the United States, a tremendous power vacuum was created. That vacuum was filled by a fundamentalist Islamic sect that called itself the *Moqaddas Sirata*, or the Holy Path.

Initially those Americans who had survived the total collapse of the nation under Mehdi Ohmshidi welcomed the *Moqaddas Sirata* because they began to restore order across the country, punishing thieves and murderers. They also brought in fuel and food, re-established electricity, water, telephone service and the Internet.

They even put radio and television broadcasts back on the air. Schools were re-opened and newspapers were printed. The American Islamic Republic of Enlightenment, AIRE, applied for membership in the United Nations, and though they were denied full membership, they were admitted in a nonvoting observer status. They were accorded membership in the OIC, the Organization of Islamic Cooperation.

But there was a very dark side to the AIRE. Churches were burned and their pastors beheaded, women were stoned to death for being raped, a young boy had his arm run over on public television as punishment for stealing a loaf of bread. Youth Confinement and Enlightenment Centers were opened where every youth from six to eighteen was incarcerated so that they could be educated in the way of *Moqaddas Sirata.* In addition, all Jewish property was confiscated and Jews were incarcerated in "Ultimate Resolution" centers.

Gradually the little group of survivors, they were now calling their operation "Firebase Freedom," began to attract others. Tom Jack was the first to join them. In the pre-O time Tom had been a SEAL who had survived more covert operations than the law of averages should allow.

Shortly after Tom joined the group they conducted a raid on the gas drilling rigs that were just off the Alabama shore. The raid was successful, the rigs were taken, and not only Fort Morgan, but all of Pleasure Island soon had a near limitless supply of natural gas. Their next operation was to steal a navy destroyer and use it to capture *Khoramashur*, a tanker ship that was filled with twenty-one million gallons of refined gasoline.

Another who joined them was Chris Carmack. In the pre-O time, Chris had been an "off the books" agent for the CIA, handling only the most difficult and sensitive cases.

AIRE destroyed the Washington Monument, the World War II monument, the monument to the Korean War, and the Vietnam Memorial Wall, the Lincoln Memorial, the Roosevelt Memorial, the Jefferson Memorial, the Einstein Memorial, and the Holocaust Museum.

In New York Harbor, Liberty Island was now bare, the Statue of Liberty being the first of the heretical symbols to be destroyed. The Gateway Arch in St. Louis had been taken down, and, on Mount Rushmore, the stone-carved faces of all the presidents had been obliterated, all this because these symbols of what had been a free America were deemed to be heretical under the Islamic law of Moqaddas Sirata.

Every artifact in the Smithsonian Institution was destroyed. In addition the books, newspapers, photographs, sound recordings, videos and movies of the Library of Congress were removed from the building and burned. Soon, the only record of what had once been the United States, the greatest nation in history, became nothing but a memory kept alive in the minds and the hearts of those who still held the country dear.

George Gregoire, a man who had been a

leading spokesman for conservative America in the pre-O time, was arrested by AIRE, and his public and televised execution was planned. Gregoire was rescued by Chris Carmack and shortly after his rescue, the conservative icon joined the group at Fort Morgan, where he agreed to give a speech to the rest of the nation. They were able to do that because Willie Stark, a member of Jake Lantz's team, was a computer genius who hacked into the satellite which would send the broadcast to every television set in the North American continent.

"Hello, America.

"Yes, I'm still here, thanks to the bravery of some real heroes. And now, I am among these heroes, men and women who have not given up, men and women who have started a new nation, conceived in liberty, and dedicated to the principles of personal freedom, self-determination, and sacred honor.

"You need not accept what has happened to you. Be aware that help is on the way. There is a new movement on this continent, building a nation called United Free America. It will be a fully armed and totally self-contained nation of free men and women. We welcome anyone who wants to come join us, to help us attain our ultimate goal.

"What is our ultimate goal?

"First, I want you to see some of my friends here.

The camera turned to show the men and women who were the heart of Firebase Freedom, and consequently, the heart of a United Free America.

"These are the brave men and women who, by their courage, determination, and dedication to the principles of honor and duty, guarantee that we will reach that goal. I will let them tell you now what our real goal is."

All smiled, and raised their fists as they shouted the motto of the UFA.

"Take Back America!"

The Beginning . . .

CHAPTER ONE

Fort Morgan, Alabama

As electricity was restored and fuel became available, life in southern Alabama was beginning to return to something that approximated normalcy. The motel-like structures that had been built inside the walls of Fort Morgan were all but abandoned as those who once occupied the temporary quarters were now moved into an area known as "The Dunes." Here were thirty-eight large, multi-story beach homes built on stilts. In addition there were two seven-story condos each with seventy apartments.

Bob and Ellen Varney owned a house here and were permanent residents, as were James and Cille Laney. The other homes and condo units were the property of absent owners, most of whom were trapped up north. That left their places empty, so Jake and Karen moved into a house next door to the one occupied by Bob and Ellen. The other members of the Phoenix Group moved into unoccupied homes so that now The Dunes had taken on all the appearances of a small community.

With abundant fuel, a steady supply of electricity, and even more importantly, security and freedom from the oppressive SPS and Janissaries of Moqaddas Sirata, Gulf Shores began to come back. Once again stores were selling groceries, most of it locally produced vegetables, fruits, milk, eggs, and meat.

On this March evening the twenty three men and women of the Phoenix Group, plus George Gregoire, gathered on the beach. A pig had been cooking all day on one of the grills, and potatoes were roasting in a fire on the beach. Red and gold sparks were riding the rising heat waves into the sky to join with the stars that filled the black velvet.

"Okay, folks, the meat's ready," Bob said, and everyone lined up as Bob began carving the pork.

"Whoa, this is good!" Deon Pratt said as he took his first bite. "Where did you learn to cook like this?"

"My dad owned a fish and barbeque market in Memphis," Bob said. "I worked for him for a while after I retired from the army, until he fired me."

Jake Lantz laughed. "You mean your own father fired you?"

"Yep."

"What for?"

"You would have had to know my Dad. He wasn't what you would call a very understanding man."

Ellen laughed. "You want to tell them why he really fired you?"

"It wasn't anything."

"Tell them."

"One day I wrapped up some fresh fish for a woman customer. I'm not that good at wrapping things, and she complained about it, said I had done a sloppy job. So my dad fired me."

"For that?"

"No, it was for what he said to the woman," Ellen said. "Tell them what you said."

"What I said was . . . 'What the hell, lady, you plannin' on mailin' those fish somewhere?' "

The others laughed.

"Well, I'll remember not to have you wrap any fish for me," Tom Jack said. "But you can bar-beque for me anytime you want."

"So, Major, where do we go from here?" Marcus asked.

"He's not a major, he's a general," Willie corrected.

"Oh, yeah, I forgot," Marcus said. "And I'm a captain. Nothing like getting in on the ground floor when you start building a new army. But that brings me back to my question. What are we going to do with this new army?"

"Well, our primary mission is the primary mission of any army, and that's to protect the people," Jake said.

"But in our case, I think you have an expanded mission," Gregoire said.

"What would that be?" Jake asked.

"The mission hasn't changed. It's to take back America."

"Well, yes, that would be the goal," Jake said. "But for now it is more of a rallying cry than a reality."

"We can make it a reality," Gregoire said.

"Tell me, George, how many other groups have you heard from that are like us?" Bob asked.

"I have heard from survivalist groups all over the country, from as far away as Washington state, and as close to us here as Pensacola, Florida," Gregoire replied. "But I know of no other group that is quite like this one. That's why I say that we can make take back America a reality. You people, that is, we," he said, making a circular motion with his hand to take everyone in, "can be the core of the movement. I think we should expand, invite others to join us."

"What do you think, Jake?"

"I know that there are pockets of military gathered on the old military posts," Jake said. "If we could get all the other military groups to join us, we could probably put together an army that was big enough and strong enough to resist anything Ohmshidi might try."

"I think we should go beyond just contacting the military," Bob said.

"What do you have in mind?"

"The birth of a nation," Bob said.

"Are you serious?"

"Yes, I'm very serious. Right now we are calling

ourselves United Free America, I say we make it a reality."

"Oh, yeah, I see it now. You're the president of UFA, so you're getting power hungry."

"Well, let's face it, Jake, it's no fun being a president, unless you have something you can be president of," Bob said, laughing.

"How would we go about doing something like that?" Tom asked.

"First thing is, we are going to have to come up with a concept. And a constitution."

"What's wrong with the constitution we have?" Chris asked.

"Nothing that a few amendments won't cure," Bob said.

"What kind of amendments?"

"I tell you what, I'll write up a few amendment proposals, and a code. Then I'll run them by all of you and see where we might go from there," Bob suggested.

"Good idea," Jake said.

"Before I go any further, I'd like to get a feel from this group. If we are going to start a new nation, then I look at you people as George Washington, John Adams, Thomas Jefferson, Benjamin Franklin, James Madison, and Thomas Paine. You're our founding fathers."

"Where does that leave me?" Deon asked. "There weren't any brothers who were founding fathers."

"That's where you're wrong, Deon. There were as many as a thousand black soldiers who were wounded at the Battle of Bunker Hill and one,

Salem Poor, performed so well that he was given a citation signed by fourteen officers. No, if we do this, we are all in this together."

"May I make the motion?" Sheri Jack asked.

"Absolutely, you may make the motion," Bob said.

"I move that we reach out to others like us, and that we band together to form a new nation."

"I second that motion," Julie Norton said.

"All in favor?"

The vote was unanimous.

"Good," Bob said with a broad smile. "Our future is laid out for us."

"Now," Jake said. "As long as we are gathered here, I've got an announcement to make, and an invitation to issue."

Everyone stopped eating and chattering, and looked toward Jake.

"Karen has decided to make an honest man out of me. So one week from now, we are going to be married. You are all invited."

Jake's announcement was met with an enthusiastic response, and congratulations.

Holy Spirit Episcopal Church, Gulf Shores, Alabama

Judge Roy Moreton had made national news back in the pre-O time by allowing the Nativity scene to be erected on the courthouse grounds. When he refused to remove it, even after a federal court order, he was arrested, and removed from the bench.

He was one of the first judges to offer his service to the fledgling group of freedom fighters once the Phoenix Rising group broke away, and it was he who issued marriage licenses to Jake Lantz and Karen Dawes. Father Ken Coats conducted the wedding at Holy Spirit, which was particularly meaningful since it was a meeting at Holy Spirit that had allowed the little group of survivalists to expand beyond their initial base at Fort Morgan, to encompass all of Pleasure Island.

After the wedding, a reception was held in the parish hall.

"Hey, Major, I've got something for you," Deon Pratt said. "It's a wedding present."

Jake Lantz was no longer a major. In fact, in a recent organization of their group, Jake had been made a general in the provisional army of United Free America, but Deon, a martial arts and weapons expert, was one of the original members of the group. And because Deon had served with Jake in the pre-O days of the US Army, he often called him major, as did the others of the original group.

"You didn't have to get us anything, Deon. Just having you here is enough."

"Oh, this isn't for both of you. It's just for you," Deon said. He was carrying a paper sack, and reaching down inside, he pulled out a can of root beer.

"Oh, my God!" Jake said. "I can't believe it! A root beer? Where did you find it?"

"It?" Deon said. He laughed. "It's not just 'it.' Tell him, Captain. Or should I say, Mrs. Lantz?"

"We now have a whole case of root beer back at the house," she said.

"It's been almost two years," Jake said. He popped the top of the can, and it began to spew out. He covered the spew with his mouth, quickly, so as not to lose any of it.

"Jake, it's hot. Don't you want it cool first?" Karen asked.

"Hot, cold, it doesn't matter," Jake said and, as he turned the can up to his lips, the others laughed and applauded.

"Where are you two going on your honeymoon?" Barbara Carter asked. Barbara was a very pretty girl with long blond hair and big brown eyes. Eighteen years old now, she was seventeen when she and 96 other youngsters were rescued from Youth Confinement and Enlightenment Center Number 25. Barbara now worked as a secretary for Jake.

"I don't know," Jake replied with a smile. "I heard about this place called Fort Morgan, which I understand is right on the beach. That might be a pretty good place to go for a honeymoon."

Barbara laughed. "It might be."

Barbara left and Jake took another swallow of his root beer. His love for the soft drink was well known, and in the pre-O time he always kept a refrigerator full of the beverage.

"When Deon told me he had found a source for that, I knew it would make you happy," Karen said.

"A source? You mean there's more?"

"Yes."

"Fantastic." Jake took another swallow, then

looked at Karen. "Are you upset that we aren't really going on a honeymoon?"

Karen laughed. "Jake, it isn't like we have to get to know each other now, is it? We've been sleeping together for three years."

"Shhh! You would say that in a church?"

"You mean you would rather me lie?"

"Ha. I guess not."

Bob Varney came over to congratulate them.

"Thanks," Jake said. He held up the can of root beer. "Did you hear? Deon found a source for this."

"This is your wedding day, but you're excited because you've got root beer?" Bob teased.

"Bob, you wouldn't tease if you knew how addicted he was to the stuff," Karen said.

"Well, yeah, but you've had almost two years to go cold turkey. You'd think it would have kicked the habit by now."

"You'd think," Jake said.

CHAPTER TWO

Taney County, Missouri

To anyone who might happen by, the little cabin that sat on top of the hill was typical of many of the structures in the Ozark Mountains of southwest Missouri. Far enough in distance from the major metropolises of the country, this area had been spared the riots and the encroachment of the Moqaddas Sirata. People who lived here were as self-supporting now as they had been 150 years ago.

The house was small, with wide, weathered-gray board siding. The asphalt shingle roof was missing a few of the shingles, and on the front porch was an old sofa with some of the stuffing and springs exposed. A wheelbarrow, without the wheel, was leaning against the front porch, and a 1998 Chevrolet Silverado pickup truck, once blue but now rusted and faded, without hood, engine, or wheels, sat on cinder blocks in the front yard.

Under the window was a flower box with carefully tended flowers. A sign in front read:

**DON'T TRY TO SELL NOTHING HERE
WE GOT NO MONEY**

The little house was a ruse. Inside the house, a hidden button would open a trapdoor in the floor that led down to an elevator chamber. The elevator went on down one hundred feet into the mountain where there was a 10,000 square foot living area, completely self-sustained with a small, nuclear power plant, a deep well, a radar alert system, cold storage of foods, with satellite Internet coverage that fed a dozen computer monitors. The numbers on the dedicated monitors reported the latest stock reports from the stock exchanges of Tokyo, London, Shanghai, Hong Kong, Toronto, BM&F, Bovespa, Australian Securities, and Deutsche Borse. In addition there was an entertainment system of more than 10,000 movies.

This was the home of Warren Sorroto, the wealthiest man in the world.

Warren Sorroto had been born Greygor Sorkosky in Hungry, in 1930. His Jewish family was killed by the Nazis, but before they were caught up in the pogrom they managed to put their son with a non-Jewish family. During the war Sorroto, who was using the name of his adoptive family, earned money by helping the Nazis locate Jews who were trying to survive by assuming new identities.

In 1947, Sorroto went to college in England.

After graduating from college, he immigrated to the United States where he began working in various financial companies, rising in importance and investing wisely until he started his own company, SIM, or Sorroto Investment Management. He began making massive amounts of money by manipulating currency. When he sold short some ten billion British Pounds, he created a financial crisis that shook England to its core, bankrupting businesses and families. But Sorroto profited to the tune of two billion dollars, in one day.

By the time Ohmshidi ran for president, Sorroto was worth twenty billion dollars, but in Ohmshidi, he saw an opportunity to make an unheard of amount of money. Sorroto manipulated the stock market, creating a crash that reflected badly on the outgoing president, who was of the opposite party, and he put a billion dollars into Ohmshidi's campaign, both by direct and bundled contribution. His Visible People Foundation and News Freedom Group managed to influence the Mainstream Media to produce and publish news stories that presented Ohmshidi in the most favorable light, but were detrimental to his opponent.

Writers for the late night talk shows were paid by Sorroto to write jokes that were critical of the man running against Ohmshidi, and when there were jokes about Ohmshidi, they lacked the cutting edge of those told about his opponent. On election day, Sorroto paid poll "guards" to stand in front of polls. He hired muscular black men, dressed them in black, military-style uniforms, and had them carry nightsticks. They were trained to profile the voters, and they were menacing, almost confrontational, to the middle-aged, white men who appeared to be affluent, while deferential to the younger voters, both men and women, to the minority voters, and to the voters who looked somewhat less successful.

When Ohmshidi won the election, mainstream media complimented him on his brilliant campaign. There were very few who realized that his election had been bought and manipulated by Warren Sorroto, perhaps because so many of them were feeding at the same trough.

As soon as Ohmshidi was elected, Sorroto began, immediately, to put his grand scheme into operation. The success of his scheme depended upon him staying in the background. Never once during the election did Sorroto give an interview in which he supported Ohmshidi. And, since the interview, he managed to keep his meetings with Ohmshidi so secret that not even Ohmshidi's chief of staff was aware of the connection.

Sorroto's first move was to convince Ohmshidi to stop all fossil fuel production, including coal, oil, and gas. He also persuaded him to stop refining, and even to halt the importation of oil or gasoline. To do so, he promised, would, by necessity, bring about the development of eco-friendly green and renewable energy.

"Just think, Mr. President. Your legacy to the world can be to free mankind of the climate destroying fossil fuels," he said.

It did no such thing, and Sorroto knew that it

wouldn't. It did, however, accomplish exactly what Sorroto wanted it to accomplish. He had cornered the market in fossil fuels and made over fifty billion dollars within a matter of months. It totally destroyed America's free enterprise system and Sorroto played it just right, riding the crest of the collapsing economy and earning another fifty billion dollars which he managed to convert into Swiss Francs and other foreign currencies, just before the final crash came. With 99 percent of Americans wiped out financially, Sorroto now had deposited in offshore accounts Swiss Francs, British Pounds, Eurodollars, Japanese Yen, Chinese Yuan, and Russian rubles, an amount of money equal to over two hundred billion dollars in pre-O currency.

Sorroto had manipulated Ohmshidi into bringing about the collapse of the nation because he planned to move in and, with a massive infusion of funds, rebuild America. While saving America, he would have himself appointed as "Director of Recovery," which position would, in effect, give him unlimited power as well as access to the recovery money. Through his manipulation, America would once more be the most powerful nation in the world, but this time with Sorroto as the supreme authority of the land. That would make Sorroto the most powerful man in the world.

What Sorroto had not anticipated however, was the action of the Moqaddas Sirata sect of Islam. Taking advantage of the weakened position of America, brought on by Sorroto's activities, the Moqaddas Sirata detonated three nuclear bombs on

American soil. That brought about an immediate collapse of the United States. Sorroto's carefully laid out plan had to be altered.

Almost immediately after the nuclear blasts occurred, Sorroto left his home in Philadelphia, retreating to the place he had already built in Missouri. Sorroto didn't live in his hideaway home alone. He had brought with him a household staff to see to his every need. Sorroto had no sexual needs. Some might think that he had no needs because of his age, but in truth Sorroto had always been asexual. His drive was for money and power, and he saw the current conditions not as a detriment, but as a stepping stone to his ultimate goal of becoming the most powerful man in the world.

Sorroto was connected to the rest of the world through the Internet, and he was able to get, not only the Moqaddas Sirata telecasts, but the outlaw telecasts as well. He had followed the change in America, had watched on television as churches were burned, and "infidels" were killed. What was happening in America didn't particularly bother him, the weaker the country became, the easier it would be for him to reassert himself and continue with his grand scheme of things. He knew that the national conversion to Islam was very thin, done only to have access to goods and services, and to avoid being killed.

Some might think it the height of conceit for Sorroto to think that he could take over an entire country, but if Sorroto decided to declare himself a nation, he would be the 50th wealthiest nation in the world. He knew, though, that if he intended to play on this world stage, he would have to have nuclear weapons.

And he had already put that into motion.

Moscow, Russia

Lieutenant Colonel Leonid Trutnev was a gambler and was now so badly in debt that it threatened his career. If word of his indebtedness and addiction to gambling got to his commander, Colonel Vladimir Shaporin, he would be kicked out of the military. Trutnev was deputy commander of the Tenth Battalion of the Tamanskya Division, and therein might be his salvation. Ivan Buzinsky, a taxi driver who had himself once been an officer in the army of the old Soviet Union, hinted to Trutnev a couple of weeks earlier that he knew how to make a lot of money.

Trutnev cut him off quickly, because he had an idea of what Buzinsky was talking about. But he had received a telephone call last night from someone to whom he owed a great deal of money, a man who was connected to what people were calling the Russian Mafia.

"I would strongly suggest, Trutnev, that you pay your debt within two weeks, or you will have more than your army career to worry about."

That cryptic message sent him into Moscow today, to find his friend Buzinsky.

"So," Buzinsky said, when Trutnev got into his cab. "You are willing to talk to me now about my offer." It wasn't a question, it was a statement.

"Yes," Trutnev said.

Buzinsky chuckled. "I thought getting a telephone call from Klokov might change your mind."

"Wait a minute. You know about the telephone call? How do you know?"

"I'll just say this," Buzinsky said. "I'm not the only one involved in this thing. There are some people who are very powerful who are also involved. And if you help us, they can help you, with much more than just money."

"Buzinsky, what is your role in this?"

"Let's just say that I am the facilitator," Buzinsky said. "I will get paid when I put you in contact with the person who can make all this happen."

"Well, let me ask you this. Does this have anything to do with the fact that I am the deputy commander of a nuclear missile battalion?"

Buzinsky laughed. "You don't think anyone would be interested in you for your good looks, do you?"

The taxi stopped.

"Why have you stopped here?"

"I think you might enjoy a steam bath," Buzinsky said.

"I don't want a . . ."

"I think you do," Buzinsky said, pointedly. "Go into chamber number one. There you will meet Boris."

"What is his surname?"

"There is no need for you to know that."

"I see." Trutnev started to pay for the ride.

"There is no charge. I think we will do business and then we will both make money."

Trutnev stepped out of the car, then looked at the two story building at 14 Neglinnay Ulista. He entered the building through the squared off corner.

Inside, the hostess at the desk was an unattractive woman with a square chin and eyebrows so heavy that they practically met in the middle. A cigarette dangled precariously from her lips, and when she spoke, Trutnev feared that it might fall from her mouth.

"Sixteen hundred rubles," she said.

"Sixteen hundred?" Trutnev gasped. "So expensive?"

"This is the Sanduny Banya. It has been here for over one hundred years. It is the most famous sauna in all of Russia."

"It looks as if it has been here for over one hundred years," Trutnev said. "All right, here is the money."

Trutnev gave the woman the money, then passed through a light blue stucco entrance hall, up one flight of stairs to the changing room. There he was served a cup of tea, then stripping down, he wrapped himself in a towel. There were four steam chambers, and as Buzinsky said, he chose chamber number one. There were four men in the steam room, but one man, with grey hair and a bushy mustache, spoke.

"Leave now," he said.

Three of the others got up and started toward the door and Trutnev started after them.

"You stay, Trutnev," the man said.

"Boris?"

"Sit," Boris invited.

Trutnev sat in the chamber, surrounded by hot steam, and he began to sweat. For a long moment neither man said anything.

"When you leave, you will find a thumb drive in the pocket of your trousers," Boris said. "Insert the thumb drive into the inventory computer of your battalion. Use it to replace the information that is on the inventory, then remove the thumb drive and destroy it."

"There was uh, some talk about money," Trutnev said.

"In addition to the thumb drive, you will find a packet of one hundred thousand rubles."

"That's . . . not enough to pay what I owe."

"You owe nothing. Your debts have been paid."

"Oh, thank you, Boris! Thank you!" Trutnev said.

"Do not fail us."

"I won't. I'll do as you say."

CHAPTER THREE

Dallas

Martin Axleman grew up in North Dallas in an affluent neighborhood. His father was an avowed socialist, and a very successful syndicated columnist for socialist publications. Graduating from high school in 1974, Axleman attended the University of Chicago where he majored in political science. After graduating from college, Axleman remained in Chicago where, in 1987, he formed a political consultancy company, Axleman & Associates. He specialized in managing campaigns for minorities, and for candidates who held extreme left-wing philosophies.

Mehdi Ohmshidi was a naturalized American citizen who had born a Muslim in Islamabad, Pakistan, but had long ago renounced the faith of his birth. He rose to national prominence as the federal prosecutor who tried the case against Masud Izz Udeen. Izz Udeen was an Islamic terrorist who released Sarin gas into the ventilation system of Madison Square Garden, killing over seven hundred Americans.

As Izz Udeen received his sentence of death, he pronounced a fatwa against Ohmshidi whom he denounced for abandoning Islam, and implored Muslims of the world to martyr themselves if need be in order to kill Ohmshidi. The fatwa against him, along with his successful prosecution of Izz Udeen, propelled Ohmshidi into politics, and that's where Axleman came into the picture.

Axleman played a major role in Ohmshidi's initial run for the United States Senate. When Ohmshidi ran in the primary, he, as well as his opponent, had to submit a petition with 750 registered voters in order to have his name put on the ballot. His opponent, Ewell Lynch, submitted 2,315 names, or more than three times the total needed. But Axleman challenged the names before the Chicago Board of Elections, and had 1,875 of the names disallowed, thus removing Lynch from the ballot.

By the time Lynch was able to prove that the names were valid, it was too late, Ohmshidi had garnered the nomination. When Ohmshidi ran in the general election, his opponent was Charles "Bruiser" Kane, a very popular sports figure who had played on the 1985 Super Bowl Champion Bears. Well into the race, a woman appeared on a Chicago radio station with the claim that she had quit working for the Bears' front office because of sexual harassment from Bruiser Kane.

Kane denied it, and his reputation was such that nobody believed the first charge, but three more women came out in rapid succession with their own charges, and even though his denials were just as adamant, people were now beginning to question him.

"I think it's hypocritical that Kane is campaigning on such things as morality, and the sanctity of marriage, but has maintained a harem all these years," one 'woman on the street' interviewee said.

Then Kane's marriage got into difficulty and he withdrew from the race, to be replaced at the last minute by a weak candidate who was never able to gain traction with the Illinois voter. Axleman won the senate seat by an overwhelming margin.

Then the Twenty-eighth Amendment to the Constitution was passed. This repealed Section One, Article Two, making any naturalized citizen eligible to be president of the United States, clearing the path for Ohmshidi to run for President.

Helped by an overwhelmingly supportive media—their support bought by Warren Sorroto—Ohmshidi was elected president, and Axleman was rewarded for his efforts by being appointed Ohmshidi's chief of staff.

It was Axleman who gave Ohmshidi his campaign theme of "fundamentally changing America." He was also the one who designed the Ohmshidi campaign logo, a green letter *O* enclosing wavy blue lines which represented clean water, over which was imposed a stylized green plant. It was also Axleman who designed the new national flag, white, with a wide red bar running from the top of the banner to the bottom. In the middle of the red bar was a white circle and in that circle, the Ohmshidi *O.*

Then, when conditions in the country deteriorated, and nuclear bombs were detonated, Ohmshidi had to flee Washington. Axleman left as well, returning, not to Chicago, but to Dallas. Always one to take advantage of any condition that would better himself, Axleman became one of the first to very publicly convert to the "Holy Path" of Islam.

At first, Axleman, who was now calling himself Amar Shihad, converted only for the conveniences the conversion offered. As he got into it though, he realized that there was a huge power vacuum in American Islam. A smart man could do well, and within a year, utilizing his political skills and the lack of any principle other than self-advancement, Amar Shihad became the Grand Ayatollah of the Dallas and Fort Worth metroplex.

He quickly realized, though, that you couldn't just be smart, you also had to be ruthless. And because Martin Axleman had always had a sadistic streak—as a boy he used to capture birds alive, then pull their beaks out—it wasn't hard for Amar Shihad to become the man that others referred to as the "Devil of Dallas."

Shihad developed a policy he called "Societal Adjustment and Realignment." The SAR program stated in the slick brochures that it was designed to "improve society by eliminating those impediments to good order and harmony."

Those impediments, as the brochure pointed

out, were Christians who had not converted to Islam, and Jews who, by Moqaddas Sirata law, were prohibited from converting. The impediments were eliminated by being killed. There were no exact records kept, but estimates were that Shihad had already been responsible for hundreds, if not thousands of deaths in the Dallas–Fort Worth metroplex. He had recently authorized another SAR operation.

The Galleria Mall, Dallas

A huge, but temporary banner had been erected in the parking lot of the Galleria Mall.

Making Lives Better With
Societal Adjustment and Realignment
Obey Ohmshidi

There were ten buses parked in the parking lot of the Galleria, five in one line and five in another; the parallel lines of buses were separated by about one hundred yards.

"Please have your identity cards ready to show the officials," a loudspeaker said. *"You will not be allowed to board the bus without your identity cards."*

"What if we don't want to board the bus?" someone asked one of the officials. All the officials were wearing black uniforms trimmed in silver. They wore the collar pins of a scimitar and severed head of the Janissaries, the elite corps of the SPS, or State Protective Service.

"If you do not board the bus, you will be shot," one of the Janissaries replied.

"Please have your identity cards ready to show the officials. You will not be allowed to board the bus without your identity cards."

There were five hundred "subjects" gathered in the parking lot, men and women. There were no children, they had already been taken from their parents and were now in the Youth Confinement and Enlightenment Centers. Gathered here were some of the few remaining Jews, Christians who would not convert, and unrepentant atheists.

They had been rounded up by the Special Operations Units. Not all Jews, Christians, and atheists had been rounded up, and there was neither rhyme nor reason to those who were. This was all a part of Amar Shihad's plan of control.

"Let them always be looking over their shoulder," Shihad said. "Will the Special Operations Unit come for them today? Tomorrow? Perhaps they will be spared."

Shihad knew that the uncertainty would play a big role in allowing him to control the population.

"Please have your identity cards ready to show the officials. You will not be allowed to board the bus without your identity cards."

The raid that gathered the subjects this time was conducted in the middle of the night. It had been six weeks since the last roundup operation. Nobody had ever heard another word from any of those who had been taken before.

"Please have your identity cards ready to show the officials. You will not be allowed to board the bus without your identity cards."

"What do they want with us?" Leah Rosewell asked her husband. "We have nothing left. They took our store, our home. We have nothing more to give them."

"I don't know," David said.

"I'm concerned," Kaye Miller said. "My sister was taken three months ago and I've not heard another word from her. It isn't like her not to write."

"I wouldn't worry too much about that," Mort said. "Mail service today is practically nonexistent. You know that."

"Please have your identity cards ready to show the officials. You will not be allowed to board the bus without your identity cards."

Leah put her hands over her ears. "I wish they would stop making that announcement over and over and over. It is driving me crazy!"

"That's why they are doing it," David said. "They want to irritate us. Maybe I can irritate them a bit."

"What do you mean?"

David held up his finger, then called over to one of the Janissaries.

"Sir?"

"What do you want, Jew?"

"I was just wondering. Will we be allowed to board the bus if we don't have our identity card?"

"You must have your identity card to board the

bus," the black-uniformed guard replied, totally unaware of the sarcasm of David's question.

"Okay, thank you. I wasn't sure whether we could or not."

"Please have your identity cards ready to show the officials. You will not be allowed to board the bus without your identity cards."

"All right!" one of the Janissaries called. "Form a single line here and board the buses!"

"There are only ten buses," a man protested. "We are too many for ten buses."

A nearby Janissary pulled his pistol and shot the protester. There were shouts and screams of fear and alarm as the protestor crumpled and fell.

"Now," the shooter said with an evil smile. "There is one less. I'm sure the buses will accommodate the rest of you. Begin boarding."

As Leah and David approached the front of the line they saw a "V" made of sawhorses. The V was splitting the line of people, some going left and some going right. A Janissary was standing just inside the V with his arms folded. He was not giving directions, but letting the borders choose for themselves.

"Which way, David?" Leah asked. "Which way should we go? Left or right?"

"You choose, Leah."

Leah watched the Janissary's face to see if she could discern any difference in his expression as the boarders were making their decision. She noticed nothing.

"Which way, Leah?" David asked again.

"To the right," she said. She had no reason to justify her choice, it was just one she made at the last minute.

When they got on the bus it was easy to see how ten buses could accommodate five hundred people. There were no seats on the bus.

As the buses got underway, everyone was ordered to sit on the floor. It was so crowded that there was scarcely room to sit at all, and the positions were cramped and uncomfortable.

"Sit behind me, Leah," David suggested. "We can put our backs together."

"No," a man behind David said. "Put your back against my back, your wife can put her back against my wife's back. That way we will still be braced, but together. I don't know how much longer we will have the opportunity to be together, we should take advantage of it."

"Yes," David said. "Yes, that is a good idea."

Others on the bus, seeing the arrangement David, Leah, and the couple behind them had made, did the same thing. The conditions were still cramped and uncomfortable, but sitting in such a way at least made it bearable.

They had no idea how long the trip would be and as they discussed it among themselves, some suggested that it might be two or three days.

"But surely if it is to be so long, they will stop occasionally to allow us to walk around, won't they?"

"I wouldn't put anything past these monsters," another said.

"Are the other buses with us?" someone asked.

"There's no way to tell. The windows are all blacked out."

The buses rolled on.

CHAPTER FOUR

After 36 hours on the bus, it finally came to a halt. They had not been given anything to eat or drink. They had not been allowed to leave the bus when the bus stopped for fuel, not even to go to the bathroom, and by now everyone on the bus had soiled their pants. The first thing to greet David, Leah, and the others on the buses when they stepped down was a large white sign inscribed with stark black letters.

Your SAR Program at Work
Ultimate Resolution Camp 35
Grand Ayatollah Amar Shihad
Obey Ohmshidi

The "camp," as the sign called it, was completely surrounded by a high, chain-link fence. There were several rolls of razor wire on the ground at the base of the fence, which was constructed at a reverse angle of about thirty degrees so that, even without the razor wire, it would be hard to climb. On top of the fence was more razor wire, and there was razor wire on the ground on the other side. In addition, there were manned guard towers all around the perimeter.

Of the ten buses that had been in the parking lot of the Galleria, only five were here now. Where had the other five gone? Had they made the correct choice in choosing the buses on the right?

"Oh, David," Leah said. "What have we gotten into? What is going to become of us?"

David reached over to take her hand in his.

"I don't know, Leah. I don't know," he said, quietly.

The buses had come into the compound and the passengers, or, as David thought of them now, the prisoners, moved around gingerly, trying to get the circulation going again after the long, cramped trip. Other than the prisoners, all of whom had expressions on their faces that David knew must mirror his own, the only other people he saw were the Janissary guards, dressed in their black uniforms.

"David," Leah said. "There is no one here except for those of us who just arrived. Where are the ones who were here? What happened to them?"

"Again, my sweet, you have asked me a question I cannot answer," David said.

"Will they let us stay together, do you think?"

"We will live together, or we will die together," David said. "I will not allow us to be parted."

"Yes," Leah said, resolutely. "We will live together or we will die together."

On the front wall was the red, beige, and blue portrait of Ohmshidi.

To one side of it were the words:

Obey Ohmshidi!

A black-uniformed Janissary stepped in front of them.

"You are all filthy!" he said. "You have soiled your clothes. Don't you know enough not to pee or shit in your pants?"

"When the bus stopped we were not allowed to leave," one of the men said, but as soon as he spoke, one of the other guards came over to him and began beating him with a club.

"You will not speak unless you are given permission to speak," the Janissary in front said. "Now, all of you, take off your clothes and go into the shower."

One of the prisoners raised his hand.

"What do you want, Jew?"

"I am a Christian," the man said.

"Christian, Jew, you are the same. You are all infidels. What do you want, Jew?" he repeated.

"Do you intend for us all to strip here, in the open? Men and women together?"

"I see no men or women here. I see only Jews. Strip, now."

Half an hour later all the prisoners were showered, and in clean clothes. Then they were led to barracks, one hundred people to each building.

Moscow

Starlite Diner first appeared in Moscow in 1995 in the garden of the "Aquarium," directly opposite the Theatre City Council. The red and silver interior of the Starlite Diner revived the atmosphere of 1950s America, with walls that are covered with pictures of iconic movie actors, such as James Dean and Marilyn Monroe, 1955 Fords and 1957 Chevrolets, as well covers of past Life magazines. The food is traditionally American, specializing in hamburgers, French fries, and milkshakes.

It is mostly a hangout for young Muscovites and Americans who live in Moscow wanting a taste of pre-O America, as well as older Russians who had a longtime enthrallment with America.

Aleksandr Mironov was one of the latter, which was very good for him, because his position as a member of the United Nations delegation enabled him to live in the country that had always fascinated him. The fact that he had also been a member of the KGB at the time did not diminish his appreciation for America.

In Moscow now, he had come to the Starlite Diner with his nephew, Colonel Vladimir Shaporin. He was surprised when Vladimir suggested that they meet here—but flattered thinking that perhaps his nephew was being nice to him.

"Get the French-fried onion rings with your cheeseburger," Mironov suggested. He chuckled. "I'm sure they are a heart attack waiting to happen, but, oh, they are delicious. And a strawberry milkshake," he added.

"I'll defer to your expertise, Uncle Aleks, and let you order," Vladimir said, once they were seated.

"Good, good, trust me, I'll make your dinner an experience you won't forget," Mironov said. He placed his order, then seeing the pictures on the wall, started pointing them out, with explanation, to his nephew.

"That's James Dean," he said. "*Rebel Without a Cause*—if you want to know America in the fifties, you must see that movie. Oh, and Marilyn Monroe, the most beautiful American actress ever. That's Johnny Cash, and that's Johnny Unitas. That's a 1957 Chevrolet, and that's Elvis Presley. Oh, and listen, that's him singing on the jukebox now."

"Jukebox?"

Mironov pointed. "That gaudily lit thing over there, from which the music is coming." Mironov sang along for a few lines. "*If you can't come around, then please, please telephone.*"

"You like Americans, don't you?" Vladimir said.

"Yes, I like them. That is, I did like them. I don't know that I could like them now. I'm not sure I understand what has happened to America," Mironov said. "I don't mind admitting it. Though, of course, during this time," he took in the photos with a wave of his hand, "the fifties and the sixties—it would not have done for me to say this. We were in a cold war then, with the threat of nuclear annihilation hanging over us all."

Vladimir drummed his fingers on the table for

a moment or two, then glanced around the restaurant to make certain he couldn't be overheard.

"Uncle Aleks, what if I told you there is still a nuclear threat?" he asked.

"Well, of course, as long as there are nuclear weapons, I suppose there is always that chance," Mironov said.

"More than just a chance."

Mironov's eyes narrowed. "What are you trying to tell me, Vladimir?"

"Uncle, as you know I am commanding officer of the Tenth Battalion of the Tamanskya Division. In a recent inventory, I discovered that five of the three-kiloton warheads were missing."

"What? Did you report them?"

"I did."

"And what action has been taken?"

"None."

"None? But, that is impossible! How can there be no action taken?"

"After the end of the Cold War the Americans gave us software designed to allow us to keep track of our inventory. That computer says that there are no missing warheads, but I think someone has hacked into the files, making it appear as if all is well."

"What makes you suspect that?"

"Because I have also kept a record of them on the property book. The property book shows five more weapons than we currently have in our inventory."

"My dear boy, that has always been the nightmare of both the American and the Russian governments."

"Not our government," Vladimir said.

"What do you mean?"

"I went to Defense Minister Basov and told him that the warheads were missing. When he asked how I knew, I told him that according to the property book, we still have the warheads. But according to the computer, and according to a physical inventory, the warheads are gone."

"You're sure it isn't simply an accounting mistake—that you didn't transfer them out and lose track of them?"

"Uncle Aleks, you lose track of your billfold, your fountain pen, your car keys—you do not lose track of nuclear warheads."

"What did Basov say?"

"He demanded that I surrender the property book and all hard copy records to him. He also told me that I was dealing with something that was none of my business. When I told him that I was responsible for the nuclear weapons under my command, and that it definitely was my business, he told me that this involved something that was way above me, and that I should forget about it—including the conversation we had."

"How big is a three kiloton weapon? I mean, how much damage could it do?"

"It's about one-fourth the size of the bomb that destroyed Hiroshima," Vladimir said. "It would larger than any nonnuclear blast in history—with the heat and radiation of a nuclear weapon. Believe me, uncle, this is not something you would want to fall into the wrong hands."

"Who else have you told about this?" Mironov asked.

"Only my deputy commander," Vladimir replied.

The waiter brought the hamburgers, fried onion rings, and milkshakes to the table at that moment. Mironov thanked him, then, smiling, picked up the hamburger and took a big bite.

"Oh, my," he said. "Try this, Vladimir. You will think you have died and gone to heaven."

"Uncle, did you hear one word I said to you?" Vladimir asked.

"I heard," Mironov said. "And I will look into it, nephew. I promise you, I will look into it."

Ultimate Resolution Camp 35

Two hundred and fifty had arrived at the camp, now there were only one hundred and eighty-seven left.

"Our experiment of keeping men and women together has not worked," the camp commandant told them, when he assembled them for the daily announcements. "Tomorrow, you are to be separated, and the women will be taken to another camp."

"No!" someone shouted. "No, please, don't do this!"

"Enjoy your last night together," the commandant said with a sardonic smile.

Those nights in the barracks the women, and many of the men, were crying.

"David," Leah said. "Do you remember what you said when we arrived at this place?"

"What?"

"You remember. You just don't want to say it, because you think I don't want to hear it again."

"You say it," David said.

"You said that we would either live together, or die together."

"Yes, I did say that."

"Then let us die together."

David took Leah's hand in his. "Is that really what you want?"

"Yes, my darling," Leah said, holding David's eyes with a steady gaze. "If we are to be separated tomorrow, I want us to die together tonight."

"Wait here," David said. "I'll be right back."

Leaving Leah on the single bed they had shared ever since arriving at the camp, David sought out one of the other prisoners that he knew was a doctor. The doctor, who was 75, was the oldest of all the prisoners. He was a widower, his wife having died even before they were all rounded up.

"Doctor Solomon," David began, but Solomon held up his hand. "I know what you are going to ask, nearly everyone here has asked the same thing. If you'll return to your wife, I'll address the subject for all of you."

David returned to the bunk.

"Did Doctor Solomon have a suggestion?"

"He's going to talk to us now," David said.

"People, please, pay attention," Doctor Solomon said. "I want to tell you a story, then, as a result of that story, offer a suggestion.

"The story I will tell you is the story of the Masada, as told by Josephus. For many years scholars believed it was fiction, but archeologists later proved the authenticity of the story.

"Jerusalem fell to the Romans in 70 A.D. but there were many Jewish zealots on Masada, a mountain top fortress, who refused to surrender, and Rome was unable to subdue them.

"But the Romans were determined to do this, so they surrounded the mountain with as many as 15,000 soldiers. They built siege camps and an earthen ramp so Roman battering rams could ascend to one of the gates. The siege lasted seven months, then the walls were breached. But when the Romans entered there was no resistance. There was no resistance because all but two women and five children were dead.

"The women told the story of how ten men were chosen by lot to kill all of the others, then one was selected to kill the remaining nine, then kill himself. In that way, only one person had to take upon himself the sin of suicide.

"According to Josephus, the Jewish leader said something that might apply here. He said, let us die un-enslaved by our enemies and leave this world as free men in company with our wives and children.

"I know that many of you have chosen to die tonight, rather than be separated from your wives.

Those of you who have made such a choice, stand by your bed. Those of you who do not wish to participate, go to the back of the room. I will take the sin upon myself to kill you, so that you not leave this world as a suicide."

"How will you do it?" someone asked.

"By ligature strangulation," Dr. Solomon said. "I will use an article of clothing as a garrote. It isn't exceptionally painful, and at any rate, it generally brings on unconsciousness within five to ten seconds, so you will be unaware of what is happening to you."

"What will happen to you, Doc?"

"I'll hang myself. Now, those who want to participate, stand by your bed. Those who don't, move to the back of the room."

Not one person moved.

"All right," Solomon said. "I'll get started."

David and Leah stood in an embrace as Doctor Solomon began his terrible task. There was no sound, neither from the victims, nor from the witnesses who were waiting for their own fate. After about five minutes, Dr. Solomon approached them. Solomon was sweating profusely, and there was an expression on his face that was unlike anything David had ever seen before.

"It isn't too late for you two to back out," Doctor Solomon said.

"We will live together, or die together," Leah said.

"Which of you shall go first?"

"I will," Leah said.

"Wait," David said. He embraced and kissed his wife. "Principle eleven of Maimonides tells us that our great reward will be life in the world to come. I will see you, my beloved, in the world to come."

CHAPTER FIVE

Dallas

Grand Ayatollah Amar Shihad was on the telephone, speaking with the commandant of the Ultimate Resolution Camp 35.

"How many of them committed suicide?" he asked.

"One hundred and four, Grand Ayatollah," the commandant said.

"And how many did that leave you to deal with?"

"Eighty-three."

"How soon will you apply the ultimate solution?"

"It is being applied now, Grand Ayatollah, even as we speak," the commandant said.

Shihad smiled, and nodded. "You are doing good work, and are truly walking the holy path," he said.

"I do this for the glory of Allah, and Moqaddas Sirata. Obey Ohmshidi, Imam."

"Obey Ohmshidi," Shihad replied.

* * *

Rosewell Apparel, Inc. manufactures, distributes,
and retails branded fashion apparel. The Company
also wholesales t-shirts and other casual wear to
distributors and screen printers, as well as operates
a retail e-commerce website.

That was the business statement of the company that David Rosewell had started, and owned. Buck Tinsley had driven a delivery truck for Rosewell Apparel for twenty years, and he thought Rosewell was as fine a man as he had ever known. When the Janissaries of the Moqaddas Sirata came for Rosewell and his wife, Buck was infuriated.

"Nothing will change for you and the other employees," Fahad Farran said. This company has been nationalized, and will now manufacture only clothes that are suitable for Muslim wear. It shall be known as the Way of the Enlightened Clothing Company. You will continue to drive as before, but now you will be able to drive, content in the knowledge that you are no longer working for a Jew."

"Nothing will change for us, the son of a bitch said," Buck said to Carter Davis, his brother-in-law. "But can I have a beer and pork skins while I watch football on the weekends? Well, let's examine that. No alcohol, so there goes my beer. No pork, so there goes my pork skins. Oops, and no football. Also, no basketball or baseball. But the son of a bitch says nothing will change."

"Do you know where the old Mary Kay building is in Addison?" Carter asked.

"Yeah, I know where it is. Why?"

"You want beer and football? I'll come pick you up Wednesday at six."

"What's going on, Carter. What's this about?"

"You just be ready by six, on Wednesday."

Because cosmetics were considered sinful, Mary Kay was no longer in business and, as Moqaddas Sirata had not yet found a use for the building, it was unoccupied.

On Wednesday nights a growing group of men would meet on the fifth floor of the building. As far as anyone driving by on the Dallas Parkway was concerned, the building looked no different on Wednesday night than it did at any other time. There were no cars parked around the building, and no lights showed from the building. Of course nobody expected to see lights, because there was no electricity connected to the building. Except on Wednesday nights.

Two of the group of men who met on Wednesday nights were electricians, and they would connect the Mary Kay building to the power grid just before the group would meet, and disconnect it when the meeting was over. The windows of the fifth floor were carefully blocked out so that no light could be seen from outside.

True to Carter's promise, there was beer available, and also football, or at least DVD's of past football games. One of the men, a Texas A&M

grad, had a DVD of the Alabama–A&M game where A&M beat the number one ranked team in the country, holding off an Alabama comeback by intercepting a pass in their own end zone in the closing one minute and thirty seconds.

After the game was over and everyone started to leave, Carter asked Buck to stay a few minutes longer.

"All right," Buck said.

Carter introduced Buck to two other men from the group; Frazier Nelson and Dean Pollard.

"Buck," Frazier said, "before we go any further in this discussion I have to know two things. One, what is your level of frustration with the way things are and two, how far are you willing to go to change things?"

"I don't have the vocabulary to tell you how much I hate the way things are now, and I'm not sure I can do anything to change things. But if there was anything I could do to change it, I would."

"Even at the risk of your own life?"

"What do you have in mind?"

"Nothing unless I have a commitment from you."

"Yeah. After what these sons of bitches did to Mr. and Mrs. Rosewell, yeah, I would risk my life.

"David and Leah Rosewell were also good friends of mine. I don't know whether they are dead or alive, but I don't intend to stand by and let this go without response of any kind. How do you feel about that?"

"Whatever you have in mind, I want to be a part of it."

"Good," Frazier said. "Two days from now, Farran is going to send you out on a job. You'll be deadheading out to Houston. But first you are going to go to just beyond the Addison Airport. Do you know Dooley Road?"

"Yes, I know the road. It comes off Keller Springs."

"Go about one hundred yards south on Dooley Road and you'll see an orange traffic cone. When you get there, stop. At exactly ten fifteen, open your trailer door, then get back in the cab and wait."

"Wait for what?"

"Wait for a signal to proceed. When you get the signal, proceed on to Midway Road, then down to 635, then on to Houston."

Buck shook his head. "I don't know what you have in mind, but it won't work. My truck has a GPS; Farran will know where I am."

"Ron Bannister does the maintenance on your truck, doesn't he?" Frazier asked.

"Yes."

Frazier smiled. "Don't worry about the GPS."

"Bannister is one of us?"

"Yes, but don't acknowledge it, not even to him," Frazier cautioned.

"All right."

"What do you know about Amar Shihad?" Frazier asked.

"I don't know much about him. I know he is the Grand Ayatollah of Dallas."

"He is the one who put the Jews into the concentration camps, including David and Leah Rosewell." Frazier paused before he spoke again. "He is also the one who is responsible for the murder of way over a thousand men, women, and children at the Dallas–Fort Worth Metroplex."

Buck whistled. "Damn, I knew he was an evil bastard, I guess I just didn't know how evil."

"Day after tomorrow the Grand Ayatollah is going to the Addison airport to take a business jet to Washington, D.C. where he is to be given some sort of award by Ohmshidi."

"What's he being awarded for?"

"It doesn't matter," Frazier said. "He'll never get the award because we are going to kill the son of a bitch just before he gets to the airport."

"How are you going to get to him? Isn't he always surrounded by bodyguards?" Buck asked.

"He never has guards, he rides alone in an open car with just his driver," Novotny said.

"Shihad isn't that stupid, is he?" Buck asked. "To travel around without body guards? Why would he do such a foolish thing?"

"He's not stupid, but he is foolish. He has become arrogant with his absolute power, and he likes to demonstrate his complete control of the city by riding around in his open-topped green Mercedes, with no guard," Frazier said. "He can't believe that anyone would actually make an attempt on his life." Frazier opened another beer. "Only we aren't just making an attempt, we're going to do it. And you are a part of the plan."

"You mean just by sitting on Dooley Road with the doors open to my trailer?"

"Yes."

Buck smiled. "I don't know how that makes me a part of the plan, but if it winds up getting that bastard killed, I'm all for it."

Addison, Texas

There were two cars in the road at the corner of Jimmy Doolittle Drive and Keller Springs. From the position of the two cars it appeared as if there had been a minor collision and they had the road effectively blocked. Frazier Nelson and Dean Pollard were standing in the road between the two cars, yelling at each other, gesticulating wildly.

That was what greeted Amar Shihad and his driver as they approached.

"Grand Ayatollah," the driver said. "Our way is blocked."

"Well, get out and tell the fools who I am," Shihad said. "Tell them to make way."

"Yes, Grand Ayatollah," the driver said.

When the driver opened the door, Frazier and Dean could be heard yelling at each other.

"You dumbass!" Frazier was shouting. "Where did you learn to drive? Haven't you ever heard of a turn signal?"

"Well if you hadn't been going so fast, you would have seen that I was turning. I had plenty of time to turn in front of you, if you hadn't been speeding."

"Driver," Shihad called. "Tell them I've no wish

to listen to their foolish quarrels. I am an important man and I have business to attend to."

The driver looked back toward Frazier and David, and an imperceptible nod of acknowledgement passed between them. The driver turned and suddenly ran to the side of the road.

"What are you doing? Get back here at once!" Shihad shouted angrily.

With Shihad's attention diverted Frazier and Dean reached through the open windows of the two cars and grabbed AK-47s.

"What? What are you—?" Shihad shouted, but his shout was cut off by the staccato bark of automatic weapons fire. Bullets crashed through the windshield of the Mercedes, punched holes in the side, and slammed into Shihad, leaving his body a bloody mess in the back seat.

Frazier and Dean left the two weapons in one of the cars, then drove off in the other. Driving quickly through the Addison tunnel, they turned onto Dooley where the saw Buck's truck sitting about a hundred yards up from the corner. The doors to the trailer were open, and there were two ramps leading up into the trailer.

Frazier, who was driving, drove up the ramp into the trailer. He and Dean got out of the car and pulled the ramps up as Carter Davis, who was waiting on the side of the road, hurried up to close the trailer doors. That done, he walked up to the front of the truck.

"Drive away," he said.

Buck nodded, put the truck in gear, then drove away. After he turned onto Midway, before he reached the LBJ Freeway, he was met by three SPS cars, their red and blue lights flashing, the warning sirens blaring.

Fort Morgan

There were, by now, several groups of freedom fighters around the country, most of them in the South. Fort Benning, Georgia, Pensacola Naval Air Station in Florida, Fort Rucker in Alabama, Keesler Air Force Base in Mississippi, and Barksdale Air Force Base in Louisiana were now in control of the patriots, occupied in the main by many of the men and women had had been stationed there in the pre-O time.

Even though Jake Lantz and the Phoenix Rising group had taken over Mobile, the capital of what they were now calling United Free America was still located at Fort Morgan.

"Why shouldn't we stay here?" Jake replied when he asked why they didn't move the capital to Mobile. "We have everything we need at the fort, it is easily defended, and it has probably gone through a hundred or more hurricanes without damage. I see no reason why we shouldn't stay right where we are.

Not one of the group who identified themselves as Phoenix Rising, disagreed with Jake.

That had been an earlier discussion. At the moment though, Jake Lantz and Bob Varney were at the Mobile airport. When Mobile was freed from the State Protective Service there were several aircraft there that were returned to their original owners. One was a business jet, a Cessna Citation 10 which belonged to Vaughan Charter. Jake and Bob had arranged for Dick Vaughan to fly them to the five military bases in order to enter into conversation with the patriots who now occupied them.

The fastest business jet in the world, the Citation 10 is a six hundred mile per hour aircraft so that wheels up to wheels down between Mobile and Pensacola was a matter of minutes only. Landing on Runway 7R, Vaughan was able to take the A5 exit, then he taxied back down the A taxiway to Base Ops. There were at least half a dozen men standing out front, waiting for them. Jake opened the door and stepped down, followed by Bob, and then by Vaughan.

A short, grey-haired man stepped forward. "I'm Hi Gurney," he said as he extended his hand in greeting.

"Mr. Gurney, I'm Jake Lantz." Jake took Gurney's hand, then introduced Bob and his pilot.

"Come on in, have some coffee with us and we'll talk about things," Gurney invited.

"Will your plane need servicing?" one of the others asked.

"No, thanks, it's good," Vaughan said. "General, I'll wait out here with the plane," he added to Jake.

"All right," Jake said.

"General, huh?" one of the men with Gurney said. "Well you two should get along fine. Hi was an admiral."

Jake chuckled. "Then you've got me ranked, Admiral. I was a major in the pre-O days. This gentleman, who is the provisional president of United Free America, appointed me general in our provisional army."

"I'm sure it was a wise appointment," Gurney said. He looked at Varney for a moment. "You have the look of a military man about you. Would I be wrong if I guessed that you were in Vietnam?"

"Three tours, Admiral," Bob said. "I was a warrant officer."

"Aviator?"

Bob nodded. "Helicopter pilot."

"And a damn good one too," Jake said. "I've seen him operate."

Gurney led them into a lounge area in the operations building where a pot of coffee and the fixings sat on a table. After a moment of filling cups and adding milk and sugar, they settled into cushioned chairs and sofas to talk.

"I'm aware of what you folks are doing over there in Alabama," Gurney said. "And I was pleased when you contacted us and said you wanted to drop by for a visit. I've been thinking that there must be a way we can help each other."

"Have you heard from any of the other people here in Florida?" Jake asked. "How many would you say support your movement?"

"I'd say most of the people who live north of I-4 support us," Gurney said. "Those south of I-4 are primarily the ones who put that bastard in the White House in the first place, and a hell of a lot of them still support him."

"Have you ever thought about breaking off North Florida from the southern part of the state?"

"I've never really given it much thought," Gurney said.

"Think about it," Jake said. "Do that. Form your own state, then come join us as a state in the UFA?"

"UFA?"

"United Free America," Jake said. "Part of the reason we're making this trip is to get into contact with other independent groups to invite them to join us."

"You think there is a chance for such a thing?" Gurney asked.

"I do. Fort Benning, Keesler and Barksdale Air Force Bases, and Fort Rucker are all controlled by patriots. And we have a destroyer, the *John Paul Jones,* that is on patrol right now in the Gulf, keeping an eye on the off-shore gas and oil platforms."

"Historically, the military bases have been in the South," Bob added. "So getting control of them shouldn't be that hard."

"And Ohmshidi has no army as such," Jake said. "All he has are the State Protective Service and the Janissaries."

"Yes, but from what I've heard, he has over a million of them," Gurney said. "And you have to give the son of a bitch credit, he has started rebuilding, he's bringing their economy back, and he has all the gold in Fort Knox to back him."

"Not all the gold in Fort Knox," Bob said with a chuckle.

"What do you mean?"

Jake laughed as well. "What our president

means is that one of our very first operations was to relieve Fort Knox of some of its gold."

"Good heavens! For real? How much did you get?"

"In the neighborhood of 50 billion in pre-O dollars," Bob said.

Gurney whistled softly. "That's a damn good neighborhood," he said.

"We're using it to back our printed currency." Bob pulled out his billfold, then took out a bill. "Here is an example of the bills. We are only printing one, five, ten, and twenty dollar bills. No coinage at all."

"This is a good-looking bill," Gurney said. The bill he was holding was a five dollar bill. "Feels good, too."

"Seventy-five percent cotton and twenty-five percent linen," Bob said, "just as in the pre-O currency. And, every dollar is backed by gold."

"I see you have Reagan's picture on the five. Who do you have on the other bills?"

"Eisenhower is on the one, Truman is on the ten, and Bob Hope is on the twenty."

Gurney smiled. "Bob Hope?"

Bob nodded. "My father saw him in North Africa during World War II, and I saw him twice in Vietnam. I don't think we've made a medal high enough to honor him."

"I can't say as I disagree with you," Gurney said.

"What about it, Admiral?" Jake asked. "Are you with us?"

Gurney nodded his head. "Damn right I am. Whatever it is you have planned, count me in."

CHAPTER SIX

Dothan, Alabama

As he shot baskets, sixteen-year-old Troy Jackson bobbed and weaved about on the blacktop pad near the chain-link fence that surrounded the grounds of the Dothan High School. Faking around an imaginary defender, Troy went high for a perfect layup. Troy had been a pretty good basketball player in the pre-O time. He had played on the eighth grade team and the JV team. He would have moved up to varsity the next year, had the country not collapsed under Ohmshidi.

He had thought his dreams of playing basketball were over, but the movement that had started down in Gulf Shores, Alabama went on to free Mobile, and was gradually moving north so that it now incorporated Dothan as well as several other nearby towns, such as Newton, Enterprise, Ozark, and Troy, even as far north as Montgomery. It was beginning to look as if he might have a chance to play varsity basketball after all.

He had just rebounded a missed three-point attempt, when he saw a truck coming very slowly up the drive toward the school entrance. The driver, a swarthy man wearing an eye patch, looked like a pirate. Troy paid particular attention to the truck because few trucks came this way, and one didn't see a pirate every day.

Troy waved at the driver. Instead of returning the wave, however, the driver looked away. Shrugging it off, Troy returned to his game. With his back to the goal, he dribbled, then pivoted around for a jump shot, getting all net. He smiled at the shot and wished that his father, who had played for Auburn, had seen this one.

"Miss Margrabe! The truck!" a girl's voice shouted.

The girl's shout, and the sudden racing of the engine caused Troy's attention to be drawn back to the truck. He saw the truck moving swiftly across the grass, heading straight toward the fence that surrounded the school. There were several young students gathered just inside the fence and they turned to look, so surprised by the strange action of the truck that they were frozen into immobility.

Troy recognized the danger at once. Dropping to the ground he rolled into a tight ball with his arms folded over his head.

The truck-bomb detonated at the fence.

Troy felt the shock wave and the heat of the explosion. He was also bruised and cut by the detritus that fell on him, but he was not seriously injured. Eleven school children and one teacher, outside at the time and close to the fence, were not so lucky. They were killed, along with two others who died when the engine block of the truck crashed through the windshield of their car, just because they happened to be driving by on Highway 231 at exactly the wrong time. In addition to those killed, twenty-six children and three adults received injuries ranging in degree from Troy's minor cuts and bruises, to four who were listed as critical.

Fort Morgan

When Jake and Bob returned from their recruiting tour that same day, they landed at the Mobile airport, then flew by helicopter across the bay to Fort Morgan. Bob and Ellen hosted the others for dinner that night, and he and Jake told his guests about their visits with other patriot groups.

"Basically they have all agreed to join us," Jake reported. "And what we have now is a military force awaiting only the command and structure that is necessary to bring them all together."

"We have an air force, an army, and a navy," Bob said.

"What is the size of our military?" Tom asked.

"We did some figuring on the plane on the way back," Bob said. "It looks like when we get everyone on board, we'll have a combined force of a few thousand."

"A few thousand? That's not a very large army," Chris said.

"Don't look at it like that," Jake said. "Look at the few thousand as a cadre around which we will build our military. Once we get things underway, I think we can use them as a magnet to attract others. I believe we will be able to develop a pretty sizeable military force rather quickly."

"Yes," Bob said. "And one of the advantages we have, over anything that the AIRE has . . . is that we actually have most of the military equipment. When the US totally collapsed, the military left behind the very latest in helicopters, Humvees, armored personnel carriers, trucks, jet fighters, bombers, even UAVs. We don't have a significant sea power yet, but we do have a navy base at Pensacola, we have a sheltered port at Mobile, and we have a ship building company in Pascagoula."

"Yeah," Tom said. "When you look it like that, I think we can hold our own if anything happens."

After dinner they watched a newscast from CMN, the Columbia Muslim Network. The program began with a full screen shot of the new national flag. The words *CMN, America Enlightened Truth Television* were keyed onto the screen, replaced by the words *Obey Ohmshidi*, then a reverent voice over intoned the opening lines.

"All praise be to Allah, the merciful. Whomsoever Allah guides there is none to misguide, and whomsoever Allah misguides there is none to guide. You must live your

life in accordance with the Moqaddas Sirata, the Holy Path. Those who do will be blessed. Those who do not will be damned.

"You are watching CMN. And now, our National Anthem."

As the music played, the national flag of the AIRE fluttered in the background, but, superimposed over the letter O, was Ohmshidi's face. It remained prominent as the music began to play, the words sung by an all male chorus.

American Islamic Republic of Enlightenment
Our people loyal and true
To Ohmshidi our Leader
We give all honor to you.
Glory to our great leader
May he remain right and strong
The party of the faithful
Ohmshidi to lead us on!
In Moqaddas Sirata
We see the future of our dear land
And to the Ohmshidi banner,
In obedience shall we stand!
Glory to our great leader
May he remain right and strong
The party of the faithful
Ohmshidi to lead us on.

When the anthem ended, the scene returned to the studio where a young woman was sitting behind a news desk. She was wearing a burqa and her face was covered so that only her eyes could be seen.

"Obey Ohmshidi.

"In Dallas today, two cowardly infidels murdered Grand Ayatollah Amar Shihad. Imam Shihad was on his way to the airport, to take a flight to Muslimabad where he was to have received the Ohmshidi Award of the Holy Path for his application of the Ultimate Resolution to the Christians and Jews of the Dallas–Fort Worth Metroplex.

"In Dothan, Alabama, today, a brave martyr sacrificed himself for Allah and the glory of our beloved Glorious Leader, President for Life, Mehdi Ohmshidi, may he be blessed by Allah. The martyr, who is now in paradise, drove a truck filled with explosives into a schoolyard.

"Several schoolchildren were killed, but it must be noted here that if the children had been in the Youth Confinement and Enlightenment Center as they should have been, none would have been killed. The fault therefore lies with those apostates and infidels who, in violation of what has been decreed by Glorious Leader, President for Life Ohmshidi, may he be blessed by Allah, have taken their children from an environment that would guide them along the path of Moqaddas Sirata, and exposed them to the heathen world."

The picture on the screen was replaced by a stylized portrait of Ohmshidi in a pensive pose, looking slightly up and to his left. The rendering was in red, beige, and blue, with the words Obey

Ohmshidi underneath. The letter *O* in both words
duplicated the new symbol.

> *"In other news, the Organization of Islamic
> Cooperation announced that every member
> nation of the OIC will support the American
> Islamic Republic of Enlightenment's petition to
> the United Nations for full status membership.
> The OIC had high praises for our beloved
> Glorious Leader, President for Life Mehdi
> Ohmshidi, may he be blessed by Allah, and
> said that to him goes the praise and credit for
> destroying the Satan that was the United States.
> In so doing, our beloved Glorious Leader,
> President for Life Mehdi Ohmshidi, may be
> blessed by Allah, removed a threat from the
> peace loving Muslim states of the world.*
> *"That is the news.*
> *"Obey Ohmshidi."*

Bob clicked off the TV. "I don't know who it was
that killed that son of a bitch in Dallas, but here's
to them," he said.

"Yeah, we could use a few more like that," Tom
said.

"I expect we have more like that than anyone
knows," Chris said.

"I expect you are right," Bob agreed.

"But how many do we have like that bastard
who killed the school kids in Dothan? I never, ever
thought I would see the time when an American
would become a suicide bomber."

"He wasn't an American," Chris said. "He gave

up that designation as soon as he signed on to this Moqaddas Sirata nonsense. And when you think about it, it isn't all that new. Even in the pre-O time we had them. It was my job to keep up with them. There's Colleen Rose, she calls herself "Jihad Jane," Daniel Patrick Boyed, Adam Gadahn, Abdul Yasin, Anwar Al-Awlaki, Omar Hammami, he was from right here in Alabama, John Walker Lindh, and David Headley, all born in America. Oh, and how can we forget Major Yusef Mahaz? How he shot up a processing center at Fort Eustis.

"Mahaz doesn't count. That was workplace violence, don't you remember?" Tom asked sarcastically.

"Yeah, I remember," Bob said with a mordant chuckle.

"The point I'm making is this," Chris said. "What we're doing now is essentially the same thing that happened during the Civil War. We are trying to establish a new nation, carving a chunk out of what was the United States. And there's no way we are going to be able to do this peacefully. There is going to be fighting, and it will be American against American."

"What do you think of that, Bob?" Jake asked. "Do you agree with Chris?"

"I'm afraid I do agree with him," Bob said.

"What I'm worried about is, if it does come down to fighting, will our people fight against other Americans?" Jake asked. "That's going to be asking an awful lot from them."

"Jake, Americans fought against Americans in the Civil War, and 'brother against brother' wasn't just an expression. There really were cases of brother against brother, and son against father," Bob said.

"But that didn't stop the killing, did it?" Tom asked.

"No. And as you know it was the most deadly conflict in our history. Estimates are that from 600,000 to 750,000 died in that war. Americans did a pretty good job of killing other Americans."

Bob's comment was met with a stony silence.

Hamburg, Germany

American passports were no longer recognized and the government of AIRE had not yet issued passports. That was no problem for Sorroto who had a Swiss passport, and his own personal Boeing 787 aircraft with more than twice the range required to fly him from Springfield, Missouri to Hamburg.

He was in Hamburg to donate ten million euros to the "Sorroto School of Business." However, he was also here to meet with Dmitry Golovin. Golovin was a Russian general with whom Sorroto had been in contact. Golovin had the authorization of his government to meet with Sorroto, because Sorroto had promised to give ten million euros, which came to 360 million rubles, to a children's hospital in Omsk, Russia.

Sorroto and Golovin walked out onto the patio outside the *Kuchenwerkstatt Gasthaus* and over to the far corner where their conversation was masked by the sound of traffic on the autobahn.

"I have five of them," Golovin said.

"How large are they?"

"Three kilotons."

"No, I mean how much do they weigh? I don't want them to be unwieldy."

"They weigh 140 kilograms."

"What is that in pounds?"

"It is about 300 pounds."

"Then one person could not handle it."

"It could easily be transported on a . . ." Golovin made a motion with his hands to indicate a two wheel loading dolly.

"Yes, a two wheeler, I understand. How much do you want for them?"

"Three billion rubles," Golovin said.

"Three billion, that's 70 million Euros. That is a great deal of money."

Golovin smiled. "What is it you businessmen say? It is a seller's market. Where else can you buy five nuclear weapons?"

Sorroto chuckled. "You have a point."

"Where shall I deliver them?"

"Just hold them for now. I'll let you know when I want them, and how I want them delivered."

CHAPTER SEVEN

Moscow

Boris Petrov and Dmitry Golovin met in the Shokoladnica restaurant.

"There are so many people here," Golovin said, "that I wonder if we should not have chosen a quieter place."

"Nonsense," Boris said. "This is the alpha and omega of chocolate, and their chocolate pancakes are the pride of Moscow. There is nothing unusual about us meeting here, and enjoying the pancakes. Were we to meet in a quiet tea room somewhere, suspicions might be aroused."

The waiter delivered the chocolate delicacies to the two men, and they began to eat with obvious enjoyment. They talked as they ate, giving no indication to anyone else in the restaurant that their discussion covered anything other than their admiration of the cuisine.

"Three billion rubles," Golovin said.

Boris smiled. "So he did not attempt to bargain?"

"He has more money than all the czars of Russia combined. It means nothing to him except as a means to an end," Golovin said.

"Has he said why he wants the weapons?"

"He did not say, and I did not ask."

"Perhaps he is acquiring them for that part of America that has broken away from the rest of the country," Boris suggested.

Golovin shook his head. "No, I truly think he wants the weapons for himself. And such a man is truly dangerous."

"If he is not dangerous to us, why should we care?"

"True, why should we care?"

"There is one man who is a danger to us," Boris suggested.

"You are talking about Vladimir Shaporin," Golovin said.

"Yes. Already he has gone to the Defense Minister with his claim that he is missing five warheads. I convinced the Defense Minister that all the warheads were accounted for, and he dismissed Shaporin. But Shaporin is not someone who can so easily be dismissed. You are going to have to take care of him, and, you must do so quickly."

"You are right. Shaporin must be dealt with. I will see to it that it is done."

Colonel Shaporin's quarters, Sharapovo, Russia

Vladimir Shaporin parked his 2008 Lada Kalina in the parking lot of the senior officers BOQ. A single officer, Vladimir found it cheaper to live in the BOQ than to find an apartment downtown, and because Colonels were authorized a two room suite, his quarters weren't all that uncomfortable.

Vladimir was beginning to have second thoughts about having told his uncle of the missing warheads. He was certain that there were people, highly placed in the government, who knew about it—and for some reason were covering it up. He didn't suspect his uncle, but he may have put his uncle in danger by bringing him in on it.

Why was the government so reluctant to do anything about it? Were they embarrassed? Were they afraid of the negative publicity the Russian government would get if news of this got out?

Or—and this, he didn't even want to think— was the reason more sinister? Were certain officials within the Russian government actually complicit in the disappearance of the warheads?

That unpleasant thought was still on Vladimir's mind as he opened the door to his room. He was surprised to see that, although he had left a desk lamp on, it was dark. For a moment he thought perhaps the power was off, but then he realized that all the hall lamps were burning.

As soon as he stepped into the room, he caught the heavy, almost acrid odor of a Sobranie cigarette. Vladimir didn't smoke, but his deputy commander, Lieutenant Colonel Leonid Trutnev did, and Sobranie was his brand.

"Leonid?" Vladimir called into the darkness. "Leonid, are you in here? What are you doing in my room?"

A lamp was turned on and Vladimir saw Trutnev sitting in a chair by the desk.

"Leonid, what is the meaning of this? You have no right to—" he paused in mid-sentence when he realized that Trutnev was holding a pistol. "What? What are you doing?"

"You should have stayed out of it, Colonel," Trutnev said. He shook his head. "Minister Basov told you to forget about it, but you didn't listen."

"Leonid, you, a traitor?" Vladimir said. He shook his head. "I can't believe you are a traitor."

"I'm not the traitor, Vladimir, you are," Trutnev said. He pulled the trigger on the pistol and Vladimir saw a flash of light, even as he felt a deep, burning pain in his chest. He experienced a sense of light-headedness for a brief instant, then, nothing.

Leonid picked up the phone and made a call.

"It is done," he said.

"Good. You are now the commanding officer of the Tenth Battalion of the Tamanskya Division."

"Thank you, sir. You honor me."

Fort Morgan

Jake, Bob, Tom and Chris were in what they were now calling the cabinet room of the old museum building at the fort. Even though everyone had moved their living quarters away from the fort, the museum building still functioned as the headquarters.

"We've gone about this sort of bass ackwards," Bob said, "in that we have built an army before we built our nation. But these are unique circumstances, and it is my belief that we are going to have to have an established military almost immediately."

"I agree," Jake said. "I'm drawing up a military structure now, breaking it down into corps areas."

"Have you given more thought to my suggestion of having one defense force, rather than an army, navy, and air force?" Bob asked.

"Yes, and I think that's the way to go," Jake said. "Tom, Chris, what do you two think?"

"I suppose I could go along with that," Tom said, "but you need some sub-division within that structure. Part of being a SEAL was the pride of unit. And if we become one conglomeration, we'll lose that pride."

"I agree," Jake said. "We'll marry the two concepts, we'll have a central command and control, but the units within will have their own identity."

There was a knock on the door, and Willie Stark stepped in.

"Yes, Willie, what is it?" Bob asked.

Willie held up a few sheets of paper. "This is what our Web page is going to look like. I printed it out so you could see it before I put it on the Internet."

"All right, let's take a look at it," Bob said.

INVITATION TO JOIN

By virtue of the fact that the voters of this country made a terrible mistake in voting for free stuff, as opposed to freedom, a dangerously incompetent president was put into office. As a result of that president's share the wealth experimentation, his world-first agenda, and his malfeasance in office, the nation once known as the United States of America no longer exists.

This has given us the opportunity to start over, to establish a new nation that is colorblind and free of hate and prejudices. Our laws will be based on common sense. We will live by, and enforce these laws. This new nation shall be known as:

UNITED FREE AMERICA

- We have learned by bitter experience that freedom must be constantly nurtured and protected from those who would take it from us, whether by force, or promise of free things to lazy people.
- We believe that it is not only the right, but the obligation, of every law-abiding citizen to bear arms for his/her defense, for the defense of the innocent unjustly attacked, and for the mutual defense of our country.
- Welfare shall be in effect only for the elderly, infirm, and those who need a temporary helping hand, and the welfare system must also:
  —Require that everyone who can work must work.

—Establish the concept that being a
    productive citizen in a free society is
    the only honorable path to take.

• The motto that for many years served the
    U.S. Military Academy shall be our motto:
    DUTY, HONOR, COUNTRY.

• If this appeals to you, if you wish to
    follow the example set for us by our
    forefathers so long ago, please respond
    to New nation@Freedom.com.

"That looks pretty good," Jake said. "But how can we get people to come look at it?"

"Don't worry about that," Willie said. "I have so many search engine optimizers that half of what anybody starts searching for will bring them to this site."

"Including the bad guys?" Tom asked. "I mean, won't this tell them what we are doing?"

"They are going to know what we are doing anyway," Bob said. "I say to hell with them, we'll just be in their face with it."

"Yeah," Jake said. "Yeah, I like that."

"All right, Willie, go ahead and get this up as quickly as you can," Bob said.

"Yes, sir," Willie replied.

"Any other suggestions?" Bob asked after Willie left.

"Yes, I have one," Chris said. "We are going to need more than an army. We're going to need something like the CIA."

"I agree," Jake said. "And since you brought it

up, I assume that means that you are willing to serve in that capacity, and organize it."

"Well, yes and no," Chris replied.

"Why no?"

"I am willing to serve in that capacity," Chris said. "But initially, I think we should have a one man bureau. And I'll be that one man."

"I'd be willing to go along with that, Chris, except for one thing," Bob said.

"What's that?"

"I've never been associated with such an organization, but I've certainly read about it—you know, James Bond and all that. And from what I've read, it's pretty dangerous. What if you get killed?"

"I'm glad you are so concerned about me," Chris said with a smile.

Bob chuckled. "Don't get me wrong, I'm not particularly concerned about you. But if you get killed and there's nobody to take your place, where will that leave us?"

"I expect Tom has done about as many spook jobs as I have," Chris said.

"Hardly," Tom said, laughing. "You've been doing this for what? Forty years?"

"Hey, hey, hey," Bob said. "Show a little respect for your elders here. I'm pretty sure I once flew Chris behind German lines. It was German lines, wasn't it, Chris?"

"I believe it was."

"Yes, I started to say I flew you behind British

lines, but as I think back on it now, I believe that was Nathan Hale."

"Right. And we know how that one worked out," Jake said.

"But I did give him that line he used. *I regret that I have but one life to give to my country,*" Bob said.

"You sure do have a way with words. No wonder you're a writer."

"You old guys are crazy, you know that?" Tom said, laughing.

"That's all right. Being crazy is what keeps us sane."

CHAPTER EIGHT

New York City

Two years earlier, when Ohmshidi's outlandish socialist policies had brought the Republic to its knees, Islamic terrorists had managed to sneak in three 100-kiloton nuclear bombs. There were simultaneous explosions of the three nuclear devices, one in Boston, one in Norfolk, and one in New York. The bomb in New York, by design, had been off-loaded from the ship, put into a rental truck, and driven to 350 Fifth Avenue, where, at the agreed upon time, it was detonated right in front of the Empire State Building.

Within the first second, the shock wave destroyed even the most heavily reinforced steel and concrete buildings including the Empire State Building, Madison Square Garden, Penn Station, and the New York Public Library. Within this initial circle more than 75,000 people were killed instantly. Those caught outside were exposed to the full effects of the blast. Those inside, though shielded from some of the blast and thermal effects, were killed as the buildings collapsed. The fireball had a maximum radius of two tenths of a mile. However, the blast effect greatly outweighed any direct thermal effects due to the fireball. An overpressure of at least 10 psi extended out for one mile, and concrete and steel reinforced commercial buildings were either totally destroyed or severely damaged out to the edge of this ring. The few buildings that remained standing on the outside edge of this ring had their interiors destroyed. Landmarks affected by the blast at this distance were the Chrysler Building, Rockefeller Center, the United Nations, and four hospitals. All of those buildings were either totally destroyed or so severely damaged that they were unusable. Most people inside those buildings were either killed by flying debris or died as the buildings collapsed. Those in the direct line of sight of the blast were killed instantly by the thermal pulse. Fatalities were estimated at 300,000 with at least another 100,000 being severely injured, many of whom died within the next six months.

By the end of the second second the shock wave had moved out another half mile, extending the destruction out to a 1.5 mile radius. The overpressure dropped to 5 psi at the outer edge of that ring, which covered an area of 4 square miles. Reinforced structures were heavily damaged and unreinforced residential type structures of brick and wood were totally destroyed. At this point the affected structures included Carnegie Hall, the Lincoln Center, and the Queensboro Bridge. All these structures were near the outside edge of the expanding ring. All windows in these structures were shattered and many interior walls collapsed.

At this point, 190,000 more people, who were inside buildings, were killed by building collapse and flying debris. Another 190,000 suffered varying degrees of injuries. Most of those outside, and not in the direct line of sight of the explosion escaped direct injury from the blast, but many were injured by flying objects. The thermal pulse, which was still sufficiently intense to kill anyone in the direct line of sight, killed another 30,000. The total number of injured was over 200,000.

This region presented the most severe fire hazard, since fire ignition and spread occurred more easily in partly damaged buildings than in completely flattened areas. At least fifteen percent of the buildings were instantly ignited, then the fire spread to adjoining buildings. Over the next twenty-four hours, fires destroyed about half the buildings.

Two and one half miles from ground zero, reinforced structures received varying amounts of damage, with those buildings at the edge being almost completely undamaged. Wood and brick buildings received moderate amounts of initial damage, with the damage becoming less significant at the outside edge of this ring. Within this ring an estimated 235,000 people were fatalities, with another 525,000 injured to varying degrees. There were many injuries due directly to the blast overpressure, however, the thermal pulse was still sufficient to kill or incapacitate those not indoors or otherwise protected. The degree of injury from the thermal pulse depended greatly on clothing and skin color. Darker clothing and skin absorbed more of the energy, giving a more severe burn. The material type and thickness also determined the severity of burns from the thermal pulse.

Damage due to fire was particularly bad in this band. The energy in the thermal pulse was still great enough to start combustible materials on fire, yet the overpressure and accompanying wind was less likely to put out the fires. Only a small percentage of the fires were started by the thermal flash of the bomb; many more buildings were damaged as the fire spread out of control since the capability to fight fires was nonexistent.

The outside band extended out for almost 4 miles from ground zero and had an overpressure of 1 psi at its outside edge. At the inner edge there was light to moderate amounts of damage to un-reinforced buildings of brick and wood. Reinforced structures and commercial buildings received light damage at most. This band extended out to the site of the unfinished Freedom Tower at One World Trade Center and the undamaged Statue of Liberty in the south, across the East River into Queens in the east, and across the Hudson River to New Jersey.

Though this ring covered an additional 30 square miles, much of this area was over water or less densely populated areas. The affected population in this ring was approximately half a million. There were almost no fatalities in this ring and only a small percentage, roughly 30,000, received injuries from the thermal pulse. Flash blindness and permanent retinal injuries from the blast extended out beyond 20 miles. But since this was a ground level explosion, the number of people who were looking in the direction of the blast and had a clear view was much less than if the explosion had taken place several thousand feet above the city.

Because this was a surface explosion, it produced much more fallout than a similarly sized airburst where the fireball never touches the ground. This was because the surface explosion produced radioactive particles from the ground as well as from the device itself. The early fallout drifted back to earth on the prevailing wind, creating an elliptical pattern stretching from ground zero out into Long Island. Because the wind on the day of the detonation was relatively light, the fallout was highly concentrated in the area of Manhattan just to the east of the blast.

Manhattan is an island connected to the rest of New York and New Jersey by tunnels and bridges. Many of those access points were affected to some degree by the blast. The Lincoln and Queens Midtown Tunnels were both in the 10 psi ring and were so badly damaged as to be impassable. The Queensboro Bridge was in the 5 psi ring and was also put out of commission. All the remaining tunnels and bridges fell in the 2 or 1 psi rings and received only moderate damage so that they remained usable.

With almost 900,000 people injured to various degrees, the task of caring for the injured was far beyond the ability of the medical system to respond. All but one of Manhattan's large hospitals were inside the 5 psi ring and were completely destroyed. There weren't enough empty hospital beds in all of New York and New Jersey for even the most critically injured. The 1 psi ring alone had an estimated 30,000 burn victims who required specialized care. In the days following the nuclear detonation, many of the injured died from lack of any medical care.

For well over a year, Manhattan was without any utilities: electricity, gas, water, or sewage. Transportation of the injured and the ability to bring in the necessary supplies, people and equipment depended upon the condition of the tunnels and bridges that connect Manhattan to New York and New Jersey; nearly all of those were destroyed, or blocked to some degree. And even when rescuers were able to get into the city, the streets and avenues were so filled with rubble that they were completely impassable.

Tens of thousands of survivors became homeless. Creation of temporary shelters was the first recovery task after all the trapped and injured had been found and cared for. True recovery for New York was still a long way off. Some areas remained dangerously radioactive and even without the radioactivity it was likely that New York City would never fully recover to its original status as the nation's leading financial and cultural center.

Now, nearly two years later, most of the material that comprised those buildings in mid-Manhattan remained piled up to depths of hundreds of feet in places. Absolutely nothing in what had once been the heart of the most advanced and bustling city in the world was recognizable.

All the commerce of New York had moved south of 10th Street, and this little inhabited end of Manhattan could have been Baghdad, Tripoli, Teheran or Kabul from the looks of it. Nearly every man on the street was wearing a *thobe*, and every woman a burka. Bryan Gates, who was dressed no differently from any other man on the street, went in to a coffee shop on East First Street. Bryan had once been a member of the CIA, but because he had been covert, very few knew of his background. His method of making a living now was as covert as it had been in the pre-O times. He "adjusted" things.

If somebody was having a problem with an officious member of the AIRE government, Bryan, for a price, would "make things right." Often a visit to the offending party was all that was needed. Sometimes a little more persuasion was necessary, and a kneecap might be broken. In those cases where persuasion was ineffective, Bryan made a more permanent adjustment.

Taking his coffee over to an empty table, he was very surprised to see an old but familiar face from his past. Aleksandr Mironov was sitting at a table on the other side of the room. When their gazes met, Mironov got up and brought his coffee to Bryan's table. Bryan stood, and the two men shook hands.

"Have a seat, Aleks. How long has it been?"

Mironov smiled. "I was assigned to the Soviet delegation to the United Nations from 1972 until 1981, when you blew my cover as a member of the KGB. I came back in 2004 as a member of the Russian delegation, and stayed until Christmas of 2008. I left right after that."

Bryan took a swallow of his coffee and looked around before he answered, quietly. "You chose a good time to leave."

"So I have observed. What has happened to your country, Bryan? What has happened to the America I loved?"

"You can see for yourself," Bryan said.

Mironov made a tsk sound, and shook his head.

"What brings you here, Aleks? I know it isn't the United Nations, they are no longer here, nor are we any longer a member."

Mironov handed Bryan a newspaper clipping.

Офицер покончил с собой

Полковник Владимир Шапорин, командир десятого батальона отдела Таманскуа был найден мертвым в своей квартире в это утро, жертвой самоубийства. Хотя Шапорин оставила никакой записки, считается, что он раскаивался за свою веру, что он потерял некоторые ядерные боеголовки, которые были в его ведении,—это убеждение, вытекающих из устаревшего метода учета.

Это хорошо известно, что полковник Шапорин не доверяют системе компьютерного учета, так как он жаловался он своему начальству.

Печальная ирония заключается в том, полковник Шапорин не потерять боеголовок. Они благополучно приходилось, и был Шапорин показал немного больше терпения, он мог бы легко показать, что его беспокойство было напрасно.

"I haven't been using Russian much, lately," Bryan said. "If you don't mind, I'm going to read this aloud, and you tell me if I have it correct."

"All right," Mironov agreed.

Bryan cleared his throat, then began to read aloud. "Army Officer Commits Suicide. Colonel Vladimir Shaporin, commanding officer of the Tenth Battalion of the Tamanskya Division, was found dead in his quarters this morning, the victim of a suicide. Although Shaporin left no note, it is believed that he was remorseful over his belief that he had lost some nuclear warheads that were in his charge—that belief stemming from an antiquated method of record keeping. It is well known that Colonel Shaporin did not trust the computer accounting system, as he had complained of it to his superiors.

"The sad irony is, Colonel Shaporin did not lose the warheads. They are safely accounted for, and had Shaporin shown a bit more patience, he could have easily been shown that his worry was for naught."

Bryan looked up at Mironov. "Did I get it right?"

"Yes."

"Aleks, I get the idea that you wouldn't be bringing this article to me unless you believed that these five warheads really are missing."

Mironov nodded. "Vladimir Shaporin was my nephew. I don't have the slightest doubt but that he was murdered. And he was murdered because he knew that the warheads were missing."

"What happened to them?"

"I think they were sold on the black market."

"To who? Someone in the Middle East?"

Mironov shook his head. "To an American."

"Good heavens, you mean the states that have broken away? They bought them?"

"No. To *an* American. One man, representing only himself."

"Who is it? What's his name?"

"I've told you as much as I know. But I have contacted someone in Russia who can help. He wants to meet with Chris Carmack."

"Chris Carmack? Why would he want to meet with Carmack? I'm not even sure he is still alive. And if he is alive, I have no idea where to find him."

"You must try," Mironov said.

"All right. I will try."

Mironov stood. "I wish you the best of luck, my friend. The lives of many, many people may depend on it."

Bryan nodded. Then, as Mironov left the coffee shop, Bryan thought about the last time he had seen Chris Carmack.

Bryan had met Chris at the Mehran Kabob Restaurant on Pennsylvania Avenue, within sight of the White House. The two shook hands, then found a table in the back of the room that was some distance separated from any other customer in the restaurant. Chris had been someone that Gates worked with in the CIA, and though he never knew about Chris's "contract killing" job, he did know that Chris had been involved in several very classified operations.

"What are you doing these days, Bryan?" Chris asked.

"Whatever I have to do to turn a buck. Or, I guess I should say, a Moqaddas."

"Do you still have inside sources of information?"

Bryan broke eye contact, and shrugged, but didn't answer.

"And if you had that information, would you sell it?"

"Chris, are you wired? Are you still working for the government?"

"I swear to you that I am not," Chris said.

Bryan smiled, though the smile was strained. "You

were trained to lie," he said. "I never did know exactly what you did for the company, but I did know that it was top secret. How do I know you haven't just taken your talent over to the SPS, or worse, to the Janissaries?"

"I was a contract killer," Chris said.

Bryan nodded. "Yeah, I thought it might be something like that."

"I'll give you another piece of news about me, that if it got out, would have my head on the chopping block, literally. You will be the only one who knows this, and the only reason I'll tell you, is to show you that I represent no danger to you."

"What would that be?" Bryan asked.

"I've already given you some information, I told you I was a contract killer. Now, I'm going to ask you for some information. If you can supply it, I will give you five thousand Moqaddas, then I'll give you the incriminating information I spoke of."

"Five thousand Moqaddas?"

"I have the money with me."

"Where did you come up with money like that?"

"First, you answer a few of my questions, if you can."

"All right, ask. I'll see what I can do."

"Where are they keeping George Gregoire? In which jail?"

Bryan shook his head. "They aren't keeping him in any jail. He is being kept on the top floor in Grant Hall at Fort McNair."[1]

---

1. *Firebase Freedom*

* * *

Shortly after that meeting, Gregoire had been rescued, and Rahimi killed. And since that time, Gregoire had made broadcasts from the center of the rebel stronghold.

Bryan smiled and hit his fist into his open palm. He knew exactly where Chris Carmack was.

CHAPTER NINE

Fort Morgan

Chris was on the balcony of his sixth-floor apartment at The Dunes condo, looking out toward the Gulf of Mexico. There was absolutely no surf today, the gulf being as flat as a swimming pool. Kathy came up behind him, then leaned into him. When she did, Chris smiled.

"You are either wearing something very thin or . . ."

"Would you believe the or?" Kathy asked, her voice low and breathy.

Chris turned toward her, and his smile broadened. "Damn," he said. "You are totally naked."

"I am not totally naked," Kathy replied. She smiled, and held out a foot. "If you would bother to look at my feet, you would see that I'm wearing slippers."

"Now why the hell would I want to look at your feet?" Chris asked, wrapping his arms around her, and pulling her naked body against him.

"Woman, what have you got in mind?" he asked.

"I don't know," Kathy said. "I suppose it depends on . . . what comes up."

Chris chuckled. "Yeah, well, something has come up."

"So I've noticed. Shall we take care of it?"

"I think that would be an excellent idea."

Philadelphia, Pennsylvania

Not one traditional university had survived the collapse of the United States. Old and storied schools like Harvard, Yale, Princeton, Penn, as well as traditional football powerhouses like Alabama, Ohio State, USC, and Christian schools such as Notre Dame, Seton Hall, Texas Christian, and Baylor were gone.

In their place were new schools based upon the religious principles of Moqaddas Sirata, schools with names like Islamic University of Enlightenment, Holy Path College, and American Islamic University. Math and science courses were still being taught, but there were no American or world history courses available. Neither were there courses in business, literature, art, or music. Medical and law courses were still available, but the law courses stressed sharia law, and the practice of medicine was limited to males only. And, as part of their instruction, they learned that women were to receive no medical treatment of any kind as it was a sin for any man, including a doctor, to look upon the naked body of a woman.

"Should such a heresy occur, both the doctor and the female patient will be put to death," the course warned.

The curriculum was heavy with classes on Islamic thought, Muslim philosophy, as well as the evils of Christianity and Judaism.

"It is our duty to convert everyone to the truth of the Holy Path, including other Muslims who have not seen the way. Those who do convert will be received as one of us. Those who do not convert will receive neither sustenance, support, or sympathy from the believer. It would be better for the nonbeliever to die quickly, for death is sure to come."

Four students of the University of Islamic Enlightenment were gathered in the one-room apartment of Ron McPherson. The students were Ron's sister Ann, Carl Mosley, and his wife, Sally. Ann and Sally were wearing blue jeans and a T-shirt, though both girls had burkas handy for when they left the room. They had gathered around Ron's computer, giving him suggestions on what to write. After a few minutes he lifted hands from the keyboard.

"I think this is it," Ron said.

"Read what you have," Carl said.

Ron ran his cursor back to the beginning of the file.

"A Message of Defiance, and a Plea for Action," Jack read.

"Great title," Ann said. "Who came up with that?"

"You came up with it," Sally said."

"Oh, no wonder I like it," Ann said with a chuckle.

Ron cleared his throat before he continued to read.

"We were born free, looking forward to a future with the innate idea that could achieve anything we set out to achieve, limited only by our intelligence and self-determination. This was the result of what had been two hundred and thirty two years of freedom in a country that was the preeminent nation in the entire world.

"But the nation that our parents, grandparents, great-grandparents, and generations past fought to build and preserve, is no more. How did this happen?

"Perhaps we can start with the universities. The education we sought to guide us into our professional careers was sabotaged by the very people who were to provide us with this education. College and University professors all across the country began a program of indoctrination of a left-wing political philosophy that exceeded the actual education.

"This platform undermined two hundred and thirty two years of awareness of duty, sense of honor, and pride of country. The result was the creation of a society that was more interested in free stuff than freedom. The United States of America did not fall victim to a foreign enemy, but to an electorate that was either too selfish, or too intellectually challenged, to carry the torch of freedom forward. We voted for a candidate who had no record of accomplishment, or even a history of gainful employment.

"When the *Titanic* struck the iceberg, Thomas Andrews, the head ship designer, was aboard. As each succeeding compartment filled with water, he was able to calculate to the minute when the ship would reach the tipping point, when there would be more compartments not contributing to the buoyancy of the ship than there were compartments that were contributing to the buoyancy. Once that tipping point was reached, the result was inevitable, the *Titanic* would go down. With the unprecedented spending, and the number of noncontributing units outnumbering the contributing units our "ship of state" reached the tipping point, and, like the *Titanic*, our Republic foundered.

"We are no longer a nation of individuals, we are a flock of sheep. We stood by without so much as a comment as our economy was wrecked while, to deal with the emergency *he caused*, Ohmshidi began to strip our rights away. And where are we today? We are subject to Moqaddas Sirata, a degrading law that enslaves our women, and robs us of our humanity.

"In the 1960s this nation witnessed the power of an aroused student population when it helped to end an unpopular war. It is time, once more, for the students to take the lead. Next Wednesday we are calling upon all students to show solidarity with our sisters, by men and women wearing a burka, and staging a sit in at every university in the country.

"Signed, Warriors of the White Camilla."

"Okay, what do we do with it now?" Sally asked.

"First thing we will do is send out an e-blast," Ron said. "I had a computer geek who agrees with us create a program for me. All I have to do is send it to one address, and it will go out to every student in every university in the country."

"How many students would that be?" Carl asked.

"Before the collapse of the United States we had twenty million university students," Ron said. "I imagine that now the number is less than five million."

Carl smiled. "But five million . . . damn! That's quite a circulation!"

Ron put the article into an e-mail file, and typed in the macro address "university," then hit send.

University of Islamic Enlightenment

Ron and Carl made a reasoned decision that they would not wear burkas on the day called for. If they didn't wear burkas, it seemed less likely that the movement, should it actually occur, would be traced back to them. They were purposely late in arriving but were rewarded as soon as they did get to school by what they saw.

Sitting on sidewalks and on the front porch of the entrances into all the academic buildings, were hundreds of students. And, because they were all wearing burkas, it was impossible, without a closer examination, to tell who was male and who was female. There was a big, hand-painted sign sticking up in the ground near the demonstrating students.

EQUAL TREATMENT
FOR
MEN AND WOMEN

"All right, look at this!" Carl said excitedly.

"I wonder if it is like this at universities all over the country?" Ron asked.

"I'll bet it is. Why should they be any different? Nobody here realizes that the movement started here."

"Attention! Attention! All students who are currently demonstrating must leave at once!"

"Don't anybody leave!" one of the students shouted, though as everyone was in burkas, it was impossible to tell who shouted.

"Attention! Attention! All students who are currently demonstrating must leave at once!"

"Stand your ground!"

The staff and faculty nearest the demonstrating students began talking quietly among themselves as they tried to decide what they should do. A couple of them went over to take down the sign, but after a couple more announcements over the public address system, telling the students that they must leave at once, it was the staff and faculty who finally left.

"They're gone! We won!" someone shouted, and the demonstraters cheered.

* * *

That evening in Ron's room, he, Ann, Carl, and Sally celebrated their victory.

"What happens now?" Ann asked.

"I don't know," Ron admitted. "We let the genie out of the bottle, from now on what happens is up to the genie."

Muslimabad (formerly Washington, D.C.)

"How could something like this happen?" Ohmshidi asked. "For the last week there have been thousands of students all across the country showing up for school, men and women, dressed in burkas, and blocking the entrances to the academic buildings. After the first day you said it would go away, but it hasn't. It's gotten larger. What started as a few hundred has grown into tens of thousands, maybe hundreds of thousands of protesters!"

"It is bound to go away, Glorious Leader," National Leader Franken said. "These kind of movements feed upon publicity. And because we control the press, not one word of these incidents has been printed, or discussed. It's as if it never happened."

"But it has happened," Ohmshidi said angrily. "And I want it stopped. That is, if you can stop it."

"Oh, I can stop it, Glorious Leader. But it will require action of the harshest kind."

"I don't care how you do it. I just want this movement stopped."

"Yes, Glorious Leader," Franken said.

After leaving the Oval Office, Franken called in several of his advisors to discuss the situation with them.

"How did they manage to coordinate it so that everyone knew when to gather and what to do?" Franken asked.

"Oh, we know how that happened, National Leader," Clint Waters, the chief of SPS security said. "A blast e-mail was sent out, going to hundreds of thousands, if not millions, of students."

"Where did the e-mail come from?"

"We haven't been able to track it back to its source, but we are on the net now so, when another one comes out, we will know about it."

Franken drummed his fingers on the table for a moment. "Can we do something more than just know about it?" he asked.

"What do you mean?"

"Can we send one out to the same people?"

Waters nodded. "Yes, we can. And I think I know where you are going with this. We can monitor the e-mails and next time one comes out, we can send one right afterward, admonishing them against the meeting."

"No," Franken said.

"No?"

Franken smiled. "I want to send an e-mail out, organizing another demonstration. Only this time we will have our men there ahead of time, and when they arrive and start their demonstration, we'll be there."

"National Leader, if we arrest that many students,

where will we put them? There are just too many for us to handle."

"Who said anything about arresting them?"

"Well, if we don't arrest them, what are we going to . . ." Waters stopped in mid-question, then smiled. "It would send a very strong message to anyone else who might try something like this, wouldn't it?"

"Do it," Franken said, standing up, then walking quickly from the room.

Philadelphia

A CALL TO ALL STUDENT REVOLUTIONARIES
If you wish to demonstrate against the
government, gather in assembly hall at
eight o'clock Monday morning.

"Did you send this, Ron?" Carl asked, showing Jack the e-mail he had printed off.

"No, I didn't send it," Ron said.

Carl smiled. "Good! You know what this means then, don't you? It means that our movement is spreading! Now, others are taking the initiative to organize demonstrations."

"I suppose so," Ron said. "But I wish they had coordinated this with us. The only way these demonstrations are going to have any effect is if they are well orchestrated. I mean, look at this. Gather in assembly hall? What assembly hall? And what are they supposed to do when they get there?"

"I don't know, but I suppose all organizations

have growing pains. The SDS, the Weather Underground, even the Vietnam Veterans against the War, all began as independent groups before they began to cooperate for a single goal. I'm told that there was one peace demonstration where 250,000 students came to Washington," Carl said.

"That's true," Ron said. "Well, what do you say we go to Assembly Hall on Monday Morning and see what's going on?"

"Good idea."

"Ron," Ann said Monday morning just before they were ready to leave. "Let's not go. I've got a funny feeling about this."

"What kind of feeling?"

"A feeling like something isn't quite right. I don't think we should go down there."

"We've got to, Ann, don't you see? We are the ones who started this movement. How would it look if we get cold feet and chickened out now?"

"It's not the same thing. Like you said, there was no coordination on this. It is haphazard at best. Let's don't go down there. It won't make any difference to the movement whether we go or not. We could just sit this one out and see what happens."

"I tell you what. You and Sally stay here," Ron said. "Carl and I will go."

"No, if you're going then I'm going as well."

"No, I'm serious, Ann. Maybe there is something to what you say, maybe this wasn't as well organized. Maybe the SPS has gotten word of it somehow. If that's the case, it only makes sense to not commit everyone."

"I agree with Ron," Carl said. "Sally, you stay here with Ann."

After several minutes of arguing about it, Ann and Sally finally decided that they would stay back.

"Be careful," Ann said. "Don't leap in right away, sort of hang back until you see what's going on. Promise?"

"I promise," Ron said.

When Ron and Carl arrived at the assembly hall, they were pleased to see that there were at least two hundred students there, and they were all standing around, talking excitedly, but with a sense of apprehension as well.

"What's supposed to happen here?" someone asked. "The message didn't say what we were supposed to do."

"Maybe someone will come speak to us," another suggested.

The confusion grew until it looked as if several were going to leave.

"Talk to them, Ron," Carl said. "We can't waste this opportunity."

"Yeah, you're right," Ron said. He picked his way through the crowd to the front of the hall, then he climbed up on the stage. Walking to the front, he held his arms up, calling for attention. The conversation quieted.

"Hello," he said. "My name is Ron McPherson, and I thank you all for coming."

"What did you call us here for?" somebody shouted. "What are we supposed to do?"

"Well, truth to tell, I didn't call you here, and I don't know who did," Ron said. "I got the same message as you, but I figure that if we are all gathered here, then we may as well take advantage of it."

Two SPS men, dressed as workmen, were in the utility room of the auditorium. They were each carrying a tool bag and, reaching into the bag, they pulled out gas masks. They said nothing as they pulled on the masks, then donned rubber gloves. One of the two men opened an inspection plate to the ventilating system. The other removed a steel container, unscrewed the lid, then, from the cushioned interior of the container, pulled out a test tube. The tube opening was sealed with a cork and, very carefully, he removed the cork, and held it up to look at the liquid.

"You sure that's enough?" the man who had opened the inspection plate asked, his voice muffled by the gas mask.

"It's Sarin. You don't need much," the first man said. He poured it into the ventilating duct, and the stream of air atomized it, then pushed it through the duct to the outlet grate. Sarin gas quickly filled the room.

"If we can organize students all across the country, we can . . ." Ron was saying, but suddenly his nose started to run. Embarrassed, he reached up to wipe it and saw that many others in the room were also experiencing a runny nose. Next, he felt a tightness in his chest.

"What?" someone shouted. "What is happening?"

Ron started having difficulty breathing, then spittle began drooling from his mouth. That was followed almost immediately by vomiting and, even though he was in distress he saw that he wasn't alone. Everyone in the auditorium was having trouble and many were already down. Ron lost all control of his bodily functions, he began to defecate and urinate at the same time. He tried to call out, but he couldn't make a sound. Falling to the floor he began to twitch and jerk, then, in a final series of convulsive spasms, he found it impossible to breathe.

Everything went black.

CHAPTER TEN

Muslimabad

Ohmshidi and Franken were in the presidential quarters of the White House, watching a newscast on TV.

The program began with a full screen shot of the new national flag. The words *CMN, America Enlightened Truth Television* were keyed onto the screen, replaced by the words *Obey Ohmshidi*, then a reverent voice over intoned the opening lines.

> "*All praise be to Allah, the merciful. Whomsoever Allah guides there is none to misguide, and whomsoever Allah misguides there is none to guide. You must live your life in accordance with the Moqaddas Sirata, the Holy Path. Those who do will be blessed. Those who do not will be damned.*
>
> "*You are watching CMN.*
> "*In a series of unrelated incidents today, more than two thousand college students died*

*at several universities when malfunctions of
their ventilation systems introduced some sort of
unknown toxin into the air supply.*

*"Officials at all the schools that were involved
say that they have looked into the problem and
made the necessary adjustments. The purposes of
the simultaneous meetings are still unknown, as
there were no survivors at any site who could
shed light on the incidents.*

*"There has been some suggestion that these
gatherings may have been meeting to protest
against the government. If that was the case,
then the cause of these accidents can easily be
surmised. The accidents were visited upon them
by Allah as punishment against those who would
turn against the Glorious Leader, President for
Life, Mehdi Ohmshidi, may he be blessed by
Allah.*

*"Because of the just punishment of Allah, it
is believed that there will be no more of these
ill-informed and illegal demonstrations against
a righteous government, and the Glorious Leader,
President for Life, Mehdi Ohmshidi, may he be
blessed by Allah.*

"Obey Ohmshidi."

Ohmshidi picked up the remote and clicked
the TV off. He smiled at Franken.

"You did well," he said. "I think, perhaps, those
who would make a demonstration against me will
get the message."

"Thank you, Glorious Leader."

"Of course there are those people down south

to worry about. Where is it? Florida? The people that call themselves Phoenix Rising?"

"It is Alabama, Glorious Leader, and now they are calling themselves United Free America. We are monitoring them closely, but they are so isolated that I think we will see little from them."

"It isn't enough merely to keep them isolated, National Leader Franken. I want them destroyed. It is not good to have any element that is so openly in rebellion. If we are to maintain absolute control over the country, then we must be prepared to put down any dissent, wherever it might be."

"I will find their weakness, Glorious Leader, and when I do, we will exploit that weakness to crush them."

"Good." Ohmshidi walked over to the bar and poured two shots of whiskey. Handing one glass to Franken. "Islam and Moqaddas Sirata prohibit the consumption of alcohol," he said. "Except for the chosen ones," he added with a smile as he took a drink.

Natchitoches, Louisiana

All up and down Parkway Street lawn sprinklers whispered as they worked, and the little bubbles of water that were clinging to the perfectly manicured grass flashed in prismatic colors. In the driveway of one house a father and son threw a baseball back and forth. Next door to the baseball-tossing father and son was a brick colonial house with four bedrooms and two and half baths. This house, like its neighbors, had a long backyard that ended at the bank of the Cane River. This was the house of John "Stump" Patterson, who, in the pre-O time had been a colonel in the U.S. Army.

Stump was standing in his backyard holding a large fork as he watched four steaks sizzling on the charcoal grill. Stump got his nickname when he played football in high school. During football practice a pulling guard was chastised by the coach for not taking Patterson out.

"Damn, Coach, I'd have more luck knocking over a tree stump," the young player said. Patterson was stuck with the name Stump, and it had stayed with him. Powerfully built, the onetime linebacker for LSU looked as if he could still put on pads and a helmet, and take the field once more for the purple and gold.

"Kitty!" Stump called into the house. "How are the baked potatoes coming?"

"The potatoes are done," Kitty said. "So is the salad and bread."

"Then we are about ready to eat. Have you heard from Arlie and Paula?"

"We're here, Stump," Arlie Grant said coming out the back door of the house at that moment. Arlie had been a lawyer in the pre-O time, but only lawyers who were proficient in Sharia Law could practice now, and Arlie refused to learn it.

Stump picked the steaks up one by one, then forked them onto a serving platter where they lay brown and glistening in their own aromatic juices.

Kitty and Paula had set the table on the patio and the four sat down for their meal.

"Damn," Arlie said as he carved into his steak. "It's been a long time since I had a steak like this."

"We wouldn't have it now if it weren't for Jimmy Barnes," Stump replied. "I talked him into butchering and selling me a whole cow."

"Ha. I'm surprised Barnes would accept Moqaddas as payment."

"He doesn't like accepting them any more than I like using them," Stump said. "But we don't have any choice."

"For now," Arlie said.

Stump was just about to take a bite of his steak, but he put the fork back down and looked across the table at Arlie.

"What do you mean, for now?"

"You've heard of United Free America?"

"Yes, who hasn't? I've been following Gregoire on the Internet. What are you getting at, Arlie?"

Arlie pulled a thumb drive from his pocket and showed it to Stump. "After we eat, I want you to take a look this."

"All right," Stump said.

Nothing else was mentioned about the thumb drive until after they had finished their meal. Then they went into Stump's office where Arlie plugged the little memory stick into a USB port, and called it up. On screen was a man, sitting behind a desk, looking into the camera.

"I know him," Stump said. "That's Major Lantz. We served together in Germany when I was a captain and he was a lieutenant."

"I know you know him," Arlie said. "That's one reason I came to you."

"How are we going to hear him if you two don't stop talking?" Kitty asked.

On screen Lantz began to talk.

> *"Six weeks from now on the fourth of July, and the choosing of that date is no accident, we are going to hold a convention at the Old Civic Center in Mobile, Alabama. You, by virtue of viewing this video, are being invited to be a part of the delegation from your state.*
>
> *"It will be our intention to expand upon what we have done with United Free America, to broaden this platform until we have created a completely self-sustaining nation, built upon the same principles that guided the founders of the United States.*
>
> *"Please make every effort to be here.*
>
> *"Thank you, and God bless America."*

"Will Louisiana send a delegation?" Stump asked when the video ended.

"Yes, we are definitely sending a delegation."

"Who all is on the delegation?"

"I'm hoping you will be on it," Arlie said. "I am being very selective as to who I contact. As Jake Lantz says in the video, I have to be very careful and contact only those in whom I have great trust, as well as those who I think will be able to make a valuable contribution. That's why I've come to you."

"Well, I'm flattered and honored, Arlie, that you would think of me."

"Will you accept the invitation?"

"Yes, I will. I'm curious though, who else is on the delegation?"

Arlie smiled. "So far, just you," he said.

Stump laughed. "Just me?"

"Yes. I thought that you might have some suggestions and, between the two of us, we could come up with just the right people."

"How many do you think?"

"The suggestion is that each state bring a delegation of ten."

"I wonder how many states are being invited."

Arlie shook his head. "I don't know how many have been invited, and of course, I have no idea how many will respond. It could be that when this is all said and done that Louisiana and Alabama will be the only two states to respond."

"I would hope that Mississippi does as well," Stump said. "It would be very hard to form a coalition between us and Alabama, if Mississippi is not a part of it."

"I'm sure they will be," Arlie replied.

Fort Morgan

Chris was walking on the beach when he saw someone coming toward him. Because Chris, and the person approaching him, were the only two on the beach, Chris went on the alert. He pulled a small pistol, a DB9, from his pocket and held it concealed by his side as he and the approaching walker closed the distance between them.

Then he recognized Bryan Gates. What was Gates doing here?

Chris and Gates had been friends for a long time, but he was pretty sure that Gates knew he was the one who killed Rahimi. Was Gates working for the AIRE government? Was he here on an extreme prejudice mission?

Gates held up both hands, palms facing Chris, as he came closer.

"You have nothing to fear," Gates said.

Chris nodded, then put his pistol back in his pocket. Smiling, he extended his hand.

"What are you doing down here, Bryan?"

"I've come across some information that somebody needs to know," Bryan said. "And I don't know who I can trust anymore."

Half an hour later Chris took Bryan to the fort museum. Bob and Jake were there, and one of them had just said something funny, because both men were laughing.

"Hey, Chris, what's up?" Bob asked when Chris came in. "Who's that with you?"

"This is Bryan Gates, an old friend of mine from the pre-O days. He has an article from *Pravda* that I think you should read.

"*Pravda*? Is it in Russian?"

"Yes," Chris said. "But Bryan and I both read Russian."

"Then read it to us."

Chris, who was carrying the article, read it to them.

"Do either of you have any insight into the article?" Jake asked, after Chris read it.

"My source is convinced that this was not a suicide," Bryan said. "My source believes that Shaporin was murdered, but Shaporin told him, before he died, that the warheads are missing."

"According to the article, the computer says they were accounted for," Bob said.

Jake chuckled. "Ask Willie how hard it is to change the computer."

"Yes, I guess you have a point there," Bob said.

"Shaporin was convinced the computer program was wrong because he kept a hard copy count of the warheads in his charge, and he found five missing. He told my source that he had gone to his commander with it, and his commander brushed him off."

"Brushed him off because he didn't believe him?" Bob asked.

"Perhaps. But Shaporin thought it might be because his commander might have had a hand in it. He thinks they were deliberately taken from the inventory."

"And you think Shaporin's commander plans to sell those weapons?" Jake said.

"I think he has already sold them."

"To who? To Ohmshidi?"

What do you know of a man named Warren Sorroto?" Bryan asked.

"Sorroto? Yeah, I've heard of him, who hasn't?" Bob replied. "Gregoire used to call him a 'spooky dude,' I believe. He's a very wealthy man who financed socialist groups, and some say he had a lot to do with getting Ohmshidi elected in the first place."

"He had more than just a lot to do with it," Bryan said. "Ohmshidi would have never been elected if it hadn't been for Sorroto."

"Is he that much of a left winger?" Jake asked.

Bryan shook his head. "To tell the truth, I don't think he really has any political position other than his own. From what I've been able to learn, he supported Ohmshidi because he knew that Ohmshidi would destroy the country, and he was counting on that."

"Why in heavens name would anyone want the country destroyed?"

"He made over a hundred billion dollars in the collapse. And now he wants all remaining vestiges destroyed so he can move in and pick up the pieces. That's why I think he is the one who is buying, or perhaps has already bought, five nukes from Russia."

"Are you telling me that Russia would sell nukes to an individual?" Jake asked.

"Remember, this isn't the Russian government," Bryan said. "This is a person, or some persons within the government, who have access to the weapons, and are willing to sell them if they are paid enough money. And believe me, Sorroto has enough money."

"What is your level of confidence in this information?" Chris asked.

"I'd say point niner niner," Bryan replied. "Considering my source."

"Yes, you keep talking about your source. But you haven't given him a name yet," Jake said.

"I'm quite sure that the name won't mean

anything to you," Bryan said. "But I'm equally sure that it will mean something to Chris. My source is Aleksandr Mironov."

"Damn," Chris said. "That's a pretty good source."

"I take it, you know this, Aleksandr Mironov?" Bob asked.

"Yes, I know him. Under the old Soviet regime he was on their United Nations staff, but that was just his cover. He was actually a general in the KGB," Chris said. "What does he tell you, Bryan?"

"Shaporin, the man who the newspaper article says committed suicide, was Mironov's nephew. According to Mironov, Shaporin came to him with this tale, less than two weeks before he died."

"Does he know who has the weapons now? Or, how they are being transported?" Jake asked.

"He either didn't know, or he wouldn't say," Bryan said. "But, Chris, he wants you to meet with someone that you know."

"Who?" Chris asked.

"Nicolai Petrovitch."

"Damn," Chris said with a little chuckle. "It's been a long time since Nicolai and I butted heads."

"Butted heads?" Bob asked.

"We were in the same business, but on opposite sides. I was CIA, he was KGB."

"Does he want to meet Chris here?" Jake asked.

"No, he wants to meet in Russia," Bryan said.

"Chris, I don't know," Bob said. "I mean, if you guys were enemies for all those years, how do you know you can trust him?"

"I'm certain I can trust him," Chris said. "In our

business, people like Nicolai and I have done a lot of things that the average person may consider immoral—and perhaps they are. But among ourselves, we do have a very strong code of conduct."

"So you are saying you want to go."

"It's more than I want to go, Bob. I've got to go. If it is Sorroto we are talking about, and if he gets his hands on these weapons, I don't have the slightest doubt but that he will detonate one of them in Mobile. If he really is planning on picking up the pieces, then he is going to want the whole continent as weak as he can make it and, that means he is going to have to get rid of us, if he can."

"He's right, Bob. If there is any way we can stop those nukes from getting over here, we're going to have to do it," Jake said.

"All right," Bob said. "What will you need?"

"Money to make the trip, then I'll need some walking around money once I get there."

"How much money?"

"Fifty thousand rubles should do it. That's just a little over fifteen hundred dollars."

"We don't have any rubles, but we have Swiss Francs."

"I'll get Willie to look up the exchange," Jake said.

"It's about the same," Chris said. "Fifteen hundred Swiss Francs will take of it. Plus airfare over there and back."

"Sheri Jack is handling our money," Bob said. "I'll get her right on it."

CHAPTER ELEVEN

"Chris, why do you have to make the trip?" Kathy asked that evening.

"I don't know anyone else, other than perhaps Bryan, who could do what has to be done."

"Why doesn't Bryan go?"

"Because Nicolai asked for me, specifically.

"What if it is a trick?" Kathy asked.

"What kind of trick? What do you mean?"

"Aren't you and this man Nicolai on different sides? Aren't you enemies?"

Chris shook his head. "Not any more. There is no Soviet Union, and there is no United States. Nicolai and I are dinosaurs from another age."

"I'm frightened for you."

Chris laughed. "Ha! You are frightened for me? Are you not the same woman who robbed a dozen banks with me?"

"That was different."

"What was different about it?"

"I was with you then. If anything had happened to you, it probably would have happened to me as well. It's easier to share danger with someone you love, than to worry about them when they are far away and there's nothing you can do about it."

"With someone you love?" Chris asked.

Kathy held up her hand. "I know, I know, we don't have that kind of relationship. You were quite clear about it when we first got together. It was just going to be a symbiotic relationship of mutual need and sharing. And I promise you, I won't mention it again."

"Why not?" Chris said, putting his arms around her. "I sort of like the idea."

Their lips met in a deep kiss.

"That was quite a kiss good-bye," Chris said.

"That wasn't good-bye," Kathy said.

"It has to be. I'm leaving in the morning."

"Oh, you can still go," Kathy said. She smiled at him, then, taking him by the hand, started toward the bedroom. "I just have a better way of telling you good-bye, is all."

Taney County

Sorroto was watching the news on America Enlightened Truth Television.

> ". . . in the southern part of Arkansas. The incident occurred two days ago when a group of rebellious infidels who have yet to accept the way of the Holy Path ambushed six members of the State Protective Service. The rebels opened fire, without warning, killing the six peace-loving SPS members, whose presence was only to ensure

*tranquility, and to make certain that the rights
of the Muslim followers are protected.*

*"Our Glorious Leader, President for Life
Ohmshidi, may he be blessed by Allah, has said
that he will not allow rebel groups such as this
one, to harass our people. Here is our Glorious
Leader, President for Life Ohmshidi, may he
be blessed by Allah, delivering a statement from
the White House."*

Ohmshidi appeared on screen.

*"All praise be to Allah, the merciful.
Whomsoever Allah guides there is none to
misguide, and whomsoever Allah misguides
there is none to guide. You must live your life
in accordance with the Moqaddas Sirata, the
Holy Path. Those who do will be blessed. Those
who do not will be damned," Ohmshidi began.*

*"Within the past few days, the infidels among
us, heathens who refuse to join with the majority
in creating a holy nation of peace, have violated
good order by holding illegal demonstrations, and
even going so far as to take up arms against us.
This is a very bold step, and it is something that
I will not allow.*

*"Recently, many of the misguided college
students, who were holding protest rallies, paid
the ultimate price when they learned the wrath of
Allah. More than two thousand students, who
were illegally gathered at the assembly halls of a
dozen universities across the country, were killed
when the ventilations systems in the halls where*

*they were meeting malfunctioned, emitting toxic
fumes. It is now well understood that Allah
smiles upon me, and looks with much disfavor
upon any who would oppose me.*

*"I have ordered National Leader Reed Franken
to put all the SPS on alert, ready to defend itself
against any further attacks. And I caution
anyone who hears this message not to think
you can attack Moqaddas Sirata with impunity."*

Ohmshidi clasped his hands together, prayer-
like, and bowed his head.

*"All praise be to Allah, the merciful.
Whomsoever Allah guides there is none to
misguide, and whomsoever Allah misguides
there is none to guide. You must live your life
in accordance with the Moqaddas Sirata, the
Holy Path. Those who do will be blessed. Those
who do not will be damned."*

Sorroto turned off the TV, and decided it was
about time he paid Ohmshidi a visit. He picked up
the telephone intending to call, but he changed
his mind. If he called, Ohmshidi might construe
that as Sorroto asking to see him. In order to
make certain that Ohmshidi would never forget
his station, relative to Sorroto, Sorroto would
show up in Washington, or Muslimabad, or whatever in hell Ohmshidi was calling it, with no prior
announcement. But Sorroto would not go to the
White House to meet Ohmshidi. He would
demand that Ohmshidi come to him.

Muslimabad

When Warren Sorroto arrived in Muslimabad, he hired a limousine to take him to the Mandarin Oriental Hotel.

"Yes, sir?" the desk clerk said, greeting him deferentially.

"I'll have the Oriental Suite," Sorroto said.

"Oh, I'm sorry, sir, but that suite is occupied."

"Tell them you are sorry, but you made a mistake. Give them a double refund, and offer them their choice of any other suite in the hotel for free."

The hotel clerk started to protest, but, even though he had never met Sorroto, he knew that this was no ordinary customer. "Yes sir," he said, picking up the phone.

Two hours later Sorroto was standing at one of the round windows, looking out toward the water when the telephone rang.

"Yes?"

"He is here, Mr. Sorroto."

"Tell him he may come up," Sorroto said. "Alone."

"But he goes nowhere without his bodyguards."

"He will either come here alone, or he can return to the White House," Sorroto said. "I really don't care which. But if he returns to the White House without seeing me, he will pay a penalty."

There was a pause at the end of the line, then the caller returned. "He'll be right up, Mr. Sorroto."

Sorroto hung up the phone without answering. He was preparing himself a martini when he heard the doorbell. Picking up a remote device he pointed it toward the door and pushed the button. The electric lock buzzed, and the door was pushed open. Ohmshidi came in.

"Would you like a drink?" Sorroto asked.

"Alcohol is banned in the American Islamic Republic of Enlightenment," Ohmshidi said.

"Bullshit. I know you drink, but have it your own way," Sorroto said. He poured his drink into a shaker. "For me, a vodka martini. Shaken, not stirred," he added with a smile. When Ohmshidi made no response, Sorroto looked over at him. "Bond, James Bond."

"I beg your pardon?"

"How the hell did you ever get elected president, knowing so little about the culture and history of this country? Never mind, you weren't elected. I appointed you." Sorroto capped off his comment by taking a swallow of his drink.

"Oh, I wouldn't say that," Ohmshidi replied. "Nobody has enough power to appoint a president."

"Really? Would you like me to demonstrate that power by removing you from office and putting someone else in?"

"No, no, I . . . uh . . . am very grateful for your support."

"Yes, I would think so." Sorroto took another drink and continued to stare at Ohmshidi, who was beginning to show his unease.

"Sit down," Sorroto said. It wasn't a request, it was an order, and Ohmshidi sat, quickly.

"What did you want with me?" Ohmshidi asked.

"I saw the news on television as to how more than two thousand students were holding meetings to demonstrate against you."

"Yes, but they were, uh, taken care of by Allah."

"Don't give me any of your bullshit, Ohmshidi. I know damn well you killed them."

"You did not think that I would allow such a thing as student protests to go unchallenged, did you? If it got out of hand it could spread and cause more problems."

"Yeah," Sorroto said. "Look, I'm not condemning you. You did what you had to do."

"Yes," Ohmshidi said with a sigh of relief. "I am glad that you understand."

"You are also aware, are you not, that resistance to your government is growing all across the South?" Sorroto asked.

"A few isolated incidents here and there," Ohmshidi said. "It's certainly not anything I can't handle. I have spoken with National Leader Franken about it."

"Franken," Sorroto said, making a scoffing sound. "Why you appointed that incompetent fool as head of the SPS, I'll never know."

"I believe that the National Leader will have little difficulty in dealing with these few upstarts."

"I'm not so sure about that. Never underestimate a person's determination to be free."

"Oh, I think that isn't a problem," Ohmshidi said. "I'm told that over ninety percent of the population has converted to Islam so that they can buy goods and services. And as long as I control that, I can keep control over everything."

"I think ninety percent is a vast overestimation. I would say that it is more like sixty percent, and damn few of those are real."

Ohmshidi smiled. "You don't understand. I don't care whether they are real or not. All that is important now is that I have control over them. And as long as I control such things as food, fuel, electricity, and the press, I do have control over them."

"Like I said, Ohmshidi, don't underestimate a person's determination to be free."

"Why are you so concerned about this, anyway? I know that all of your money is in offshore accounts. What difference does it make to you what happens here?"

"It makes a difference to me, because I have plans for this country's future."

Ohmshidi's face reflected an expression of concern.

"You have plans for this country's future?"

"Yes."

"Do your plans include me?"

"Oh yes, they most definitely include you," Sorroto said. "I wouldn't have made you president in the first place, if I didn't want to use you."

"Use me?"

"Yes, Ohmshidi. I intend to use you."

CHAPTER TWELVE

Fort Morgan

Bob was sitting at his computer. For a moment he drummed his fingers on the desk, creating a drum cadence, then, putting his fingers back on the keyboard he resumed his writing.

Langley pulled his long gun out of the saddle holster, and started walking into the canyon, leading his horse. The horse's hooves fell sharply on the stone floor, and echoed loudly back from the canyon walls. The canyon made a forty-five degree turn to the left just in front of him, so he stopped. Right before he got to the turn he slapped his horse on the rump and sent it on through.

The canyon exploded with the sound of gunfire as Dingus Cahill and the Bennetts opened up on what they thought would be their pursuer. Instead, the bullets whizzed harmlessly over the empty saddle of the

riderless horse, raised sparks as they hit
the rocky ground, then whined off into empty
space, echoing and re-echoing in a cacophony
of whines and shrieks.

Bob had written more than 200 Westerns under
at least 40 names, and even though there were no
more Westerns being written, for the simple
reason that there were no more publishers, Bob
found some comfort in doing what he had been
doing for fifty years.

He was about to start a new paragraph when
Jake knocked quietly, then stuck his head in
through the door.

"Mr. President, do you have a moment for us?"
Jake asked.

Bob chuckled. "How about calling me Bob?
And who is us?"

"Tom Jack is with me."

"Sure, come on in."

"Writing?" Jake asked.

"Yes," Bob answered. "I know, people probably
think it's foolish of me to continue to write, especially since there are no legitimate publishers left.
But it's something I used to tell my students whenever I would speak at a writing conference. A real
writer cannot not write, no matter whether he or
she sells or not. Real writers have a divine discon-
tent that drives them to write. So . . ." Bob pointed
to the screen. "Colt Langley rides again."

"What's Colt Langley doing now?" Jake asked.
He had read several of the published Colt Langley

novels, and had been reading this novel as Bob was writing it.

"He's got the three bad guys holed up in a dead-in canyon, and he's going in after them," Bob said.

"Three against one?" Tom asked. "How do you plan to get him out of that?"

"Hey, Tom, you don't know anything about Colt Langley, do you?" Jake asked. "He is one badass dude, I tell you. Why he's killed . . ." Jake looked at Bob. "How many has ole' Langley killed, anyway?"

"Before the publishers all went out of business, there were 40 Colt Langley books, and he generally killed at least six or seven in each one."

"Even if it was only six in each book, that would be 240," Jake said. "So you see Tom? Three bad guys? They'd better be saying their prayers, because they're goin' down."

Tom smiled. "You're right, Colt Langley is one badass dude.

"I'm pretty sure you didn't come here to talk about Colt Langley," Bob said.

"No. I thought you might like to know that we heard from Louisiana. They will be sending a delegation. And, an old army buddy of mine is going to be with them. Colonel Stump Patterson."

"Stump? That's not his real name, is it?"

"If I remember, his real name is John. But I never heard him called anything but Stump. We were together in Germany."

"Germany," Bob said with a smile. "If that doesn't bring back good memories. My favorite tour for the whole time I was in the army was when I was in Germany. I would have extended my tour if I hadn't gotten orders to Vietnam. I was a single officer then, and on flight pay. What could be better?"

"Where were you in Germany?" Jake asked.

"I was stationed at Conn Kaserne in Schweinfurt. There was a bar on Niederwerrner Strasse called the Scotch Bar. A very pretty young *fraulein* named Uta used to hang out there a lot. She's twenty-one, twenty-two maybe, you know, just the age to be perky and—wait. Damn! She'd have to be at least seventy-two now! Never mind."

Jake and Tom laughed.

"I was with D Troop of the 3rd Battalion of the 7th Cavalry," Bob said. "We had our own pipe and drum corps. I'm sure you've heard of us."

"Yeah, yeah," Jake teased. "I got enough of your 'Garry Owen' crap when I was in. I know all about Custer's Own, believe me."

"So, Louisiana is coming. How many states does that make now?"

"Eight," Jake said.

"Are we going to move our capital to Mobile?" Tom asked.

"No, I don't see any reason why we should, do you?" Bob asked.

"No, I don't. Sherri and I are just getting settled in here. We're on the sixth floor of The Dunes, on the north side. There's not a better view on the entire island."

"Tom Murchison, my best friend in the world bought that unit," Bob said, wistfully. "We'd been friends since the third grade, but as adults it was always a long distance friendship. He only got to come to his unit one time before he got cancer and died."

"I'm sorry. It makes me feel bad to think that I'm able to take advantage of that."

Bob smiled. "Well, you've both got the same first name. And knowing Tom as I did, if the cancer hadn't killed him, seeing what Ohmshidi has done to the country would have."

"Too bad he didn't get to enjoy his place. It sure is beautiful."

"How do you know he isn't enjoying it?" Bob asked. "Truth is, sometimes I feel his presence, just like I feel the presence of the men I served with in Vietnam—men whose names are now on the wall. *Were* on the wall, I mean," Bob corrected, bitterly. "We thought their names would be preserved for a thousand years; who would've ever thought that some low-assed bastard would take the wall down?"

"Well, at least we have the satisfaction of knowing that one of our own killed the son of a bitch who did that," Jake said.

"That would be Chris. Has anyone heard from him?" Tom asked.

"I don't think we are likely to hear from him," Bob said. "If we are lucky he will just show up and tell us that the job has been done."

"You know who Chris reminds me of?" Jake asked.

"Who?"

"Your Western hero, Colt Langley." Jake made

the shape of a pistol with his hand, made the sound of firing, then lifted his extended index finger to his lips as if blowing away the gun smoke.

"Have gun, will travel," Jake said.

"That was Paladin," Bob said. "Or more accurately, Richard Boone."

"Who?" Tom asked.

"A TV show back in the late fifties and early sixties," Bob said.

"You people are old!" Tom said, laughing.

"At my age the only alternative to being old is being dead," Bob said. "I'll take being old. Tell me, by the way, have we heard anything from Virdin? His ship is still on patrol, isn't it?"

"Yes, he's guarding the off-shore gas rigs," Tom said.

"Do you think he has everything he needs? I mean, he's only one destroyer."

Tom chuckled. "This isn't the navy you remember, Bob. The *John Paul Jones* has more fire power than the entire Japanese fleet that attacked Pearl Harbor. Believe me, he more than has enough to handle anything that might come up."

At sea on the John Paul Jones

It was just after sunrise and in the east the sun was spreading color through the heavens and painting a long smear of red and gold on the surface of the sea. On the bridge, Captain Stan Virdin was drinking coffee as he took in the beautiful sunrise. Because Virden enjoyed classical music, and because he thought it had a calming effect on the crew, he had the Intermezzo from *Cavalleria Rusticana* broadcast throughout the ship by way of the 1MC.

The *John Paul Jones* had been built as an *Arleigh Burke* class destroyer, and was among the largest destroyers built in the United States. The *Arleigh Burke* class destroyers were the most powerful surface combat vessels ever put to sea. The *John Paul Jones* was a multi-mission ship with a combination of an advanced anti-submarine warfare system, land attack cruise missiles, ship-to-ship missiles, and advanced anti-aircraft and anti-missile weaponry.

When the United States collapsed under Ohmshidi, the American Islamic Republic of Enlightenment took its place and reestablished the military. The destroyer *John Paul Jones* was renamed the *Shapur 1* by the navy of the AIRE, but when the ship was recaptured by the patriots of Firebase Freedom, it was once again called the *John Paul Jones.*

The current mission of the *John Paul Jones* was to protect the offshore gas and oil drilling rigs that the patriots of Firebase Freedom had captured. Those rigs were now producing gas and oil for the use of the patriots who were in open revolt against the AIRE.

"Calling myself an admiral, when we only have one ship, would be a bit of self-aggrandizement, wouldn't it?" Virdin had replied, when he was offered that rank by Bob Varney. I'll be satisfied with the rank of captain."

So it was as Captain Virdin that he took his ship out on patrol.

"Captain, we have surface contact, small vessel approaching at thirty-five knots, bearing one, niner, zero," the radar operator said.

"Thirty-five knots? Damn, that's practically flying," Virdin said. He raised his glasses and looked slightly west of south, but he saw nothing.

"Mr. Pearson, launch the UAV copter," Virdin ordered.

"Aye, sir."

On deck preparations were made to launch the small, unmanned helicopter.

Stand clear of the rotor blades! the 1MC announced.

The craft took off, then started toward the contact. In the CIC room Virdin and the others watched the monitor.

"There it is," someone said.

The contact was a small patrol boat. The boat sprouted four machine guns and what looked like torpedo tubes, and it was heading toward the gas wells, going so fast that it was throwing up quite a rooster tail behind it. Suddenly one of the guns began firing at the UAV.

"Cap'n, we're being fired on."

Virdin pushed a button. "Weapons?"

"Weapons, sir, Lieutenant Langley."

"Do you have the coordinates of the surface contact?"

"Aye, sir."

"Take it out."

"Aye, sir."

Thirty seconds later a Tomahawk missile was launched, and Virdin watched the trailing smoke as it headed toward the horizon. All eyes were glued to the monitor until there was flash of light, then black, as the patrol boat was hit.

There was cheering in the CIC.

"Signalman, send the following message to Phoenix. Sighted armed patrol boat approaching defense area. When we sent a UAV out for further observation, the UAV was fired upon. Patrol boat engaged and sunk."

"Aye aye, sir," the signalman replied.

"Secure from weapons, make ready to recover the UAV."

Fort Morgan, Alabama

When Willie Stark received the message from the *John Paul Jones*, he picked up the phone and called over to headquarters.

Barbara Carter, an attractive eighteen-year-old girl and recent escapee from the Youth Confinement and Enlightenment Center Number 251, took the call.

"Headquarters, Firebase Freedom, this is Barbara."

"Barbara, this is Willie. Is the General there?"

"Just a minute, Captain Stark, and I'll get him."

"Captain Stark? I thought we were beyond that."

"Not when I'm on duty," Barbara replied. It was

an open secret that Barbara and Willie had been seeing each other on an increasingly regular basis.

"You won't be on duty tonight," Willie teased.

"I'll get the general for you," Barbara said. "And we'll see about tonight, tonight," she added, with a smile in her voice.

Jake was talking with Bob Varney and Tom Jack when Barbara knocked on the door, and when Jake looked up at her, she spoke.

"Captain Stark is on the phone, sir."

Jake picked up the phone. "Yes, Willie, what is it?"

"Sir, I just got a FLASH message from Captain Virdin."

"Wait a minute, Willie, I'm going to put you on speaker phone," Jake said. He pushed the button so Bob and Tom could hear as well. "All right, go ahead, what is the message?"

"Sighted armed patrol boat approaching defense area. When we sent a UAV out for further observation, the UAV was fired upon. Patrol boat engaged and sunk."

"Thank you, Willie," Jake said as he punched out of the conversation.

"Did he say he sunk the boat?" Bob asked.

"That's what he said."

"Well, you can't say he isn't decisive. I hope it was a patrol boat, and not some fishing boat."

"Bob, I know Virdin, and I've known him for a long time," Tom said. "If he says it was a patrol boat, you can hang your hat on it."

"Has he always been this decisive?"

"He is someone who was born for command," Tom said. "He isn't afraid to make a decision, but I certainly wouldn't call him rash."

Bob nodded. "All right, good," he said. "He is the kind of man we need in leadership positions if we are going to make this thing work."

CHAPTER THIRTEEN

Moscow

Although Chris had come into "The Company" in the last two years of the Cold War, he had been quite active in his dealings with the Soviet Union, and during those days, Nicolai Petrovich had been his counterpart. Even as the two men represented opposing governments, Chris and Nicolai managed to develop a respect for each other's skills and professionalism and once had actually worked together to defuse what could have been a very dangerous situations. In this cooperation, both had been taking personal risks because many of the things they did would not have been approved by either government. That degree of shared danger gave them a sense of intimacy, as if they were together against the rest of the world.

Nicolai was retired, but Chris knew that Nicolai could get the information he needed. The only question was, would he?

"It has been a long time, my friend," Nicolai

said when Chris called. "And now, with the—unpleasantness—over between our two countries, we can call ourselves friends."

"We were always friends, Nicolai," Chris said. "We were just doing our job."

"Yes, and we did our jobs better than most," Nicolai agreed. "So, tell me, my friend, why, after all these years, do you contact me now?"

"I wanted to give you my condolences on the death of our mutual friend Vladimir Shaporin."

By expressing his condolences, Chris was telling him that he was here in response to Nicolai's request for a meeting.

"Yes, thank you. I am looking forward to seeing you again."

"It has been a long time since I was in Moscow."

"You must see the statue of Peter the Great while you are here. It is a favorite of many tourists," Nicolai said. "I am sure you will enjoy your trip. And, if you get a chance, stop in to see me."

"I will," Chris said.

A time and temperature sign in front of the Park Kultury metro station read *1900—20 degrees.* Realizing that the temperature was expressed in Celsius, Chris estimated the conversion to be just under 70 degrees Fahrenheit. He walked down Krymsky Val Ulitsa to Kaluzhskaya Ploshchad and the giant Lenin statue. Directly opposite the statue of Lenin was the entrance to the Oktyabrskaya metro station. There, Chris took the orange-colored radial line exactly one stop to the Tretyakovskaya station. Leaving the train and reaching the street, he turned left past a McDonald's, crossed the road and stepped into a pedestrian alleyway. Following the alleyway to the Moscow river, he crossed the pedestrian bridge, then, at a point near Gorky Park, stopped to look back toward the small island in the middle of the river. There, rising more than three hundred feet high, was a statue of Peter the Great, standing in the bow of a sailing ship. Though there was nothing aesthetically pleasing about the statue, it was, nevertheless, impressive in its awfulness.

"You are American?"

It was a female voice and looking around, Chris saw a very pretty woman, olive complexioned, with dark hair and big, brown, almond-shaped eyes.

"Yes," Chris said.

The woman smiled and thrust her hip out provocatively. "If you are visiting our country, you need a Russian girl to show you a very good time," she said. "I can do that, and it will not cost you very much."

There was an older couple nearby and they looked over at the young woman with an obvious expression of disapproval. They had been on the metro with Chris and had been speaking German. When the young Russian woman solicited Chris, they turned and walked away.

"You are very pretty," Chris said. "Thanks, but no thanks."

The young woman pushed her lips out in a

pout. "Oh, I am very disappointed," she said. "Nicolai said you would be interested."

"What did you say?" Chris asked, hearing the name Nicolai.

"Come with me, Mr. Carmack," the young woman said. "I will take you to him."

"I'll be damned," Chris said. He laughed. "I had almost forgotten how to play the game."

"My name is Tanya," the girl said as she turned and looked back for him to follow.

The neon sign in front of the club read: PIRAMIDA. Inside the club two very incongruous themes competed—one of ancient Egypt, and the other futuristic fantasy. It was as if this bar was a manifestation of the entire Russian culture, still struggling to emerge into a lifestyle the old Communist society would have called decadent. It was an improbable combination of genres, complete with space-uniformed waiters and a DJ who played loud music from the lap of a giant pharaoh.

Two strippers were gyrating to the music. The place was packed and Tanya reached back to grab Chris's hand as she led him through the crowd. More than once, a very beautiful young woman would find an excuse to rub her body against his as they worked their way through the crowd.

"Leave him alone—he is all mine," Tanya shouted, first in Russian, then in English.

Nicolai Petrovich was sitting in a booth in the back corner. Beside him was a young blond girl, as beautiful as Tanya. When they reached the booth, Tanya introduced her.

"This is Natalie," Tanya said.

Natalie smiled, and extended her hand. "I am pleased to meet you. And this is Nicolai." Natalie pouted at Nicolai. "I am afraid he did not give me his last name."

Nicolai laughed. "You don't give last names to beautiful young women in a place such as this," he said. He looked at Chris. "And your name, sir?"

"It is Christopher."

"Ah, yes, the man who discovered America," Nicolai said. "Tell me, Chris, would you like to see these two beautiful young women perform a sex act for us? They offered to do it for me, but I did not want to pay as much as they ask. So, I told this one to find another person to divide the cost."

"You will like it, I promise you," Tanya said. Moving over to Natalie, she stuck her hand down into the scoop neck of the blonde's top to grab her breast. Leaning toward her, she kissed Natalie, full on the lips.

"Come," Nicolai said. "We must see this show."

Getting up from his seat, Nicolai started after Natalie and Tanya, who were holding hands as they walked in front, leading them toward the stairs at the back of the club. Chris followed.

"Do you need another to watch the show?" a man from one of the nearby booths called out.

"I found them, they are mine," Nicolai replied. "But you are welcome to come watch, if you will pay for it all."

"I thought you would let me watch for free," the man said, and all who were in his booth laughed.

When they reached the top floor, both Natalie and Tanya removed their tops, even as they were walking down the hall, so that the few they encountered were treated to the sight of their near nakedness. The four stepped into a room, then closed the door behind them. Tanya turned on music, then she and Natalie put their tops back on.

"I hope you didn't mind the little charade," Nicolai said.

Chris smiled broadly. "Believe me, I didn't mind it at all."

"I didn't think you would," Nicolai said. He pointed to the two girls. "Tanya is my daughter, Natalie is her very good friend." He laughed. "However, they are not *that* kind of friends," he added. "It was just a way of getting you up here so we could talk."

"Natalie will watch the window and I will watch the door," Tanya said.

"Nicolai, I thank you for agreeing to help me," Chris said.

"At first, I wasn't going to help," Nicolai said. He shook his head. "I don't know what has happened in your country. I hear that America is no more."

"That is true," Chris said. "Our country has been destroyed by incompetence and arrogance."

"But this man, Ohmshidi, he was elected, was he not? By the same democracy that you Americans have always been so proud of?"

"It's as Benjamin Franklin said," Chris replied. "'When the people find that they can vote themselves money, that will herald the end of the republic.' I'm afraid that is what happened, and Ohmshidi was the result."

"Tell me, Chris, where are the men like Truman, Kennedy, Reagan, Khrushchev, Gorbachev, and Yeltsen? Those were men, my friend. They stood at the abyss and kept the world from destroying itself."

"We lived through some historic times, you and I," Chris said. He wasn't sure where Nicolai was going, so he made his response as vague as possible.

"Since you first contacted me, I've done some looking around. Alek was right. Colonel Shaporin did not commit suicide," Nicolai said. "He was murdered by Lieutenant Colonel Leonid Trutnev, his second-in-command."

"You know this for a fact?"

"Shaporin discovered that five nuclear warheads were missing," Nicolai said. "When he tried to find them, he was ordered killed. The warheads are being sent to South America."

"To South America? To what country in South America?" This was a surprise to Chris, who didn't expect them to be going there.

"Not to a country," Nicolai said. "To one man."

Chris nodded. Now this wasn't a surprise. Bryan had already told him that he believed the nukes were being bought by Warren Sorroto.

"Have they been sent yet?"

"I don't think so. I don't know when they are

being sent, and I don't know how. But I know where we can find out."

Sharapovo

The sign on the frosted glass door read: LEONID TRUTNEV, COLONEL, COMMANDANT.

Nicolai had paid the young private at the front gate of the military compound 2,500 rubles to let them into the headquarters building. Once inside, they used a sock-covered flashlight to cut down on the glare as they searched through the filing cabinets. They had been inside the office for only five minutes when Nicolai let out a little exclamation of victory.

"I found it!" he said, looking at the documents in a file folder he was holding. "They were loaded onto a fishing trawler—the *Andre Pashkov*, Russian flagged, 62 feet long, IMO number 8606862. They are to rendezvous at 0900 Zulu on 1 July with a Venezuelan destroyer called the *Felipe Gomez* at latitude minus 15.792254 longitude minus 84.550781."

Chris punched the numbers into his satellite phone, then sent it by text message.

"Inside the building! Come out now!" a voice shouted.

Moving quickly to the window, Chris looked between the blinds. There were at least twenty soldiers standing outside, all pointing their weapons toward the building.

"Damn, this doesn't look good," Chris said.

"This way," Nicolai suggested, pointing to a door at the back. "It leads to the furnace room."

Chris stepped through the door with Nicolai, but just before they left, Nicolai tossed a NFDD (noise and flash diversionary device) grenade back into the room. They heard it go off just as they reached the furnace room. Immediately after the flash-bang grenade went off, the soldiers arrayed around the front of the building opened fire. For fully one minute unabated gunfire continued from the automatic weapons the guards were using.

Because of the season, the coal-burning furnace was cold. But the coal bin was filled with coal, awaiting the winter. Nicolai tossed a thermite grenade into the pile of coal. Within a matter of seconds the coal bin was on fire and flames leaped from the burning coal onto the wooden walls of the bin, then to the walls of the building itself.

"We have to get out of here now," Nicolai said.

The two stepped through the outside door of the furnace room, then dashed through the dark to the car they had left parked behind the building. Just before they reached the car two soldiers appeared. The soldiers opened fire and Nicolai went down.

Chris, armed only with a pistol, fired back, dropping both the soldiers. He hurried over to Nicolai.

"Nicolai, my friend," he said.

"Go," Nicolai said. "Leave me."

"No," Chris said. Scooping the Russian up, Chris pushed him into the backseat of the car, then getting behind the wheel, he started it, driving away just as three soldiers appeared in front of him.

"Halt!"

Instead of stopping, Chris accelerated. The soldiers opened fire on the car and bullets smashed through the windshield and Chris lay down in the seat, steering without looking. He felt the impact of hitting one of the soldiers, then he sat up just in time to miss the building. He started toward the gate but saw two men pushing a barricade across the road. Chris turned the wheel so that the fast moving car was headed directly for the soldiers. At first they tried to speed up closing the barricade, but seeing the car coming fast toward them, they abandoned their efforts and leaped to safety just as the car sped through.

Chapter Fourteen

Chris was driving through the dark, without lights, doing more than ninety miles an hour. Once he opened up a little distance from the camp, he slowed the car until he reached a curve in the road. A long, high growth of shrubbery edged the road at this point and he steered the car behind the shrubbery, then stopped.

There was another car in front of them, but this was by design because according to their plan, whether they had encountered difficulty or not, they were going to change cars here.

Tanya got out of the other car and ran back.

"Papa!" she shouted.

Chris got out of the car then ran around to open the back door.

"You are a good driver, my friend," Nicolai gasped.

"Papa!" Tanya said again, this time a cry, more than a shout.

"Don't worry, daughter, I have been shot worse

before," Nicolai said. "Chris has shot me worse before."

"I've never shot you, Nicolai."

"No? Well, no matter, I have been so many times shot that I can no longer remember who has shot me."

"Can you walk?" Chris asked.

"With help, I can walk."

Chris helped Nicolai from the car then, supported by Chris and Tanya, Nicolai managed to walk to the other car.

"Put him in here," Tanya said, opening the trunk.

Chris helped Nicolai get into the trunk, then was surprised when Tanya pulled a false bottom down so that he was completely hidden.

Even as they were getting into the car two military cars, coming from the Sharapovo camp Chris and Nicolai had just left, drove by very fast on the road on the other side of the hedgerow, not having seen the two cars parked in the dark. Tanya pulled up onto the road behind the speeding military cars, then started back toward Moscow at a normal speed.

"I'm sorry about your father, Tanya," Chris said.

"As Papa said, he has been shot before," Tanya said. "My father is very strong. I think he will be all right."

Chris chuckled. "He is a tough old buzzard, all right, I agree with you on that," he said.

Ahead, they saw a military car pulled across the road to block traffic. Chris pulled his pistol.

"No, wait, put the gun away," Tanya said. "It will

be better to bluff our way through. Reaching into her purse, she pulled out a tube of lipstick. "Put a little smear on your mouth," she said. "Then reach behind and unsnap my bra."

Chris did so and Tanya wriggled out of her brassiere. Then leaving the top three buttons of her blouse open to expose her bare breasts underneath, she lay the bra across her lap.

She slowed the car, then stopped as they approached the roadblock. A young soldier, carrying a flashlight, came toward them. "Cover your face with your hands," Tanya said as she rolled the window down.

When the soldier reached the car, he shined his light inside.

"Why have you stopped us?" Tanya asked.

"Isn't it late for you to be out driving?" the soldier asked.

"The kind of business I am in is best conducted at night," Tanya said.

"What kind of business would that be?" the soldier asked.

Smiling seductively at him, Tanya turned her body in such a way as to open a gap in her shirt, allowing the soldier to see her bare breast. Unabashedly, the soldier shined the beam of his light on her breast, which was exposed all the way to the nipple.

"If you were not such a young virgin boy, you would not have to ask that question," Tanya teased.

"I am not a virgin!" the young soldier responded adamantly.

"Oh? Too bad," Tanya said. She took the soldier's hand and placed it just inside her blouse, on her bare breast. "I do virgins for free."

"What's going on there, Khristenko?" the other soldier called to him.

Khristenko cleared his throat. "Nothing, sergeant, I am just examining the car."

"You," Khristenko said to Chris. "Why is your face covered?"

"He is an important businessman who lives in Moscow. I think his wife would not want to see him with a girl like me," Tanya said. "Are you going to arrest us? When did the army start enforcing such laws?"

"Put your hands down," Khristenko ordered.

Chris lowered his hands and the soldier shined the light on his face. The bit of lipstick smear was clearly visible in the beam.

"Why, you are an old man!" Khristenko said accusingly. "You should be ashamed for being with such a young woman."

"Darling, old men are my best customers," Tanya said. "Now, are you going to let us go, or arrest us?"

Khristenko stepped back from the car and waved them on. "They are of no importance," he called to the other soldier.

The other soldier shined his flashlight on the car as it passed, and Tanya gave him as big a smile as she had Khristenko.

"We need to get your father to the hospital," Chris said as they drove away.

"No, not a hospital, they would ask too many

questions. I know a place to take him. They do a good job and they ask no questions."

"Good."

"Did you get what you needed."

"Yes."

"I am glad. If my father would die from these wounds, I would not want his death to be in vain."

"I'm not going to die from bullet wounds." Nicolai said and, turning, Chris saw that the back seat was down and his friend was crawling through from the trunk. "But if I had stayed in there much longer, I might have suffocated."

Fort Morgan

"General, we have a text contact from Chris," Willie said, coming into the office Jake shared with Bob.

"What does it say?"

"Five nuclear devices were loaded onto a fishing trawler—the *Andre Pashkov,* Russian flagged, 62 feet long, IMO number 8606862. They are to rendezvous at 0900 Zulu on 1 July with a Venezuelan destroyer called the *Felipe Gomez* at coordinates latitude minus15.792254 longitude minus 84.550781."

Jake plotted the coordinates. "That's just off Guatemala. And oh nine hundred, zulu, that would be fourteen hundred our time, day after tomorrow."

"That gives Virdin plenty of time to get there with the *John Paul Jones,*" Tom said.

"Yes, we'll order him there to sink the ship," Jake said.

"No," Bob said. "Why sink the ship? Let's board the ship and confiscate the nukes. Do you have any idea what that would do to our military status? We would instantly become a nuclear power, one of only nine such nations in the world."

"What if something goes wrong and they decide to set off one of the bombs? It would take out the *John Paul Jones* and its entire crew," Jake said.

"These are Russians, not Islamic extremists," Bob said. "I don't think there is much danger of them setting off the bombs and killing themselves."

"I think Bob's right," Tom said. "And if you can get me aboard the *John Paul Jones*, I'll lead the boarding party onto the Russian trawler, and we'll take the nukes."

"All right, Tom, I'll get you on board. Willie, contact the *John Paul Jones* and tell them what we're up to," Jake said.

"Yes, sir."

"What will you need, Tom?"

"Deon, if he'll agree to go with me."

Jake chuckled. "Once Deon gets word of this, you'd have to tie him down to keep him back. I think you can count on him going with you."

"You're damn straight I'm going," Deon said when he was apprised of the mission. "When do we leave?"

"As soon as we can get our gear together and say our good-byes," Tom said.

* * *

Tom and Sheri were standing out on the balcony of their sixth floor condo in The Dunes. From here they had a tremendous view of the Gulf, and the offshore drilling rigs that Tom had helped liberate.

"I know you have to do it," Sheri said. "But I don't have to like it."

"Sheri, there's no doubt in my mind, but that these nukes are meant to be used on us. We can't let that happen."

"But do we have to try and capture them? Can't we just sink the boat they are on?"

"I have the authority to do that, and if I see that we can't take them, I'll do that. But they are on a fishing trawler. I doubt that the people with them are military, because from all we've been able to gather, none of this is sanctioned by the Russian government. And even if the people with the nukes are military, how many can you get on a fishing trawler? This will be a piece of cake. We have the advantage of surprise, and probably numbers. Don't worry about it."

"I have to worry about it, because you damn sure won't."

Tom smiled. "I don't need to worry about it. You are worrying enough for both of us. And consider this. It's like Bob said. Taking these weapons will give us a huge edge over the AIRE. Enough of an edge that it might even keep them from any military action against us."

"I don't have to tell you to be careful, do I?"

"I don't know, maybe you should, otherwise I might not be."

Sheri smiled. "All right, don't be careful. See if I care."

"Well, if that's the way you feel about it."

"Be careful," Sheri said, kissing him.

The next day Tom, Deon, and eight more men were delivered by an SH-60 helicopter to the *John Paul Jones*. The helicopter touched down on the after helo-pad and as Tom stepped out he was met by Stan Virdin.

"Tom," Captain Virdin said with a warm smile. "Welcome aboard."

"It's good to be here," Tom said.

"Come on to the wardroom," Virdin invited. "We'll discuss great and weighty things."

"Captain Virdin, this is army Captain Deon Pratt."

"Captain Pratt, I'm pleased to meet you. Please join Commander—" Virdin started, then he stopped and looked at Tom. Just exactly what is your rank in this new military we're putting together?"

"Why, didn't you know, Stan? I'm an admiral now."

"Is that a fact?" Virdin asked skeptically.

"I think that's what Jake called me. Or was it 'asswipe'? I know it started with an *A*."

"Now that, I *can* believe."

"Actually the subject hasn't come up. I guess

I'm like the NCIS, I'll just assume whatever rank I need for the job."

Virdin chuckled. "Now, that's the kind of rank to have."

Deon looked around the wardroom at the paneled walls, the leather chairs, the long, polished table. "Damn, you officers live fine, don't you?"

"What do you mean *you* officers?" Tom asked. "You're an officer too, now."

"Yeah," Deon said, a broad smile spreading across his face. "Yeah that's right, I am an officer now, aren't I? I had to work for a living for so long that sometimes I forget."

The steward brought coffee, and after he left, Virdin got down to business.

"Okay," he said. "I was told you would bring me up to speed once you were on board. You're on board, so what's going on?"

Tom showed Stan the coordinates they had received from Chris Carmack.

"We are to proceed to this place at flank speed. There we will intercept a fishing trawler, the *Andre Pashkov*, Russian flagged, 62 feet long, IMO number 8606862. The *Pashkov* plans to rendezvous at 0900 Zulu on 1 July with a Venezuelan destroyer called the *Felipe Gomez* at those coordinates. We are to interrupt that rendezvous and take on board the cargo being carried by the fishing trawler."

"Hmm, the cargo must be pretty important," Virdin said.

"Five nuclear warheads," Tom said.

"Damn! Nukes? Look, this isn't a bunch of Islamic terrorists who are so eager to go see their seventy-two virgins that they'll set one of those bombs off, are they? I mean, you did say they are Russians."

"Yes, they are Russians," Tom said. Then he added, "We think."

Virdin walked over to a sideboard, opened a drawer, pulled out a bottle of liquor and poured a splash into his cup.

"Since when were navy ships authorized liquor on board?" Tom asked.

"Medicinal," Virdin replied. "You *think* they are Russians?"

"We're pretty sure."

"Pretty sure?" he asked.

Tom nodded. "Yeah, well, we're pretty much sure."

Virdin drank his coffee. "That's . . . reassuring," he said.

CHAPTER FIFTEEN

Fort Morgan

Although Abraham Lincoln used the technology of the telegraph to follow significant battles during the Civil War, he had to do so in the telegraph room of the War Department because the White House had no telegraph service. Franklin Roosevelt was the first president to actually have a war room. FDR's war room, adjacent to the Diplomatic Reception Room, consisted of little more than tables, chairs, telephones, and maps with acetate covering to allow situation updates to be posted by grease pencil.

Thanks to Willie Stark, and the geeks who had come on board since the freedom movement had started, the onetime Fort Morgan museum was filled with an array of technical equipment. President Bob Varney, General Jake Lantz, Willie Stark, Karen Lantz, Julie Norton, Sheri Jack, and Barbara Carter were in the improvised war room observing a live satellite video feed of the operation against the *Pashkov* and the *Gomez*. Over six large high-definition flat-screen television screens, they watched as the SH-60 lifted from the deck of the *John Paul Jones*.

"*Phoenix,* John Paul Jones *CIC, over.*" The sound came, clearly, from a large speaker.

"*John Paul Jones* CIC, this is Phoenix," Willie Stark replied.

"*Call when you have visual from Mad Dog.*" Mad Dog was the call sign from the Blackhawk helicopter.

"Roger."

In addition to the video coming from the deck of the *John Paul Jones*, they could also see video coming from cameras mounted on the external stores service system of the helicopter, and they could hear the radio transmissions between the CIC (Command Information Center) and the strike force.

"*John Paul Jones*, CIC, this is Phoenix. We have a visual."

Even as Willie Stark reported his visual, the TV screens that were displaying the video camera feeds from the helicopter showed the Russian trawler and the Venezuelan destroyer on the ocean below. The two vessels had come together.

"*Phoenix, this is Mad Dog, do you have the video?*" Tom asked from the helicopter.

"We have the video, Mad Dog," Bob replied. "Ask your pilot to make one low pass over the two ships, then give me a freeze frame. I'd like to get a look at what they are carrying."

"*Will do.*"

Then a moment later, Tom's voice came back. *"Beginning the pass now."*

On the screen that was receiving video from the helicopter, the horizon suddenly tilted sharply to the left as the pilot made a ninety degree turn.

For just a moment Bob had a flashback, and he could feel himself back in the right seat of a UH-1D. Subconsciously his hand moved the cyclic stick to the right, and, through a deeply imbedded ghost memory, his foot applied pressure to the right anti-torque pedal.

Through the camera lens, Bob, Jake, and the others watching saw the aircraft level out, then head straight for the Russian trawler. The helicopter was so low that, when it approached the boat it had to climb, slightly, to keep from crashing into it. Then the horizon dropped away so that only sky could be seen, and Bob could practically feel the collective stick under his armpit as the pilot had put it into a rather steep climb.

"Freeze frame coming up," Captain Virdin said from the *John Paul Jones.*

The picture on the screen changed from sky to a still picture of the deck of the boat. There were six men on the deck of the *Pashkov* and they could be seen so clearly that everyone who was watching the video could actually pick out moles and imperfections on their faces.

"There they are, Bob!" Jake said.

Bob saw, too, what they were looking for: five oblong tubes, each marked with the international symbol for radioactive material.

"Do they look like soldiers to you?" Bob asked.

"No, they don't."

"Whoa! We're taking fire here!" Tom's voice suddenly called.

"From the trawler?" Bob asked in surprise.

"No, from the rendezvous ship . . . the Gomez*!"*

"Captain Virdin, do you have the *Gomez* in sight?"

"Aye, aye, Mr. President." Virdin's voice came back over the speaker.

"Take it out. I say again, Take it out," Bob ordered.

Onboard the John Paul Jones

"Lieutenant Lester, what kind of activity do you see?" Virdin asked.

Lester was looking at the Venezuelan ship through his binoculars.

"Sir, they've fired at the helo, and they're clearing away their missile tubes."

"Sound general quarters," Virdin ordered.

Hitting a button that sounded a klaxon throughout the ship, the boatswain's mate of the watch brought the silver call, cupped in his right hand, to his lips and let fly a long shrill whistle. His voice then barked over the 1MC.

"Now general quarters! Now general quarters! All hands, man your battle stations!"

Again, the klaxon sounded, and again the boatswain mate's whistle rose in pitch, then fell.

"Now general quarters! Now general quarters! All hands, man your battle stations!"

The CIC, below decks just below the bridge, bristled with radar screens, infrared imaging screens, computer monitors, and an array of switches and dials. Virdin picked up the phone. "Weapons!" he barked.

"Lieutenant Langley, sir. Weapons manned and ready!"

"Missiles incoming, sir!" one of the CIC operators called out.

"Weapons, engage!"

The ship echoed with the sound of the four Phalanx weapons firing. Several thousand rounds per minute of forty millimeter shells lashed out toward the two incoming missiles. Both missiles were destroyed.

Virdin picked up the phone.

"Weapons?"

"Weapons, aye. Lieutenant Langley, sir."

"Launch Tomahawk."

"Aye, aye, sir."

Fort Morgan

Because of the live-feed video cameras, Bob, Jake, and the others were able to watch the attack from the helicopter's perspective. They watched the Tomahawk missile, riding on a column of flame, streak toward the Venezuelan destroyer at supersonic speed.

As the missile impacted, the ship exploded in a tremendous ball of fire. The explosion caused instantaneous condensation of the air around it, so that the shock waves that formed could actually be seen emanating out from the fireball. The helicopter flew through the smoke, then did a very sharp one-hundred-eighty degree turn to get another look.

The ship was burning profusely, and going down by the bow.

The helicopter then made another pass toward the fishing trawler and seven men could be seen standing on the deck with their hands over their heads.

"General," Bryan said. "If you can get me patched through to that boat, I think I can get them to cooperate."

"All right. Willie, can we do that?"

"Yes, sir, we can do it through the *John Paul Jones*," Willie replied.

"Captain, Virdin, open your channel to us. We're going to try and speak to the captain of the Russian trawler."

"Give me a couple of seconds, General. We'll try and reach them on 156.8 megahertz, that's the international distress."

"Captain, this is Bryan Gates. Open that channel and I'll call them."

"All right," Virdin said. Then, a moment later, *"Mr. Gates, go ahead, the channel is open."*

"Внимание Пашков. Вы должны позволить нам на борт вашего судна. Если вы будете сопротивляться, вы будете потоплены."

Bryan translated for the others. "I told them that they must allow us to board their vessel. If they resist, they will be sunk."

The reply from the captain of the *Pashkov* came in English.

"A fishing boat we are, in international waters. It is no right you have to come aboard." The voice spoke with a Russian accent.

"As you see, General, he speaks English. You can take it from here."

"Pashkov, we are coming aboard to relieve you of your cargo," Jake said. "Make no resistance or your boat will be sunk. Commander Jack, are you on this push?"

"Aye, aye, sir."

"You can take over from here."

Onboard the helicopter

"Captain of the *Pashkov,* this is the helicopter on your port side," Tom said. "Move all of your men to the front of the boat. Stand there with your hands in the air. We are coming aboard. If any of you resist us, we will shoot all of you."

"We will not resist," the heavily accented voice replied.

"Good move," Tom said. Then to the pilot, "Take us to the rear of the boat, then come to a hover so we can jump down."

The pilot followed Tom's instructions, moving to the rear of the fishing trawler then holding it in a hover that allowed the door gunner to keep the crew of the boat covered while Tom, Deon, and the rest of his men dropped down onto the rear deck. When all were aboard, the helicopter pulled away.

Tom and the others kept their weapons pointed toward the Russians.

"All right, who was I talking to? Which one of you is the captain?"

"He is Captain," one of the crewmen said. "To me you were talking because English I can speak."

"Are you military?"

"No. We are fishermen."

Tom pointed to the five enclosed tubes. "I suppose those are fishing poles."

"That is cargo we were to deliver."

"Cargo? Is that what you are calling it?"

The interpreter said something to the man he had pointed out as the captain of the vessel. The captain spoke, then the interpreter translated.

"We were paid to come to this place and meet the *Gomez*. There we were to transfer the medical cargo."

"Medical cargo? Is that what you think it is?"

"Yes. As you can see, it has the medical markings."

"Have you opened one of the containers?"

"We were told not to. There is," he made a circular motion with his hand, "as in Chernobyl."

"Radioactive material. You're damn right there is," Tom said. He spoke into his radio. "*John Paul Jones*, come in."

"*John Paul Jones.*"

"Send a gig over. You can take us and the cargo back."

Clicking off the radio, Tom walked over to

look at the tubes. They did have both medical and radiological markings on them.

"We are taking this with us."

"No," the captain said, speaking in English.

"Well now," Tom said with smile. "So you do speak English. Playing a game with me, were you?"

"I have taken money to deliver this. I cannot let you take it."

"Looks to me, Captain, like you don't have any choice," Tom said. "The ship you were supposed to give it to went down. What will you do with this if you take it back?"

The captain and the others spoke among themselves for a moment, speaking in Russian so Tom had no idea what they were saying.

"How much were you paid?" Tom asked.

"Five hundred thousand rubles."

"That's a lot of money just for delivering radioactive markers for medical use, don't you think?"

"We were told not to ask questions."

"Commander, the Captain's gig is coming abeam," one of Tom's men said.

"Captain, I have a solution to your problem," Tom said. "All you have to do is tell your people that you did deliver your cargo to the *Gomez*. I'm sure that the sinking of the *Gomez* will be world news soon enough. Your people will just assume that the ship went down after you made your delivery. That way, you can keep the money you were given, and nobody need be the wiser."

The Russian captain spoke to the others, then

there were smiles and affirmative nods. The Russian captain, also smiling, spoke to Tom.

"Yes," he said. "Yes, that is a good idea. Shall my men help you load the items?"

Tom returned the smile. "Yes, thank you. I appreciate that."

CHAPTER SIXTEEN

Fort Morgan

"Are you worried that only eight states are sending a delegation?" Karen Lantz asked, as she affixed stars to the collar of her husband's khaki shirt. Although the others had been referring to him as general, it was not until today, that he would actually don the uniform and insignia of a general.

"No, I'm not worried. I think that's a good start, and I believe that as we began to organize, other states will join us," Jake said easily.

"I'm not so sure," Karen replied.

"Why aren't you sure?"

"Well, think about it, Jake. They just declared themselves free from one union, why would they want to enter another one?"

"M.A.S.," Jake said.

"M.A.S.?"

"Mutual assured survival," Jake said. "If we all

band together, it is much less likely that AIRE will be able to do anything."

"You are probably right. Here you go, General Lantz," Karen said with a smile as she held the shirt out toward him.

"What do you think about our new uniforms?" Jake asked.

"They are sort of drab, aren't they? Tan?"

"Ha," Jake said. "Bob said this is exactly like the khaki uniforms he used to wear when he was in the army. He'll probably tear up with nostalgia when he sees me."

"We're about to find out," Karen said.

"What do you mean?"

"Here's Bob now."

Karen answered the door before Bob Varney could ring the bell.

"Hi, Bob, come on in. Want some coffee?"

"By inviting me for coffee, I assume you are telling me that Jake isn't quite ready."

"Come on, Bob," Jake said from just inside the house. "I'm a general now. Generals don't have to hurry for anyone."

"So you mean that even now, when we have the opportunity to start everything all over, we're still going to keep the tradition of Generals being late?" Bob asked with a little chuckle.

"Not for too long. I'm ready now," Jake said.

"Are we flying over?"

Jake shook his head. "Marc says we need a new pitch change link for the tail rotor, so I called Gary. He's going to run us across the bay in his boat."

"Good idea."

"Is Tom Jack going with us?" Jake asked.

"Tom is chomping at the bit, I don't think we can keep him away," Bob said.

"Tom, Deon, and the others did a good piece of work with that Russian trawler," Jake said.

"Yes, they did," Bob said. "Willie and Marcus said the weapons aren't armed, and I guess that makes sense. I don't suppose you would want to take a chance on shipping them while they are armed."

Jake chuckled. "It's not something I'd want to do. I wonder if that Russian crew actually knew what they were carrying."

"I don't know," Bob said. "But they were paid half a million rubles. They had to be a little suspicious."

"We've got them in one of the casements down at the fort, and we've sealed the casement shut. It's going to take quite an effort to get any of them out," Jake said.

"Good. I think that by intercepting them, we may well have prevented any more detonations here, and by here, I'm referring to all of what was the USA," Bob said.

"I believe you are right."

"Now, the question is, do we let anyone know that we have them? Just having them is a tremendous projection of power, whether we use them or not," Bob said. "At any rate, I'm not ready to let the secret out, yet. Not even to those who will be joining us."

"I agree. Besides, look at Israel. They have

never acknowledged having nuclear weapons, but everyone knows they do have them," Jake said.

"Or at least, they think they have them. And so far, that has been just as effective."

Jake picked up his long narrow cap. "Did you wear this kind of hat?"

"Oh yes," Bob answered.

"What do you call them?"

Bob smiled. "They are garrison caps. The men had another, not quite so nice a word for them, and I'd rather not say it in front of a lady."

"Well, aren't you a gentleman?" Karen said. "But I was in the army for six years, there aren't many words I haven't heard."

"I'm ready if you are," Jake said as he put the cap on.

"Knock 'em dead," Karen said as she kissed Jake good-bye.

"You're sure you don't want to come with me?"

"I'm the Secretary of State. We don't have a vice president and that means with President Varney gone, I have to run the country."

"Oh Lord, we're in trouble now," Jake teased.

Tom was out front, hitting golf balls, lofting them over the beach and dropping them into the surf.

"Hey, when are we going to organize our first national golf tournament?" Tom asked. "We've got twelve golf courses here, it's not like we don't have a place for it."

"What about we put you in charge of it?" Bob suggested.

"Fine, as long as I get to play in it. I've always

wanted to play in a national tournament. Okay . . . it's a little nation . . . but it'll still be a national."

"It may not be all that small after today," Jake said. "We have nine states meeting to organize."

"Do you think they will all sign on?" Tom asked.

"I think they are probably predisposed to," Bob answered. "Otherwise I don't think that many would have responded."

Bob used his golf cart to drive the three of them across the Fort Morgan Highway to the Gulf Shore Marina. At one time the marina had been very busy, not only as a home base for pleasure craft, but also for deep sea fishing boats. Gary Bryant was the captain of such a boat and he had been an active participant in the Firebase Freedom movement, providing them with fresh fish in the early days of the movement when just surviving was a priority. He had also driven the boat for the assault team that had attacked the first offshore gas rig.

Since fuel was no longer as critical as it had once been, the marina was gradually returning to its original level of business and when Jake, Bob, and Tom walked out onto the pier they saw three boats preparing to go out. One of the boats was Gary's *Red Eye*. He was waiting for them when they arrived.

The men greeted each other, then climbed aboard Gary's boat. One minute later they were speeding across the bay toward Mobile.

* * *

The automobile traffic in Mobile had nearly returned to its pre-O days. Vehicular traffic was coming back because three fourths of the cars in Mobile had been converted to run on natural gas which, as the wells were just offshore from Alabama, was in almost unlimited supply. Patriots had also taken control of, and reopened, the oil refineries in Mobile, Pascagoula, Mississippi, and Baton Rouge, Louisiana. Drilling was restarted in the Citronelle Oil Dome just outside Mobile. In addition, the offshore oil rigs just off the coast of Louisiana were once again producing crude oil.

From the port, Jake, Bob, and Tom caught a taxi to the Mobile Civic Center where they saw a huge banner stretched above the doors of the Civic Center.

Welcome to the UNITED FREE AMERICA CONSTITUTIONAL CONVENTION

There were several cars, and many more people milling around out front, some handing out printed material.

"What are they handing out?" Tom asked.

"Copies of the proposed constitution," Bob said.

"The one you wrote?"

"I can't take credit for all of it," Bob said. "I'm going to have to share authorship with Thomas Jefferson. All I did was add three amendments."

Because Jake and Bob had a major role in organizing the convention, they would occupy seats on the dais in the theater. There were two larger areas in the Civic Center, the expo hall and the arena, but they were too large.

"We want enough people that we have a good representation for all the participating states," Bob pointed out. "But we don't want so many as to make the meeting unwieldy."

The reconstituted Mobile Symphony Orchestra was playing music, at the moment it was *Claire de Lune* by Debussy. The soothing strains of the music had a calming effect on the gathering delegates.

There were television cameras in the auditorium, and the broadcast was being sent, not only by satellite, but by Internet. It was calculated that as many as twenty million, all across the continent, would watch, some with covert support, others with open antagonism, but all with interest in this event that could change America.

A voice-over intoned the opening of the proceedings.

"From the Civic Center in Mobile, Alabama, we bring you a live broadcast of the United Free America Constitutional Convention.

"Join with us as we take these first steps to lift our battered nation up from the depths of despair to a rebirth of freedom. Ladies and gentlemen, Mr. Tom Jack."

Because Bob Varney was President of Pleasure Island and Mobile, it fell upon him to conduct the meeting, and he was introduced, by Tom Jack. Tom smiled, and waited until the applause died before he began speaking.

"One year ago, like many of you who are

watching this broadcast, my wife and I were living under the hobnailed boot of oppression. We had our means of making a living taken from us, we had our freedom of religion, and freedom of speech taken from us, we became, literally, prisoners of a society that is certainly the equal, if not even more oppressive, than the Nazi regime of Germany in the last century.

"But we heard about a group of patriots who were defying the evil of Moqaddas Sirata, so we rode our bicycles seven hundred and fifty miles to join this group. When we arrived here, we met men and women who will go down in history, not as founders of a new country, but as saviors of the old, saviors of the nation that we grew up in, loved, and served.

"The man you are about to meet is one of the principals of that movement. He served our country in Vietnam where he was awarded the Distinguished Flying Cross, the Air Medal with the "V" for valor, the Purple Heart, and the Bronze Star. He is also an accomplished author whose books many of you have read.

"And now, it is my honor and privilege to introduce one of those heroes, the provisional president of United Free America, Robert Varney."

There was a generous round of applause as Bob stepped up to podium and looked out over the attendees.

At that moment Bob had a sudden flashback to the days of pre-O. Bob had been a novelist, and quite a successful one. He had also been a frequent speaker at writers' conferences all over the country. He was a good and entertaining speaker, and he had fond memories of the writers' workshops. He missed them, as he missed writing, and as he missed the times he and Ellen would go into New York for meetings with his editor or agent.

"My fellow patriots," he began. "On this day we will make history. As did the founders of the United States so long ago, we offer our support for this movement, with a firm reliance on the protection of Divine Providence, and to this end we mutually pledge to each other our lives, our fortunes, and our sacred honor. In this time and in this place, we will be laying the foundations of a government of freedom, individual liberty, and self-reliance.

"I propose that we, herein assembled, adopt the Constitution of the United States as it stands, but, with these added amendments. And, as I read them off to you, please follow me on the handouts you have received."

There was a rustle of movement as the delegates picked up their paper to follow along as Bob read.

"Amendment Twenty-nine repeals the twenty-eighth amendment, which allowed naturalized citizens to be elected to the office of President of the United States. It was that amendment that resulted in the disastrous election of Mehdi Ohmshidi, and the subsequent destruction of America.

"Amendment Thirty; public expression of religion—There shall be no law to inhibit the expression of religion in a public place, nor shall anyone be compelled to participate in the public expression thereof.

"Amendment Thirty-one; term limits—The president shall be limited to one six-year term. Members of the House of Representatives are limited to two two-year terms. Members of the Senate are limited to two four-year terms. There shall be no perks provided for members of the government that are not provided for the citizens at large.

Amendment Thirty-two; repeal of Amendment Eighteen—there will be no income tax. There will instead, be a value-added tax on all goods and services. The federal government will be responsible for maintaining the military. States, which can also apply sales tax, will be responsible for police, schools, and roads.

Amendment Thirty-three—there will be no federal programs such as welfare, aid to dependent children, or food stamps. If individual states want such a program, they shall be responsible for them.

As Bob read each amendment, those in the audience responded with applause.

After the reading of proposed amendments, the meeting broke out into ten different discussion groups, each group with at least one voting member from each state. All ten panels would discuss all six amendments. In addition each panel had a specific proposal to discuss, the idea being that after an in-depth discussion they would bring to the whole body their recommendation as to whether the amendments, and the other proposals being discussed, should be approved, or disapproved. After a long day of spirited discussion, the conference attendees gathered in the dining hall for dinner.

CHAPTER SEVENTEEN

After dinner, Jake Lantz stepped up to the podium. The silver stars on his collar flashed as they caught the overhead light.

"In a speech that Ohmshidi gave before he was elected president, he gave us a glimpse into his political agenda. This is what he said."

Jake picked up a sheet of paper and began reading from it.

"*I see a world united! A world at peace! A world where there are no rich and there are no poor, a world of universal equality and brotherhood.*

"*Such a world will surely come, my friends, but it will never be as long as we are divided by such things as religion, patriotism, the greed of capitalism, and the evil of so-called honorable military service. There is nothing honorable about fighting a war to advance one nation's principles over another. One world, one people, one government!*"

Jake lay the paper down.

"One man warned us of this, one man started beating the tocsin long before anyone else perceived that we were aboard the Titanic, on a collision course with an iceberg.

"To say that we should have listened is an understatement. Life is full of 'we should have' and 'if only.' Ladies and gentlemen, we have that oracle with us today, and it gives me great pleasure to introduce our keynote speaker, Mr. George Gregoire."

There was generous applause at the introduction, and George Gregoire stepped up to the podium, smiling at his audience. He stood there for a moment, then lifted his clinched right fist high into the air.

"I have a new dream!" he shouted. His shout was met with applause.

"Hello, America. I say hello America, because I know that, through the technical acumen of our dedicated electronic wizards that, despite all efforts to prevent it, this signal is going out all over the continent. And to those of you who are huddled in your homes in such places as New York, Illinois, and California, with the windows blocked out so you can watch us without fear of being discovered by the evil under which you are being forced to live, what we do here today is as much for you as it is for those who are gathered here for this historic conference. Do not think for one moment, my brother and sister Americans, that we do not have you in our thoughts, and in our prayers.

"Back in 1927 Norman Thomas, a declared Socialist, said the American people would never vote for socialism. But he said that under the name of liberalism the American people will adopt every fragment of the socialist program.

"Bit by bit, we saw that happening as Socialists, environmentalists, those who were more interested in free stuff than freedom, those who thought their vote for a social experiment would be cool, and those who were totally uninformed, voted into office Mehdi Ohmshidi. We all know the disastrous results of that.

"As he tried social experiment after social experiment, such as attacks on fossil fuels, sharing the wealth, and gutting the military, our country became less and less stable. As Ohmshidi literally bowed to foreign leaders and acted with hesitancy and weakness in the face of our enemies, our country became more threatened. And as Ohmshidi continued with his failed socialist policies, all the while blaming the deteriorating conditions on his predecessor, our country became less able to sustain itself. With social instability, military weakness, and fiscal unsustainability, the result was inevitable. We witnessed the total collapse of a Republic that had stood as the beacon of the world for two hundred and thirty-two years.

"Jews and Christians have seen their property taken from them, their families destroyed, and even as I speak there are Jews and Christians confined in concentration camps, which are called Ultimate Resolution camps. We have seen beheadings, stoning deaths, and mutilations brought about by agents of Moqaddas Sirata.

"I am here to tell you that today is the turning point. Dedicated and courageous men and women are met here today to begin, piece by piece, to rebuild that republic, starting with the states here represented. It is my firm belief that this noble effort will expand until once again there will be on this continent a movement, inspired by God, that will pass above amber waves of grain, cross purple mountain majesties, and extend from sea to shining sea, an America reborn, an America that once again embraces the ideals, the honor, and the universal brotherhood of our founding fathers.

"Take back America!" he shouted.

"Take back America!" the audience shouted, as one.

Racine, Wisconsin

Brad Little watched Gregoire's speech, then he went into his bedroom and started looking through the closet until he found what was looking for. He held the cap in his hand, looking at it for a moment before he put it on. The legend across the front of the hat read: Vietnam Veteran. He started toward the front door.

"Brad, where are you going?" his wife asked. "Don't go outside with that hat. You'll get in trouble."

"I'm going down to the VFW hall," Brad said.

"You know the VFW is closed."

"Yes, and I can't get a beer. But I can damn sure go down there and remember."

When Brad pulled into the parking lot of the VFW, he recognized the car of Miner Cobb, a retired master sergeant. Brad walked over and got into the car with him.

"Did you see Gregoire's speech?" Brad asked.

"Tell me something, Brad. How the hell did we let this happen?" Cobb asked.

"People bought in to the hope and change . . . they thought voting for Ohmshidi would be historic, who can say?"

"There's Porter and Carlew," Cobb said. "What are they doing here?"

"Same thing we are, I suppose," Brad said. "And as long as we're doing it, seems to me like we ought to be doing it together."

Junction City, Kansas

Althea Jennings had been Miss Teenage Kansas the year Ohmshidi was elected. There was no Miss Teenage America because the "prurient display of the female form" was banned. Althea had been in beauty pageants since she was a very young girl. She had not considered the events to be a prurient display, she had considered the events to be healthy, fun, and, a possible path to a college scholarship.

Now, whenever she went outside she had to cover herself so that she looked like a walking tent. And she couldn't go anywhere without a male relative which made it very difficult for her, because she had no brother.

As soon as Gregoire's speech ended, Althea went into her room and dug through the cedar chest until she found her bikini bathing suit. She put it on, looked her reflection in the mirror for a moment, then fell across her bed and wept.

Never, in her worst nightmare, could she have imagined anything like this could happen in America.

Muslimabad

"How is it that he is still alive?" Ohmshidi yelled at the television screen. "We should have killed him the moment we captured him."

"Glorious Leader, if you recall," National Leader Reed Franken said, "I suggested as much. But it was Rahimi's idea to make a public spectacle of his execution, and while we waited, Gregoire escaped."

Inexplicably, Ohmshidi smiled. "But every dark cloud has a silver lining, and whoever rescued Gregoire killed Rahimi."

Franken smiled as well. "Rahimi's days were numbered anyway, Glorious Leader. I had observed how he was encroaching upon your authority, and I was about take care of the situation myself."

"Yes, well, Rahimi is no longer a problem. But Gregoire is still a problem," Ohmshidi said.

"I think, Glorious Leader, if you will authorize

it, that we should make a few demonstrations of our power and authority," Franken said.

"What sort of demonstration?"

"I think, perhaps, a few military incursions into what they consider their territory. I will start with Arkansas, since that is where they attacked us."

"Yes. And make the raids," Ohmshidi paused for a moment before he finished his sentence, "painful."

"Yes, Glorious Leader, I shall."

The Convention Center, Mobile

When the convention reconvened on the following day, Bob went down each topic to get a report.

The first spokesman gave a report on free trade. "It is our belief and recommendation that each individual has the right to offer goods and services to others. The only proper role of government in the economic realm is to protect property rights, adjudicate disputes, and provide a legal framework in which voluntary trade is protected. All efforts by government to redistribute wealth, or to control or manage trade, or impose restrictive regulations, are improper in a free society. This, we submit as approved."

One by one each additional committee rendered their reports. "We oppose any government intrusion into the production of fossil fuel. We believe that wherever oil, coal, or natural gas can be found, it should be extracted, refined, and sold without governmental restraint."

"We oppose anything similar to the Federal Reserve System and believe in free market banking."

"In order to foster a productive work environment, we will allow unions to exist, but would oppose any law requiring membership in unions to work. We also propose that government workers be prohibited from either forming a union, or joining unions already formed."

"We declare that that education should be the responsibility of individual schools with maximum parental input. Prayer should be allowed in school, but no student should be forced to participate in the prayer."

"We are adamantly opposed to any sort of government sponsored health care. Health care should be determined by a free market. Emergency, and lifesaving medical procedures cannot be denied due to a lack of funds."

"Retirement planning is the responsibility of the individual, not the government. There should be no government-sponsored Social Security system."

"There should be no governmental impediments to free trade. We oppose tariffs and will not trade with any country that imposes tariffs, or otherwise introduces an unfair trade practice."

"The citizens of this nation shall have the power of initiative, referendum and recall to be applied to everyone in public office, to include all elected and appointed government officials. The judiciary at all levels, whether voted upon or appointed, are subject to this process. We believe that repeal can, and should, be used as popular checks on government."

"We believe, and by our actions herein demonstrate, that should the government become destructive of individual liberty, it shall be the right of the people to alter or to abolish it, and to agree to such new governance as to them shall seem most likely to protect their liberty."

CHAPTER EIGHTEEN

The first items to be voted on were the amendments, and though there was spirited discussion for and opposed to the amendment that would establish term limits it, as did the other amendments, passed.

With the new amendments passed, the other proposals were voted upon. Nine of the ten proposals were passed by acclamation. The only one that encountered difficulty was the one dealing with Social Security.

"Mr. Chairman," James Laney said, raising his hand and calling from the floor. "Permission to speak?"

"The chair recognizes the delegate from Alabama," Bob said.

"Mr. Chairman, I have paid into Social Security since I was twelve years old. I don't consider Social Security as being any kind of a welfare program. It is a promise and an investment, and I don't think it's right to take it away."

Stump Patterson was recognized.

"Like Mr. Laney, I paid into the Social Security system for many years. I also served in the army for twenty-four years. But my army retirement, like my Social Security retirement, was paid into a government that no longer exists. And because that government no longer exists, the accounts for Social Security, for military and civil service retirements no longer exist. There is no money available, therefore there is no Social Security to take away."

The question as to whether or not to establish a Social Security system was tabled for further discussion.

It was decided to keep the current officers in place until one year after the new country was formed, at which time a national election would be held, and that kept Bob Varney on as provisional president.

One of the most contentious discussions arose over what to call the new country. There was a strong movement to name the country Fredonia, and because George Gregoire sponsored that position it had a lot of support.

"Fredonia has a connective history with the founding of the United States," Gregoire said when he presented his argument. "It was a name first coined by Dr. Samuel L. Mitchill in 1803 when he wrote his *Proposal to the American literati, and to all the citizens of the United States,* to employ the following names and epithets for the country and nation to which they belong, whereby they may be aptly distinguished from the other regions and peoples of the earth:

1. Fredonia, the aggregate noun for the whole territory
2. Fredonian, a sonorous name for a citizen of Fredonia

But it was no less than the new president who spoke in favor of the name United Free America. "We all know that when we say United Free America, what we actually mean is the United States of America. We have always called ourselves Americans, and with this name, we can continue to call ourselves Americans.

"I believe that we are all in agreement that what we want now is an interim country, a placeholder if you will, until once more our land will stretch from the Canadian border to the Gulf of Mexico, and from the Atlantic to the Pacific Ocean. We have no ambition for a new country, or a new name. We exist for one purpose only, and that is to take back America."

Bob's speech was met with a standing ovation, and, before the vote was taken, Gregoire asked for permission to speak one more time.

"Ladies and gentlemen of this historic convention, I withdraw my support for the name Fredonia, and move that we adopt the name United Free America by acclamation."

The move was seconded, and by acclamation.

"The task before us is clear," Bob said as he

addressed them at the conclusion of the convention. "We must now return to our respective states to report to the people what we have done here. Then, with the full knowledge and support of those whom we represent, we will reconvene on the fifteenth of October, to organize our Republic. I am going to call upon Father Ken Coats to give a closing prayer.

Father Coats, the same man who had performed the marriage for Jake and Karen, stepped up to the podium, wearing the vestments of his office. The gathering grew quiet, as he intoned his prayer.

"Our Eternal Father, through whose mighty power our fathers won their liberties of old, grant, we beseech thee, that we, and all the peoples of this new endeavor, may have grace to reestablish these liberties in righteousness and peace for the benefit of all. Amen."

During the time Mobile was under the dominance of the State Protective Service and the Janissaries, the Moqaddas Sirata had published a newspaper called the *Way of Enlightenment.* When Mobile was freed, the publishers of the paper, who had stolen the paper from its original publishers, were run off, and a new newspaper, the *Journal of Freedom* was started. The *Journal of Freedom* published an article telling about the convention just completed where a new nation was born, and a new constitution developed.

IS A NEW NATION TO BE BORN?

On July Fourth (the date was purposely chosen), the old and historic city of Mobile added yet another page to its long and illustrious list of historical achievements. The states of Alabama, Arkansas, Georgia, Louisiana, Mississippi, North Florida, Tennessee, and Texas have declared themselves free, and forever unencumbered from the entity that now calls itself the American Islamic Republic of Enlightenment.

Representatives from these states met in Mobile for the purpose of drawing up a constitution for same. The hopes and prayers of an anxious people will be with these men and women as they undertake the arduous task that lies before them.

God be with them, and God bless their efforts.

Philadelphia

Ann McPherson had watched the telecast the night before of the constitutional convention of United Free America. She had not been back to school since her brother, and many of her friends had been killed in the auditorium. Although the news reports said that it was an accidental release of toxic fumes, she knew, with a certainty, that Jack, Carl, and the others had been murdered.

For several days after that awful tragedy Ann had been so shaken by what had happened that she seldom left the apartment. Then, this morning there was a loud knock on her door. There was something frightening about the knock; it wasn't the light and inquiring tap of a friend, it was loud and aggressive.

Taking a deep breath and drawing herself up, Ann answered the door. She saw two, black-clad Janissaries standing there.

"Miss Ann McPherson?" one of the men asked.

"Yes."

"Come with us, please."

"May I ask what this is about?"

"Come with us, please," the man repeated.

Ann was handcuffed and taken to what had been in the pre-O time, a precinct of the Philadelphia Police Department. Once there she was taken into an interrogation room where the handcuffs were removed, and she was told to sit down.

Then, the two men who had brought her here left, and Ann was alone in the room.

She looked around the room, which had three bare walls, painted a pale green. The fourth wall was a mirror, and Ann had seen enough crime movies and TV shows that she knew the mirror was a one-way window.

She was glad the handcuffs had been removed, and as she waited, she rubbed the redness on her wrists that the cuffs had caused.

She drummed her fingers on the table, and waited.

She looked around for a clock, but there

wasn't one. They had taken her watch when they brought her here, so she had no idea how long she had been here.

She waited.

It felt as if her legs were going to sleep, so she got up and began pacing around the room. She could see herself in the mirror, and she realized that she was seeing exactly what those unseen eyes on the other side of the mirror were also seeing.

Finally she returned to her chair, then put her clasped hands on the table and stared, pointedly, at the mirror.

She waited.

She thought of her brother, killed, no, murdered, along with two hundred others at the auditorium. She wondered how he would act if he were here, and she imagined that he would probably flip a bird to the mirror. The thought of that tickled her, and she smiled.

Almost immediately after that, the door opened and a black-uniformed Janissary came in. He was an average-sized man who had a splash of color above his left pocket. They were ribbons, like the kind of ribbons she used to see worn on the uniforms of soldiers. He sat down across the table from Ann.

"I am Major Fatih. And you are?"

"You mean you brought me down here and you don't even know who I am? Good, then you have obviously made a mistake."

Fatih reached across the table and slapped Ann, the move coming so quickly and so unexpectedly that she didn't even have time to duck. Her cheek turned red from the blow.

"I will not put up with insolent comments from a woman," Fatih said, harshly. "You will apologize for your insolence now."

"I'm sorry," Ann said in a small, frightened voice.

"What is your name?"

"McPherson. Ann McPherson."

"Miss McPherson, what did you find humorous?" Fatih asked.

"I beg your pardon?"

"Just before I came in, you were smiling. Why were you smiling?"

"I don't know," Ann said. "I wasn't even aware that I was smiling. It must have been a nervous reaction. Believe me, I find nothing humorous about this situation. Why am I here?"

"I will ask the questions. Why didn't you go to the assembly hall with your brother?"

"There was no reason for me to go."

Major Fatih removed a folded sheet of paper from his pocket, unfolded it, then slid it across the table.

A CALL TO ALL STUDENT REVOLUTIONARIES
If you wish to demonstrate against the government, gather in assembly hall at eight o'clock Monday morning.

"Do you deny that you saw this e-mail?"

"I saw it."

"Did you and your brother send this e-mail?"

"No."

"Is this e-mail the reason your brother went to the assembly hall?"

"I suppose it is."

"If your brother went, why didn't you go with him?"

"My brother was interested in politics. I am totally apolitical."

"Why have you no interest?"

"I am a woman. Such things are not for women. It is our duty to be a good wife and a good mother. As women, we exist only for the procreation of the species, nothing more."

"And yet, you are not married. Why is that you are not married?" Fatih asked.

"I am true to Allah, and if I am to marry, it must be to someone who shares my faith."

The interrogating Janissary nodded his head, and drummed his fingers. Then without another word he got up and left the interrogation room. A few minutes after he left, the same two men who had brought her here came back in.

"Am I free to go now?" Ann asked.

Her question was unanswered as the handcuffs were put back on her.

"What's happening? Why can't I go? I answered all the questions."

Still not responding, the two men led her into the back of the building where there were several holding cells. She was put into one.

The cell was depressing. It had one bunk, and an aluminum lavatory and toilet bowl sticking out from the back wall. Because the cell was completely open, she knew that she would have to perform any toilet functions without privacy.

Ann lay on the bed and wept quietly.

Later that same day, Sally Mosley was brought into the jail and put into the adjacent cell. Ann said nothing until the guards were gone then she moved quickly to the bars that separated their cells.

"Sally, they brought you here, too?"

"Yes," Sally said.

"What have you told them?"

"I've told them nothing. I told them I didn't know anything about the meeting."

"Did they believe you?"

"I don't know," Sally said. "I told them that I was a woman, and that whatever my husband did was his business."

Ann started to say something, then she saw a very tiny microphone at the top of one of the bars. She put her finger to her lips, then mouthed the word "bug" without speaking aloud.

"That is true," Ann said. "Those who question us are men, and do not understand how we are blessed by Allah to be women, and because we are women, we are uninterested in things of a political nature. Perhaps, after they do more investigation, they will realize that we are innocent of any wrongdoing. Allah be praised, I think this is how it will be."

"Yes, Allah be praised." Sally said. "I have another blessing from Allah."

"Oh?"

"I am with child."

Ann's eyes grew wide, questioning whether this was part of the playacting they were doing, or whether Sally was telling the truth. Sally nodded yes.

"Oh, Sally," Ann said, sticking her hand through the bars to grasp the hand of her friend. "Did Carl know?"

"No. I did not know I was pregnant until I was told by my neighbor. She is a wise woman who has assisted many women bear their children. She has said that she will assist me."

"Oh, but do you think that's wise. I mean shouldn't you . . ." Ann started to ask if Sally shouldn't see a doctor, but even as the question was forming, she cut it off. Sally couldn't see a doctor, because women were not allowed medical care, except for that provided by another woman. And, as women were not allowed to practice medicine, that meant that any woman who had an actual malady, such as cancer, heart disease, stroke, or any other major disorder, had to go untreated. "Shouldn't you pray to Allah that your pregnancy be an easy one?"

"Yes, I do pray that my pregnancy be an easy one," Sally said. Ann noticed that Sally did not say "pray to Allah," and she knew exactly what Sally meant.

CHAPTER NINETEEN

Sikeston, Missouri

Dr. Taylor Urban's office was on the corner of New Madrid and Center Street. The office had been there for over fifty years, first with Dewey Urban, Taylor's father, and now with Taylor. There had been a decided change in the practice beginning from the moment the "Ohmshidi Care" bill was passed establishing socialized medicine and putting all doctors on the public payroll.

The workload for doctors increased, then, when nearly half of the doctors quit their practice, the workload increased exponentially. Taylor Urban didn't quit, it wasn't about the money for him. It never had been about the money. He treated patients because he felt as if he had been born for that purpose.

After the United States collapsed under Ohmshidi, to be replaced by the American Islamic Republic of Enlightenment, there was an even more drastic change in the practice of medicine. All women doctors lost their license to practice and it became law that male doctors could no longer treat female patients.

Dr. Urban refused to follow that decree, and he let it be known that he would treat female patients. He established a second office in the back of a store that sold muslim clothing for women, such as abaya and jilbab, hijab and scarf, kurti and tunic. Because the store specialized in clothing for women, it did not immediately arouse suspicion that there were always women going in and out.

Then, one day in late July, Dr. Urban had Blanche Percy, a single young woman in her early twenties, sitting on the padded table. Blanche was topless, and Dr. Urban was feeling her breasts to search for lumps. It was at that precise moment that the door to his "secret" examining room burst open and four armed Janissaries burst in.

"Here, what is the meaning of this?" Dr. Urban demanded, indignantly.

"You and the whore are both under arrest," the leader of the Janissaries said.

"This woman is my patient!" Dr. Urban said. "How dare you break into my office like this! And how dare you call this innocent young lady a whore!"

Blanche Percy was ordered to cover herself. Then both she and Dr. Urban were taken to jail.

Blytheville, Arkansas

Merlin Lewis was an extrovert. He greeted everyone effusively, even people who were on the other side of the street, often calling them by name. He was a heavy-set man with white hair and an almost perfectly round birthmark on his face. Many years ago Lewis had been a star football player for the Blytheville High School Chickasaws. Then, he went by the nickname of Bull, the sobriquet earned by his bruising defensive play.

On this morning, Lewis went into the SPS headquarters which was located on Walnut Street in what had once been the police station. The desk clerk looked up and, recognizing him, said, "You here to see Captain Mahaz?"

"Yes, please."

The desk clerk picked up the phone and punched a number. "Your informer is here."

A moment later Captain Mahaz came out to see him.

"What do you have for me?"

"You said you wanted me to tell you when there would be a gathering of twenty or more people, violating holy law?"

"Yes."

"A group of old army and air force veterans are meeting for a picnic and softball game at Walker Park. Their wives will be with them, and I expect there will be at least thirty or more. And, I'm told they will be serving barbecued pork at the picnic."

"When is this to be?"

"Tomorrow at noon."

Walker Park

"You're blind as a bat, Wilson, if you think I was out at second base. I beat that throw by a mile."

"Carmichael, it took you two minutes to run from first to second. I was standing there, holding the ball, waiting for you. Hell, I would have had time to go to the latrine and back while I was waiting for you to run from first to second."

The others laughed at Wilson's comment. The softball game having just been completed, Army beat Air Force nine to seven, the men and women were now filing by the food table. The table was amply supplied with potato salad, baked beans, and sliced meat, which, according to the sign was "barbequed goat."

In fact, the meat came from a couple of pork shoulders, cooked the day before on a farm outside of town so that the telltale aroma wouldn't give it away.

"Damn, this is good . . . goat," someone said, and again there was laughter.

Wilson was the first to see the military truck drive into the park. "What's that deuce and a half doin' here?" he asked.

"Oh!" a woman said. "They know about the pork!"

"What pork," Carmichael said. "It's goat. Remember, if they ask us anything, it's goat."

Twelve SPS men climbed down from the back of the truck. All were armed and they started across the park toward the group of picnickers.

"I'm frightened," one of the women said.

"I'll go talk to them," Wilson volunteered. He

started toward the group of SPS men, holding up his hand as he approached.

"I don't know what you think is going on here, but I assure you this . . ."

That was as far as Wilson got, before the SPS men raised their automatic weapons and began firing.

Wilson was the first to go down. Men shouted in alarm, and women screamed as the SPS men continued to fire. Some of the victims tried to run, but the SPS men chased after them, and shot them down. Then, with every man and woman down, the SPS troopers went around the park, firing a bullet into the head of each person, just to make certain they were dead.

After that, they stepped over the dead bodies to go up to the table and help themselves to the food that was there. Nearly every SPS man who had taken part in the raid was from the local area. They had grown up eating barbequed pork so they knew, immediately, what they were eating. They had the cover, though, of the sign saying that the meat was goat, so not one man commented on it. Instead, they just enjoyed the food.

Article in the *New York Socialist Islamic Times:*

Raid on Arkansas Infidels

In the small town of Blytheville, Arkansas, located in the northeast part of that state, a group of infidels defied both holy law and Moqaddas Sirata yesterday, by gathering in a public place to consume pork.

The Qur'an prohibits the consumption of pork. "Forbidden to you (for food) are: dead meat, blood, the flesh of swine, and that on which hath been invoked the name of other than Allah." [Al-Qur'an 5:3] The above verse of the Holy Qur'an is sufficient to satisfy a Muslim as to why pork is forbidden.

That as many as twenty-eight nonbelievers would openly violate this sacred law was an insult to the Prophet Mohammed, and required quick and effective action.

The SPS in Blytheville, under the command of Captain Ahmed Mahaz, rising up in support of the righteous, conducted a raid on the sinful gathering, ridding the righteous people of Blytheville of the sinners within their very midst. Thirty-nine paid the supreme price for their perfidious act.

Obey Ohmshidi.

Sikeston

When Dr. Urban was brought into court, he looked around for Miss Percy who, he had been told, would be tried with him. She was nowhere to be seen.

"Where is Miss Percy?" he asked the bailiff.

"Dead."

"What? What happened to her?"

"She was executed."

"But she wasn't even tried!"

"Why waste time with a trial? There were four witnesses who saw her naked in your office. The judge summarily sentenced her to death and she was beheaded this morning."

"No!" Dr. Urban said. He bowed his head and pinched the bridge of his nose. "No!" he said again.

"All rise!" the bailiff shouted. "This court of shariah law is now in session, the honorable Imam Tahir presiding."

The gallery rose as the judge, wearing a dark bisht came into the courtroom. Not until he was seated did the gallery sit down.

"Sit there," the bailiff said, pointing to a single chair behind a table.

Dr. Urban noticed two things right away. There was no lawyer at his table, and there was no jury.

"Where is my lawyer?" Urban asked the bailiff.

"Silence in this courtroom," Tahir said, glaring across the bench at Dr. Urban.

"Your Honor, my lawyer hasn't arrived yet. And neither has the jury," Dr. Urban said.

"I told you to be quiet, infidel," Tahir said. "I have dismissed your lawyer and the jury. You may represent yourself, and I will act as both judge and jury."

"But that's not right!" Dr. Urban protested.

"It is right, because I say it is right. Now, sit down and don't say another word until you are given permission to speak."

Dr. Urban sat down as ordered, then he

thought again of the young woman who the bailiff said had been beheaded this morning. Was he the cause of that, simply because he had agreed to treat her?

"Prosecutor may make his case," Tahir said.

The prosecutor, wearing a thobe, was sitting at a table across from Dr. Urban. He stood and began speaking.

"This man was observed by four witnesses to be treating a female patient. This is against our law, and in a perfect example of why it is, and should be, against our law, the four witnesses observed the female to be nude from the waist up, and this man," he pointed dramatically toward Dr. Urban, "was openly fondling her breasts!"

The prosecutor shouted the last five words, and he got a gasping reaction from those in the gallery.

"I was not fondling her breasts! I was examining her for cancerous lumps!" Dr. Urban shouted.

"You will be silent!" Tahir shouted.

The prosecutor, showing by the expression on his face his disdain for Dr. Urban, continued with his presentation.

"One of the worst of evil deeds is in openly defying the law of Allah, as taught to us by his messenger Mohamed, peace and blessings of Allah be upon him." The prosecutor pointed to Dr. Urban. "The malevolence of this heretic despoiled a young woman and caused her to commit a sin which according to Mohamed, peace and blessings of Allah be upon him, demanded that he be put to death.

"There can be no lesser penalty for this man." The prosecutor sat down and the judge looked toward Dr. Urban.

"You may speak in your defense."

Dr. Urban stood up. He was going to repeat his denial that he was "fondling" Blanche Percy's breasts, but he had already shouted that out. He knew the judge had heard him, so, for a moment, he was at a loss for words, so he stood quietly for a long moment.

"Speak, or be seated," Tahir ordered.

"Your Honor, when I took the oath of my profession, I made a pledge. It is a pledge that I committed to memory, and with your permission, I wish to repeat it here."

"Does prosecution have any objection?" Tahir asked.

Dr. Urban had to hold himself in check. What did the judge mean, asking if prosecution has any objection? What right does the prosecution have to object?

"I have no objections, Your Honor," prosecution replied.

Tahir turned his attention back to Dr. Urban.

"You may speak."

"Thank you, Your Honor. This was the oath I took. 'I solemnly pledge to consecrate my life to the service of humanity. I will give to my teachers the respect and gratitude which is their due. I will practice my profession with conscience and dignity. The health and life of my patient will be my first consideration. I will respect the secrets which are confided in me. I will maintain by all means in my power, the honor and the noble traditions of the medical profession. My colleagues will be my brothers. I will not permit considerations of religion, nationality, race, party politics or social standing to intervene between my duty and my patient. I will maintain the utmost respect for human life, from the time of its conception, and even under threat I will not use my medical knowledge contrary to the laws of humanity. I make these promises solemnly, freely and upon my honor.'

"I submit, Your Honor, that it was in following the obligation of this oath, that led me to provide medical services to the young woman."

Dr. Urban sat down, and the prosecutor jumped up almost immediately

"Imam, the accused now stands convicted by his own words. Nowhere in that oath he just recited, did he mention Allah. Any oath, not taken to Allah, is heresy."

The prosecutor sat back down, a triumphant smile on his face. The judge looked over at Dr. Urban.

"This court finds you guilty as charged. You will be taken from this place to the prison at Tanner, and there you will remain until I decide how best to administer your ultimate punishment. This court is adjourned."

CHAPTER TWENTY

Gaffney, South Carolina

They were meeting in a building at the corner of East Meadow and North Johnson Street. Sarhag (Colonel) Saladin had come down from Muslimabad to talk with the "Special Operations Team." Ten men, all Janissaries, had infiltrated the South Carolina Defense Corps and, over the last six weeks, had earned the trust of Captain Ray Lumsden, the SCDC commander for the local area. They had trained under Lumsden, and had been accepted as active duty members of his company.

"Obey Ohmshidi," Saladin said.

To the man, all ten Janissaries responded with the Moqaddas salute, a closed fist, across their chest.

"Obey Ohmshidi."

The men were not wearing their black and silver uniforms, but a uniform of gray, much like the work uniforms of truck drivers and warehouse workers.

"Lumsden does not suspect anything?" Saladin asked.

"He suspects nothing, Sarhag," Jay Malone said. Malone was his birth name and although he and the other nine Janissaries had taken on Muslim names, for the purpose of this operation, which was being called "Mohammed's Hammer," they were using their birth names.

"There are eighteen of us who were trained by Lumsden," Malone said. "Eight are locals, who were sincere in joining the rebels."

"Have you a plan to handle them?"

"Yes, Sarhag. We believe that Lumsden will be sending us out on a scouting mission without one of his regulars, tomorrow. When he does, we will kill the ones who have not joined us, then we will return to the camp and kill Lumsden and the others. They will suspect nothing."

"Good. I will stay here in Gaffney until the mission is accomplished," Saladin said. "When you are done, call me on the cell phone. Obey Ohmshidi."

"Obey Ohmshidi," the Janissaries replied.

Firebase Cassandra, Cowpens National Battlefield, South Carolina

The firebase was set up on the very grounds where Colonel Daniel Morgan and his American Continental troops defeated Lieutenant Colonel

Banastre Tarleton and his British Regulars during the Revolutionary War. The roads into what had been a national park in the pre-O time were now so deteriorated that they were practically impassable by vehicle. This location was specifically chosen for that reason, as well as its historical significance.

South Carolina had declared itself as seceded from AIRE, but, because there were still people who were leery about joining another federation, it had not sent a delegation to the convention in Mobile. There were also people within the state who opposed secession and so much of the fighting within the state had been infighting.

The Firebase leader, Captain Ray Lumsden, had named the camp after his one-year old daughter, Cassandra. The young girl's pictures, posing with and without her mother, were plastered all over Lumsden's quarters. Camp Cassandra had been in position for just over a month now and, Lumsden was proud to say, the team was functioning exactly as it was supposed to. Pouring himself a cup of coffee, Lumsden sat down at his field desk, then opened up the laptop computer to establish a link with the satellite. Once the link was established, he keyed in his operational readiness report.

SECRET

Operational Readiness Report
Electronically Filed
From: FireteamCassandra@SCmil.com
To: Ops.condepcom@SCmil.com
16 July—1320 Z

Eighteen (18) locals have been recruited, armed and intensive training has been conducted. Although patrols around the firebase have been run with Cassandra personnel in charge, the bulk of the patrols have been made up by locals. Effective at 1100 Z today, I sent out the first patrol that was 100% indigenous.

Lumsden, Ray R
Cpt Team Ldr

In the field with the operational team

Walter Dent had been appointed to the rank of Sergeant by Captain Lumsden, and he was leading the eighteen-man team. Their mission for today was to set up a roadblock on Hands Mill Highway, to stop what the latest intelligence report said would be a convoy of SPS weapons.

"All right, we'll set up here," Dent said. "We'll drop a tree across the road, that will stop them and . . ." Dent saw Malone and several others moving away. "What are you doing? We're going to be setting up here, not . . ."

"Allah Hu Akbar!" Malone shouted, and the nine men with him turned their weapons on Dent and the seven with him. Most of the men had put their weapons down as they were preparing to cut down the tree so they were completely defenseless. Dent and the seven men with him went down under the gunfire.

When the stopped shooting the air was heavy with the acrid stench of gun smoke.

"All right," Malone said. "Back to the camp. We have some infidels to kill."

Dent, who had been hit in the shoulder, lay perfectly still until Malone and the others left. He heard Malone say that they had infidels to kill. He checked the others and found that all were dead. He had brought a radio with him when they started on the patrol, but it was gone. He searched the others for a radio or cell phone but couldn't find one.

Dent knew he had to warn Captain Lumsden and the others, but how? Tearing off a piece of his shirt, he stuffed it into the bullet hole to stop the bleeding, then started back toward the compound. Malone and the others had a head start, but he had to try.

Firebase Cassandra

"Cap'n Lumsden, you in here, sir?"

Looking up, Lumsden saw Sergeant Haverbrook sticking his head through the opening of the CP tent.

"Right here, Hav, what's up?"

"The patrol's comin' back, sir."

Lumsden glanced at his watch. "They aren't due back until sundown. Why are they coming back so early?"

"I don't know, sir. Kincaid was up on the tower and he saw them. But there's only ten of them."

"Ten? Didn't we send out eighteen?"

"Yes, sir, we did."

"They must've run into trouble."

"Yes, sir, that's what I'm thinking. But why didn't they radio for support?"

"I don't know," Lumsden said. "Let's go meet them."

As Lumsden and Sergeant Haverbrook started toward the edge of the compound, Lieutenant Cummins joined them. The rest of the team was playing volleyball.

"What do you mean it was out, you dumb shit? It hit just inside the line!"

"What the hell, Tyndol, do you think the North Carolina state line is the boundary?"

The response met with laughter.

"Yeah, all right, I know what I'm dealing with now," Tyndol said. "Next time I'll spike it right down your throat."

"Oooh, Tyndol, you're bad, you're baad," someone said, and again there was laughter.

"Who's that in charge?" Lumsden asked as the approaching patrol came closer. "That's not Dent."

"No, sir, it isn't," Haverbrook said. "It's Malone."

"Malone? What's he doing in charge?"

"Dent must've gone down."

They waited until the patrol was within ten yards of them.

"Malone, what happened?" Lumsden called out. "Where's Dent?"

"Open fire! Kill them all!" Malone shouted.

The members of the patrol brought their weapons around and started firing. Lumsden,

Haverbrook, and Cummins went down in a hail of gunfire. Those playing volleyball looked up in surprise, wondering what was going on. They were shocked to see the patrol running toward them.

"No," Tyndol shouted. "Don't run! Form a defense perimeter!"

Tyndol was yelling at the patrol, because he thought the attack had come from outside the camp and, ever the instructor, he was trying to get the patrol into position to repulse.

The patrol opened up on the unarmed volleyball players.

"My God, they've turned on us!" Tyndol shouted, realizing his error too late. He was one of the first to go down. The patrol swept over the unarmed Americans, killing them with grim efficacy. Within less than a minute, all twelve members of Firebase Cassandra were dead.

Malone pulled out his cell phone and punched in the telephone number for Salidin.

"Obey Ohmshidi," Salidin answered.

"Obey Ohmshidi. This is Jamal," Malone said, using his Muslim name. "*Allah hu akbar!* It is done."

Walter Dent had watched the entire massacre, unable to do a thing to prevent it. He stayed hidden until Malone and the others left, then he went into the camp, hoping to find someone alive. He knew, even before he started looking, that it would be fruitless. He had watched, helplessly, as Malone and the others finished off each of their victims with a shot to the head. He realized that he was lucky they hadn't done the same thing to the other members of the patrol.

Going into Captain Lumsden's office, he found a radio, and put through a call to Major Tobin. As he was waiting for Tobin to come to the radio, he saw, on the wall, a picture of the little girl after whom the camp was named, and he felt a lump in his throat.

"This is Major Tobin."

"Captain Lumsden is dead," Dent said. "Everyone is dead."

CHAPTER TWENTY-ONE

Philadelphia

Ann McPherson and Sally Mosley had been in jail for six weeks now, and Sally was beginning to have serious bouts of morning sickness, with vomiting, diarrhea, and weight loss.

"I have read about this," Ann said. "I think you are having something called *hyperemesis gravidarum*. It is a particularly virulent type of morning sickness. You should be in a hospital."

"Women are not allowed to go to the hospital, you know that," Sally replied, her voice so weak that it could barely be heard.

"Then you need to get out of jail so you can go home. You need rest, and you need to keep yourself hydrated."

"Believe me, I want nothing more in the world, than to go home. But there is nothing I can do about that."

"Maybe you can't," Ann said. "But I believe I can."

* * *

"Let me understand this," Major Fatih said, after Ann was brought to him. "You are willing to confess your guilt?"

"Yes, I have prayed to Allah, and I feel that I must do this if I am to be blessed."

"All right, what do you confess?"

"The first thing I confess is that Sally Mosley is innocent. She knew nothing about what her husband, my brother, and I were doing."

"How is it that she could not know? She was married to Carl Mosley."

"Yes, she was married to him. But I was sleeping with him."

Fatih looked up in surprise at the words. "You were committing adultery with another woman's husband?"

"Yes."

"Why are you confessing this now?"

"Because she is in the cell next to my cell and as I see her there, the guilt of what I have done is heavy on my heart. I have prayed to Allah, and I believe I must confess these sins so that when I go to heav . . . I mean paradise, I will do so with an unburdened heart."

"But you will not go to paradise," Fatih said. "You have committed the sin of adultery. You will go to hell."

"Then, if I am to go to hell, I will know that, by confessing my sin and clearing Sally's name, I will leave this earth having done the right thing."

The White House

That evening Ohmshidi and Franken were in the Yellow Oval sitting room of the presidential quarters, watching television. On a table between them was a silver platter filled with *naan berenji,* a rice and poppyseed cookie. Earlier, Franken had told Ohmshidi that the news program tonight would be of special interest, and that he might enjoy watching it.

Ohmshidi picked up a cookie and began eating as the program opened with a full screen shot of the new national flag, The words *CMN, America Enlightened Truth Television* were keyed onto the screen, replaced by the words *Obey Ohmshidi,* then a reverent voice over intoned the opening lines.

> *"All praise be to Allah, the merciful. Whomsoever Allah guides there is none to misguide, and whomsoever Allah misguides there is none to guide. You must live your life in accordance with the Moqaddas Sirata, the Holy Path. Those who do will be blessed. Those who do not will be damned.*
> *"You are watching CMN."*

The newscaster, a bearded man, was staring directly into the camera.

> *"And now, the news. Our viewers may remember last month that there were a series of seemingly unrelated incidents where, in a dozen university assembly halls across the nation, more than two thousand students who*

had gathered to praise Allah, were mysteriously killed. At first it was believed that the deaths were purely accidental, caused by toxic fumes which were the result of some abnormality in the ventilation system.

"Upon further investigation, however, the Janissaries, working under the guidance of our Glorious Leader, President for Life Mehdi Ohmshidi, may he be blessed by Allah, have discovered that the two thousand deaths at a dozen universities were, in fact, not unrelated incidents. They were, instead, wanton acts of murder, committed by Ron McPherson and Carl Mosley. McPherson and Mosley were themselves killed, caught up in their own nefarious activity. Now it has been learned that Ann McPherson, the sister of Ron McPherson, not only took part in the murders, but also committed adultery with Mosley.

"Equally guilty was Carl Mosley's wife, Sally.

"Both women have been tried and sentenced to death by beheading. So that their heinous crimes be made a lesson to any others who might consider such a thing, their beheadings were taped and are now presented as a public service.

"Obey Ohmshidi."

The picture on the screen showed the two women bound and gagged, standing side by side. Their eyes were open wide, and their faces reflected the fear of the moment.

Standing to one side was a bare-chested and

muscular-looking man. The man was wearing a black hood.

"*Allah hu akbar!*" someone shouted off camera, and the muscle-bound man made a wide, sweeping swing of the scimitar against the neck of Sally Mosley. Her head was completely severed and her body, with blood gushing from the stump of her neck, fell forward. Her head rolled away from the body.

The executioner stepped up to Ann, who closed her eyes tightly.

"*Allah hu akbar!*"

Again, the executioner swung the scimitar. This time the head came forward, but the body fell backward.

Laying down the scimitar, the executioner grabbed the two heads by the hair, then held them up, allowing the camera to come in close, focusing on them one at a time.

"These *naan berenji* are very good," Ohmshidi said, picking up a second cookie. "Have another."

"Thank you, Glorious Leader," Franken said.

"*Major Ahib Fatih, in charge of the Janissaries who broke this case had this comment to make,*" the news-caster said.

The picture on screen was that of Fatih.

> "*Let this be a lesson to all who would violate the law of Moqaddas Sirata. We will find you, and we will punish you.*"

"See to it that Major Fatih is given a medal," Ohmshidi said.

"Yes, Glorious Leader."

Now the picture onscreen was of a somber-looking walled compound.

"You are looking at what was once a cotton oil mill, now converted into a prison in the town of Tanner, just outside Sikeston, Missouri.

"At the moment its only prisoner is Dr. Taylor Urban. Urban, in violation of Moqaddas Sirata, was discovered to be treating women patients. When investigators went to the scene to question Dr. Urban, they found him with a woman, fondling her naked breasts. Dr. Urban was placed in prison until Imam Tahir could make a final decision as to his case. It is now known that Imam Tahir has made that decision, and Dr. Urban will be required to pay the ultimate penalty. His execution, as was the execution of the two women just shown, will be watched by millions of viewers. Here is a statement from Imam Tahir."

The picture on screen changed to that of a man with dark hair and beard, wearing traditional Muslim clothing.

"It is my sincere belief that public executions play an important role in preventing future violations of the law. Therefore it is my sentence that on August first, at one o'clock in the afternoon, local time, Dr. Urban will be beheaded. His beheading will not be the mere tape of a previous event, but will be televised

*as it is happening. I think the impact of seeing
such a thing happen in real time will do
much to bring the rest of the country under
the just laws of Moqaddas Sirata. Obey
Ohmshidi!"*

The next images to show on the screen were of
the Civic Center in Mobile, Alabama.

*"These pictures were lifted from the pirate
broadcast of the heretical rebels who are
illegitimately meeting in Mobile, Alabama.
These apostates are making the false claim
that they are founding a new nation. But the
government of the American Islamic Republic
of Enlightenment does not acknowledge this. We
show you these pictures, only so that our viewers
may be aware of the traitors who are in our very
midst."*

The picture on the screen showed several men
and women greeting each other in front of the
Convention Center. The camera moved in on
the sign.

Welcome to the UNITED FREE AMERICA
CONSTITUTIONAL CONVENTION

"Why are they showing these pictures?"
Ohmshidi asked angrily. "Get them off the screen
at once. And warn them never to show such pictures again!"

Franken made a telephone call and within seconds, the pictures of the constitutional convention taking place in Mobile were gone from the screen.

"Uh, and that concludes our broadcast," the clearly nervous news anchor said. *"Obey Ohmshidi."*

Fort Morgan

After the constitution with the additional amendments and the platform were voted on and adopted came the business of getting a new country started. Bob was chairing the meeting, which consisted of Jake and Karen, Tom and Sheri Jack, Deon Pratt and Julie Norton, Marcus and Becky Warner, Chris Carmack and Kathy York, James and Cille DeLaney, and Willie Stark.

"You, here, represent the core group . . . the ones who started everything. So I don't believe there can be any discussion of organizing the nation of United Free America without your participation."

At that moment, Barbara Carter stepped into the meeting room. "Excuse the interruption, but there is a phone call for General Lantz."

"Tell whoever it is that I'll call back," Jake said.

"It's Governor Wallace from South Carolina," Barbara said. "He said it was urgent."

"Take the call, Jake. We won't get started until you get back," Bob promised.

Jake nodded, then excused himself.

A moment later he came back into the room with a pained look on his face.

"What is it, Jake?"

"A rebel firebase in South Carolina was just wiped out."

"State Protective Service?"

"No, it was locals."

"Locals?"

"Evidently they had recruited, armed, and trained some locals, and they turned on them," Jake said.

"Damn, that doesn't sound good, to have your own people turn on you. How reliable is this information?"

"Very reliable. It seems that before they attacked the firebase, they turned on their own men who wouldn't join them. One of them survived, then got hold of Major Tobin who is the area commander. Tobin took a team over to check it out and found them all dead."

"How did you hear about it?"

Jake nodded toward the other room. "That was the governor of South Carolina on the phone. He wants to talk to you, by the way. He left a number for us to call."

"All right, have Willie make the connection, and pipe it in here on the speaker phone."

No more than a minute later, Willie knocked on the door.

"Mr. President, General, I've got Governor Wallace on the phone."

"Thanks, Willie." Bob pushed the button on the speaker. "Governor Wallace, Bob Varney here."

"Thank you for taking my call," Wallace said.

"I'm sure you've heard what happened here. We lost several good men today."

"Yes, we just got the word," Bob said. "I'm sorry for your loss, and for the families of the men who were killed."

"The reason I wanted to talk to you, Mr. President, is because I'm wondering what sort of military support you can give us."

"Are you asking to join our federation?" Bob asked.

There was a long pause at the other end of the conversation. "I wish I could say that. I wish we had been able to send a delegation," he said. "But right now our state is very heavily divided . . . almost half didn't want to secede in the first place. And there is no stronger evidence for that than the fact that Captain Lumsden and his team were killed by other South Carolinians, men that we had armed and trained. And of the sixty percent or so who were willing to secede, there is almost an even split against joining any other federation.

"What I was hoping for was, perhaps, a military aid program of some sort, you know, allies, like England and the US during World War Two."

"I'm going to let General Lantz handle that question, Larry," Bob said.

"Governor, this is Jake Lantz."

"Yes, we just spoke, it's good to speak with you again."

"Here is our problem, Governor. As I'm sure you may realize we have only just begun to consolidate our scattered military assets into one cohesive army. So committing troops right now isn't

practical. I hope that soon we will be able to do
that. In the meantime I have a suggestion. We
have quite a large inventory of UAV Predators. If
you are willing to allow it, I can establish a UAV
presence over your state."

"Yes!" Governor Wallace said. "Yes, thank you!
That would be wonderful!"

"All right, I'll get that set up."

"Governor, it's me again," Bob said.

"Yes, Mr. President?"

"I know that you don't think you can convince
your entire state to join us, but we plan to meet
again on October 15th. Perhaps you might send a
nonvoting delegation to that meeting to observe."

"Yes, I would love to," Governor Wallace said.
"October 15th, Mobile?"

"Yes."

"We will have a delegation there, and again, I
thank you."

"You are very welcome, Governor," Bob said.
"And, in the meantime, see what you can do to
convince those who are opposed to the notion
that joining with us, in full partnership with the
other states, might be a good thing for you to do."

"I am fully convinced," Governor Wallace said.
"And I will see what I can do about bringing others
on board, at least enough to give us a majority."

CHAPTER TWENTY-TWO

When the conversation ended, Bob punched the speaker off, then looked at Jake.

"Where are you getting the Predators? Fort Gordon?" he asked.

"Yes, we have fifteen of them there."

"Good. It sounds like you've got the situation well in hand. So let's get back to business here. How are we going to organize our government?"

"What's wrong with the way we were organized?" Ellen asked. "And by we, I mean the United States."

Ellen Varney was a retired school teacher who had taught Geography, History, and Civics. She had also been very much a political wonk and saw the danger Ohmshidi represented when he first started running.

"Be more specific," Bob said.

"I'm talking about the three branches of government. Executive, legislative, and judicial. And the legislative branch should be bicameral."

"Bi what?" James asked.

"Bicameral," Ellen explained. "Two bodies of the legislature, a house and a senate."

"Sounds good," Tom said. "For the president, are we going to have an electoral college, or direct election?"

"Since we adopted the U.S. Constitution as our constitution, we are locked into an electoral college," Bob said. "Article Two, Section One. It would take an amendment to change it, and that wasn't one of the amendments we proposed."

"I think the electoral college would be better, anyway," Jake said. "In order to run a national election, someone would have to have real name recognition. George Gregoire is about the only person we know with that kind of reputation, and I think he would serve us better as our spokesman, than our president."

"And I think he would agree with you," Chris said.

"I think Bob should be our George Washington," Tom said.

"I can keep my own teeth, can't I?" Bob asked, and the others laughed. "Look, I don't mind serving as president while we are getting everything started, but I would like the position to be temporary. When we are actually ready to hold our first election, I don't intend to run."

"Maybe we can get you to change your mind," Jerry said.

"Uh-uh," Bob replied. "I will pull a General Sherman on you. If nominated I will not run, if elected I will not serve."

"Damn," Jerry said with a laugh. "Did Sherman really say that?"

"He did indeed."

"I'd say that is a pretty definite no, wouldn't you?" Karen said.

"All right, Bob, we won't nominate you."

"What about a flag?" Sheri asked. "We can't have a country without a flag."

"We've got one," Jake said. "It's called the Stars and Stripes."

"No, we're a new country, we should have a new flag," Kathy said.

"Why? Most of us here served the Stars and Stripes with honor and pride," Jake said. "I wouldn't like to see it cast aside."

"Yeah, and if you all remember, when we buried Sergeant Major Clayton Matthews the Third, he was holding the flag over his heart," Deon said.[2]

"May I tell you what I think about the flag?" Bob asked.

"Sure," Jake said. "After all, you're our president. And even if you aren't going to run again, who would have more right?" he added with a chuckle.

"Like most of you, I served the Stars and Stripes, and I never stood a retreat ceremony where I faced the flag, saluting as it was being lowered, without feeling so much pride that it choked me up. But, the Stars and Stripes stands for the United States as it was, and as we hope to reestablish. Fifty states, united as one nation.

---

2. *Phoenix Rising*

"That's not what we are right now, and, while I think the Stars and Stripes should be one of our most important icons, we don't yet have the right to fly it. In fact if we were to do so, I believe it would be disrespectful. It is what we will strive for and it shall be our goal to once again unite all our states under that banner. But until we do so, what we need is an interim flag around which we can rally."

"Yeah," Jake said. "I hadn't thought of it like that, but you are right. Maybe we should have a new flag. Do you have any ideas?" Jake asked.

"No, I don't."

"Julie, why don't you come up with an idea?" Deon asked, speaking to the beautiful young black woman who had been a medical clerk in the pre-O army. "You're always drawing pictures, and you're damn good at it."

"Oh, I don't know," Julie said. "That's a pretty big order, I mean, to design a flag for a whole country? That's quite a responsibility."

"Julie, you and I go back a long way together," Karen said. Karen had been a nurse in the same hospital where Julie had worked. "And in all the time I've known you, you have never been one to shy away from responsibility. And I have seen your art work as well. You can do this, there is no doubt in my mind."

"All right," Julie said with a nod. "I'm pretty sure I can come up with a design, but even if I do, I couldn't actually sew the flag."

"I'll sew the flag," Ellen said.

"Yes, that's a good idea. You're really good at that," Bob said. "So, Julie, you and Ellen will be our Betsy Ross," Bob said. "Or would that be Betsy Rosses?"

"I'll be the Betsy, Ellen can be the Ross," Julie joked.

"I do have a recommendation for something to add to the flag," Bob said.

"What?"

"Add the words, *Deo Vindice*," Bob said. "It means God is our Protector."

"Good idea," Jake agreed.

Bob smiled. "Jake, you being a Yankee, probably wouldn't know this, but *Deo Vindice* was the motto of the Confederacy."

"Will you have a problem with that, Julie?" Jake asked.

Julie smiled. "Not at all. I may be black, but I'm from Georgia. I'm so Southern that when I was born the doctor slapped my hammock with a candied yam."

The others laughed.

"Anyhow, I've heard that there were blacks who fought for the South," Deon said.

"That's absolutely true," Bob said. "It's not all that well known because it isn't politically correct. And that's a shame, because that steals honor from those brave black men who did fight. Nobody knows exactly how many, but there are estimates that from several hundred to several thousand blacks served with the Confederate forces during the war."

Jake shuddered. "Let us hope that this experiment doesn't end up in another civil war as bloody as the first."

"That's the hope and prayer of us all," Bob said. "But I can't see Ohmshidi letting us just walk away. What happened in Arkansas and what just happened in South Carolina is evidence of that."

"Yeah," Jake said. "I don't think any of us want to go to war, but if it comes down to fighting a war or give away our freedom, then I, for one, am ready for the fight."

Jake's solemn pronouncement was met with a long, studied, silence, finally broken by Julie.

"I'll get started on coming up with a design for the flag," Julie said.

Later that same afternoon Jake, Bob, Tom, Deon, and Chris began to organize the military. Jake and Bob already had received commitments from every military base they had visited earlier, but they were well aware that there was much more that could be added to the mix.

"The truth is, we only visited five bases, but we have over forty military installations within our borders, and I would estimate at least one hundred thousand men and women residing here, who were on active duty when the US military collapsed. I think it would be a safe bet to say that over ninety percent of them would be willing to serve. Within two months, we could reconstitute a military that is at least equal to anything AIRE can put together," Jake said.

"In terms of a conventional military, yes. But AIRE has a head start on us with the SPS and the Janissaries," Tom said. "And right now, they seem to be carrying the load."

"We have another asset," Jake said. "We have at least three hundred Predator Drones that can be deployed. I don't know how many the AIRE has."

"Probably not nearly as many as we have, but they are built in Southern California, which means they can build what they need," Bob said. "On the other hand, we have aircraft assembly plants here in Mobile, and in Georgia. With reverse engineering it wouldn't be hard at all for us to build enough drones to stay ahead of them, especially since we have a head start."

"And, we have nukes," Jake said.

"Yes, we have nukes," Bob agreed.

"And AIRE doesn't," Jake said. "So we don't have that problem to deal with."

"Just because AIRE doesn't have any nukes, that doesn't mean we don't have anything to worry about," Chris said.

"Why, do you think they might reconstitute the nukes?" Bob asked.

"No, I don't believe that any of the people who have the skill required to disassemble and reassemble the nukes would be willing to do that," Chris said. "But if Sorroto was able to buy five of them once, I've no doubt but that he can do it again."

"If he does buy them, will he give them to Ohmshidi, do you think?"

"No, and the more I think about it, I don't

think he was going to give them to him the first time either," Chris said. "I'm afraid that the truth is even more frightening. Sorroto is a megalomaniac. If he acquires the weapons I believe he will keep them for himself. And he may be more likely to use them than Ohmshidi would."

"You're right, that is more frightening," Bob said.

Taney County

Sorroto was on a satellite telephone call to General Dmitry Golovin.

"May I remind you that I paid for a product that was not delivered? And I paid quite well, as I recall," Sorroto said.

"Oh, but the product was delivered," Golovin replied. "We followed your instructions to the letter. You said that the product was to be delivered to the *Gomez*. It was delivered to the *Gomez*. That was the extent of our instructions. Once the product reached the *Gomez* it was, for all practical purposes, in your hands."

"The *Gomez* has disappeared without a trace. Nobody has heard a thing from it."

"Perhaps the captain of the *Gomez* decided to go into business for himself. That was quite a valuable cargo he was carrying."

"No, he wouldn't have done anything like that. I paid him enough money to buy his loyalty."

"Well, I have read of something called the Bermuda Triangle," Golovin said. "It could be that the ship got caught up in that mysterious area and has gone to join Flight Nineteen."

Sorroto was quiet for a moment. "I want to reorder," he finally said.

"I am afraid that product is no longer available."

"I am willing to forget the previous, uh, difficulty," Sorroto said. "I am willing to pay the same amount I paid the first time, even though I never took delivery of the product."

"You don't understand," Golovin said. "There was a unique set of circumstances which made the product available the first time. I'm afraid those circumstances no longer exist."

"Do you suppose you could duplicate those circumstances if I doubled the purchase price?"

Sorroto heard a little gasp from the other end of the phone. "Did I understand you to say that you would double the purchase price?"

"Yes. But this time I will find a more secure method of delivery."

"I think we might be able to do some business together," Golovin said.

Fort Morgan

Julie and Ellen kept their work on the flag a secret for the two days it took them to design and sew the flag. Then they presented their flag, a red banner with a blue horizontal bar, intersected in the first quarter of its length by a vertical blue bar. There were eight white stars, representing the eight states that had attended the constitutional convention, six stars in the horizontal bar and two additional stars in the vertical bar. The motto *Deo Vindice* was in the lower right quarter of the banner.

The flag was unfurled at a dinner hosted by Jake and Karen and it received instant applause and acclaim.

"You know what I think?" Jake said. "I think we should find a factory that will make a thousand of these flags and we'll pass them out, first come first served. Then, as people see them and want them, they'll buy more until they become ubiquitous."

Karen laughed. "Ubiquitous? Well, I'm proud of you, Jake, showing off your vocabulary like that."

"The first thing we need to do is get them out to the military bases," Jake said. "Nothing instills a sense of pride and duty in a soldier like seeing the flag of their country."

"And, we need to get a couple out to Virdin and the *John Paul Jones*," Tom suggested.

Bob nodded. "Yes, it would be a good idea to show our flag at sea. We'll also put it on our container vessels so we can show it in foreign ports."

CHAPTER TWENTY-THREE

They didn't have to go too far to find a company that manufactured flags. There was already such a company in Hattiesburg, Mississippi, and they were not only thrilled to get the order, they turned out a thousand flags in less than a week.

"Oh, they are beautiful!" Ellen said when she saw them. "So much more professional looking than the one I sewed."

Bob laughed. "Well, do you suppose it is because they are professional flag makers?" he asked. He folded, carefully, the flag that Ellen had sewn. "But I intend to keep this one. It was the very first one, and it will always be special."

"Yes, it will be, won't it?"

The next day Jake and Tom took the flag out to the *John Paul Jones*, which was on station about twenty-five miles off the coast. Jake sat down on the helipad on the afterdeck.

"Damn!" Tom said. "Next thing you know, you'll be carrier qualified," he teased.

"Now that is a fine looking flag," Virdin said. "Though I must confess to being partial to the Stars and Stripes."

"We all are," Tom said. "But Bob laid it out for us. We'll fly the Stars and Stripes again, when we have taken America back."

"Good point," Virdin said. He held the flag in his hand. "What do you say we raise the flag."

Fifteen minutes later, with all hands on deck, two petty officers attached the flag to the halyard of the ship's truck.

"Ship's company, present arms!" Virdin called.

As the ship's company rendered the hand salute, the bugle call *To The Colors* was piped over the 1MC while the flag was run, briskly, up the flagstaff. The flag reached the top, caught the breeze, then filled and spread out displaying the colors. The hand salute was held until the final note of *To The Colors* sounded.

"Order, arms!" Virdin called. Then, "Ship's company, dismissed."

"Do you have to go back right away?" Virdin asked. "Or can you take dinner with us?"

Since both Jake and Tom were of a military background, Virdin didn't have to explain that "dinner" referred to the noon meal.

Jake and Tom gathered with the other officers in the wardroom where they were served beef stew.

"Sorry we don't have a better meal prepared, but we weren't expecting company," Virdin said.

"Nonsense, this is a fine meal," Jake said.

"Too bad you weren't here for breakfast. We had foreskins on a raft," Lieutenant Langley said.

"You had what?" Jake asked.

Tom laughed. "You would probably call it SOS. The only difference is, the navy version uses sliced beef instead of ground beef."

"Tell me," Virdin said. "What's happening back on the beach?"

For the rest of the meal Jake and Tom filled Virdin and the other officers of the wardroom in on the latest news, from the incorporation of the other military bases, to the constitution convention.

"Our next gathering of delegate will be on October 15th," Jake said. "Then we will unite as one nation, rather than what we are now, a disunion of seceded states."

"I thought we were already a nation," Virdin said. "I mean we have a flag and everything."

"Well, let's just say that we will be a bigger, and more united nation after the convention." Jake said.

"I got an e-mail from Joel Limbaugh," Chris said the next day as he and Jake were walking on the beach.

"Joel Limbaugh?"

"He was one of the Arkansas delegates who came here."

"Oh, yes, I remember the name. What was the e-mail about?"

"It was a request for me to visit Blytheville."

"Blytheville? Isn't that where the SPS slaughtered a bunch of innocent people at a picnic?"

"Yes. That's why I'm going."

"Oh?"

"Jake, you know who I am, you know my background. Joel knows as well. In the pre-O time, he was an administrative aide to Senator McKenna. McKenna was on the Senate Intelligence Committee."

"What does Mr. Limbaugh want of you?"

"I imagine he wants to make use of my particular talent."

"I see. Have you told Bob yet?"

"I'm not going to tell him. One of the things I have learned in my profession is that it is sometimes better to keep the higher-ups blissfully ignorant of specific events. That gives them deniable plausibility. Bob represents the civilian side of our community. You represent the military side. I think you have to know, but it's better if Bob doesn't know."

Jake nodded. "All right, I'll give you that. But if you disappear for a while Bob is going to miss you. How do you cover that?"

"We'll tell him that I'm going to New York to meet with some people."

"All right, Chris. You've done this kind of work before, I'll leave all the details up to you. Anything you need?"

"How many Claymore mines do we have?"

"How many do you need?"

Blytheville

Chris was told to be at the Coffee Cup café at exactly 0800 where he would eat breakfast. As soon as he entered, he saw a big man with a full head of white hair, standing just outside the kitchen. "Have a biscuit!" the big man said and Chris had to react quickly as a biscuit came sailing across the room to him.

"Biscuits! Who wants a biscuit?" the big man shouted.

"I do!"

Chris stood there for a moment as he watched biscuits sailing across the room, the big man throwing them to customers.

"Find a table and have a seat!" the big man called out to Chris. "We don't stand on ceremony here at the Coffee Cup." He threw another biscuit toward Chris who caught it, even though he wasn't expecting it.

As Chris walked toward an empty table, another customer came in.

"Oliver Deermont," the biscuit thrower said. "Come on in, come in out of the cold."

"Cold?" Oliver said.

"Oh, I don't mean cold weather. I mean the coldness of an indifferent society. Nothing like that here, in the Coffee Cup."

"I guess not," Deermont replied. "You never shut up long enough for anyone to be indifferent."

The others in the café laughed.

Chris's instructions were to turn his glass upside down, and lay his spoon across the top, and that's what he did. He had been told by Joel that if he did that, he would be contacted by Harold "Curly" Latham. Chris did as directed, then he pulled the menu from between the napkin dispenser and the sugar, salt, and pepper shakers.

Chris was dressed in coveralls and wearing a cap that read "Gristo Feeds." He looked like any other farmer in the café, including the man who, less than a minute after Chris took his seat, stepped over to the table. This had to be Curly Latham, who, evidently, was already in the café waiting for Chris. Curly was not wearing a hat, and he didn't have curly hair. In fact, he had no hair at all.

"Hello, Chris, I'm glad you could take breakfast with me," Latham said. "I know you are on your way to Memphis, and I wouldn't want to hold you up."

"No, that's quite all right, you aren't holding me up, my meeting in Memphis isn't until this afternoon," Chris said, smiling up at the man. There was no meeting in Memphis, in fact until Latham brought it up, Memphis hadn't even been on his mind. But Chris picked up on it, and followed the conversation. Neither Chris nor Latham had ever met before but if anyone in the café happened to overhear them, they would think the two men were old friends of long standing.

"Oh, Jill said to say hello to Alice and the kids," Latham said.

"I'll do that."

There was neither Alice nor children, but like the small talk about Memphis, Chris responded appropriately, in order to maintain the façade of two old friends greeting each other. They continued to talk about such things as hunting, the weather, and children's illnesses. As they were talking, Latham put a piece of paper into the napkin dispenser. A moment later, Chris removed the paper. Nothing of any importance was said until finally, at the end of breakfast the two men stepped up to the cash register to pay for their meal.

"Take care," Latham said as they started out. "And don't forget to tell Alice that Jill sends her regards."

"I'll do that."

Chris waited until he returned to the car before he read the note.

Your targets are Ahmed Mahaz and Merlin Lewis. Mahaz is the captain in charge of the local SPS company. You just met Merlin Lewis. He is the big man who owns the Coffee Cup. Don't let Lewis's friendly demeanor fool you. He is a snitch for the SPS, and is personally responsible for the deaths of at least one hundred citizens of Blytheville. Do not contact me again. Destroy this note as soon as you read it.

Chris decided that Merlin Lewis would be his first target. He did nothing until dark, then he waited behind the café between the Dumpster and the brick wall of the building. When Lewis came out of the café that night, Chris raised a CO_2 pellet pistol, aimed and pulled the trigger. The sound was no more than a quiet puff, but that was all that was needed to send a curare-tipped pellet into Lewis's neck.

Chris watched as Lewis reached up to grab his neck, then took two more steps before he fell. Then, using a pair of tweezers, he extracted the pellet from Lewis's neck and dropped it into the trash Dumpster.

Chris waited two more days before he went into the SPS headquarters building.

"Yes, what do you want?" the desk sergeant asked.

"I, uh, wonder if there is a reward if I report something," Chris said.

"What do you have to report?"

"Is there a reward?"

"That's not for me to say. That's for Captain Mahaz."

"May I speak to Captain Mahaz?"

Chris well knew who Mahaz was. Unlike many of the SPS and Janissaries, Yusef Mahaz was not a recent convert to Islam. He had been a lifelong Muslim who had been given a commission in the pre-O army, precisely because he was a Muslim. It was believed, by the army, that Mahaz would be a good liaison officer for them. His duty assignment had been to teach the other soldiers about the Muslim culture to "engender an understanding" between the religions.

But one day Major Mahaz showed up at a processing center in Fort Eustis where he began shooting. He killed thirteen and wounded twenty-nine others. Not until he ran out of ammunition did he stop shooting. Then he lay down his weapons and put up his hands, shouting *Allah hu akbar* as he was taken into custody. One of Ohmshidi's first acts was to grant Mahaz a complete pardon.

Chris waited for a moment, then the clerk came back. "The captain will see you," he said.

"What do you want?" Mahaz asked, sharply, when Chris stepped into his office.

"A friend of mine, Merlin Lewis, told me that I should come see you," Chris said.

"How could Merlin Lewis tell you that? He is dead."

"Yes, I heard he had a heart attack out behind his place," Chris said. "And that's too bad, because he promised to introduce me to you. He said that you would pay money for information."

"Sometimes I will. It depends on the information."

"I know where a group of Christians will be having a worship service."

"Nonsense, all the churches have been closed," Mahaz said.

"Ah, but this isn't in a church. It will be held in a tent in a field out of town."

"When and where is this to be held?" Mahaz asked.

"Is this information worth money to you?"

"One hundred Moqaddas," Mahaz said.

"Only one hundred? I was hoping for more than that."

"One hundred now, and if we find the Christians having a service in a tent, it will be worth four hundred more afterward."

Chris smiled, and nodded his head. "Yes, yes,

five hundred Moqaddas. That is very good. Shall I come here for the money?"

"Afterward," Mahaz said.

"Yes, afterward," Chris agreed.

"Now when and where is this to be held?"

"Go west of town, to E. County Road, 180. You will see a tent, just to the left of the road. That's where they will be. The service starts at eight o'clock tomorrow morning."

Mahaz nodded, then counted out the one hundred Moqaddas. "Come back tomorrow afternoon and I will give you the rest of the money."

"Thank you," Chris said. "Thank you very much."

It took Chris the rest of the day to get everything set up. First he had to erect the tent, and because it was a relatively large tent, it was no easy job for one man. He had to do it by himself though, because he couldn't take a chance on using anyone else. There would be no cars parked around the tent and he was a little concerned about that, but he realized that anyone who actually would attend such a service wouldn't want their cars there so that they could be identified.

When the tent was erected, he set the Claymore mines all the way around the perimeter of the tent, rigging all of them to be fired by a radio signal. The last thing he did was put a CD player in the tent, and set it so he could turn it on by radio signal. He returned early the next morning, and waited.

At about eight fifteen a car and an army truck

arrived. He saw Mahaz get out of the car, then twelve men, all dressed in the black and silver uniforms of the Janissaries, climbed down from the truck.

Chris hit a button to start the CD playing.

"I'm going to ask you, each and every one today, to give your life to Jesus! If you haven't been baptized, we'll go down to the ever-living water today so you can give your soul to the Lord. If you have been, then come on down and re-dedicate yourselves in front of all your brothers and your sisters."

The sound changed then to a hymn, being sung badly, and without music accompaniment.

> *"Shall we gather at the river,*
> *where bright angel feet have trod,*
> *with its crystal tide forever*
> *flowing by the throne of God."*

Mahaz held his finger to his lips, then signaled to the others to completely surround the tent. All the while they were getting ready, the singing from inside the tent continued.

> *"Yes, we'll gather at the river,*
> *the beautiful, the beautiful river;*
> *gather with the saints at the river*
> *that flows by the throne of God."*

"Now!" Mahaz shouted, and he and the 12 black-clad men with him, begin firing into the tent, with their weapons on full automatic.

Chris let them fire for fully ten seconds before

pushing the button on his remote. The button triggered sixteen Claymore anti-personnel mines, critically arranged all the way around the circumference of the tent, to detonate as one. The sound was earsplitting, and thousands of steel balls tore through all four sides of the tent, slamming into the flesh of the twelve janissaries, ripping their bodies into bloody pulps. All twelve Janissaries, plus their leader, Mahaz, died instantly.

CHAPTER TWENTY-FOUR

It was Tom Jack who introduced the idea of rescuing Dr. Urban. "I grew up in Sikeston," Tom said. "Dr. Urban was my doctor."

"All right," Jake agreed. "If you can come up with a plan that you think has a chance of working, I'll authorize the mission."

"I would like Deon to go with me," Tom said. "We work pretty well together."

"Everybody works well with Deon," Jake said. "That's why I chose him to be a part of my team when we first came down here. But it seems to me like this is likely to be a pretty high-risk mission, and right now, you and Deon are the only two snake-eaters I have, and I don't want to risk you both on the same mission.

"I tell you what, though. We've had some pretty good men sign up with us since we started building our military. Why don't you see Willie, he's got everyone's background on the computer. I'm pretty sure the two of you could come up with a strike team."

"Thanks," Tom said. "I'll see what he has for me."

"Snake-eaters?" Barbara asked, after Tom left.

Jake chuckled. "It's a generic term for anyone trained in special forces, whether army, navy, marines, or air force. As part of their survival training, they would catch, and eat, snakes."

"Oooh," Barbara said, with a shudder. "Remind me never to go on a picnic with a snake-eater."

"I want to go," Willie said.

"Oh, Willie, I don't think so," Tom replied.

"Why not? You think I like being nothing but a computer geek all the time. I am a soldier, I have had training, you know. It's not like I'm some kid off the street just wanting a little adventure."

"Willie, if something happened to you, Jake would never forgive me. Hell, I wouldn't forgive myself. Yes, you are a computer geek which, right now, makes you one of the most valuable members of this entire operation. Jake gave me authority to pick the team I want, and I'm not going to make a definitive statement that you can't go, because I consider you too much of a friend to do that. But I hope you have enough common sense to withdraw the request."

Willie drummed on the desk for a moment, then let out a disgusted sigh. "All right," he said. "All right, I withdraw the request. But I am telling you right now, I have no intention of being nothing but a computer geek for the rest of my life."

"Thank you, Willie. Now, I'm going to take nine

men with me. I'm going to need two helicopter pilots, an NCO as my second-in-command, and eight men, former SEALS or special forces army, as my fighting men. And, I'll want an Apache crew to provide cover for us. So what I want you to do is give me at least two men for each position, and let me study their background, then I'll make the final selection."

"All right," Willie agreed.

Later that same day Willie brought a file folder to Tom, with several printed pages inside. There was one page for each man, as well as a photo.

"These are men we can get hold of quickly," Willie said. "Some are in Mobile, some are in Pensacola, and there are even a few who are in Gulf Shores. I don't think you can go wrong no matter who you pick."

"Thanks, Willie."

"Oh, and I got something else you might find interesting."

"What's that?"

"I've got a complete layout of the prison where they are holding Dr. Urban."

"What?"

Willie showed Tom another folder. "Yep. Dimensions, entrances, guard towers, it's all there."

"Willie, you are a genius!" Tom said, smiling broadly as he took the folder. "Wait a minute, I know this place. This is the old Tanner Cotton Oil Mill. I thought you said it's a prison."

"It is now," Willie said. "They've converted it."

"Well, I'll be. I've known this place for my entire life, but I never did see the inside. I guess I will now."

Using the layout of the prison, Tom developed a plan of attack. The plan called for a Blackhawk helicopter to put the assault team on the ground, and an Apache helicopter to provide fire support. That meant he would need at least four helicopter pilots, and he decided he would let Jake select them.

The ground assault team would be his responsibility so he began looking through the list of names Willie had given him.

The first name was James Algood. He read the information Willie had supplied for him.

1. Algood, James. A sergeant first class before the collapse of the U.S. Army, Algood was a Special Forces soldier who, in Afghanistan, led the assault team that rescued three American soldiers who had been captured by the Taliban. For that action, Algood received the Distinguished Service Cross.

2. Andrew Kearney, also a Special Forces soldier who has worked with Algood. Kearney, who was a staff sergeant before the collapse of the U.S. army, is the recipient of a Silver Star for gallantry in action in Afghanistan.

3. Paul Cooper and David Lewis were both members of the Marine Corps Special Forces, both of whom received the Bronze Star with the "V" device for valor.

The last three men Tom selected were Jubal Cates, Ken Gilmore, and Jerry Ferrell. Now all he needed was to get his assault team assembled, then run do a couple of dry runs of his plan.

UAV Remote Flight Control, Fort Gordon, Georgia

Major Joseph Rowe and Captain Hal Madison arrived for their duty tour at 0350, ten minutes before they were scheduled to relieve the team before them.

"Two creams, one sugar, isn't that right, Major?" Madison asked as he stopped by the coffee table.

"Yeah, thanks," Rowe replied.

The two men they were about to relieve were in the "cockpit" of the MQ9 Reaper unmanned aerial vehicle. The cockpit of the aircraft was in a building at Fort Gordon, but the aircraft they were flying was actually 175 miles away, cruising at an altitude of 10,000 feet on a radial of 310 degrees, twenty-five miles southeast of Firebase Swift Strike.

The pilot, Captain Bill Kirby, was flying the aircraft just as if he were actually onboard, with stick, rudder and throttle. The Mission Management Computers, consisting of two internal navigation and global positioning systems, were operating in conjunction with an embedded GPS receiver for enhanced navigation performance and faster satellite acquisition. All the flight data was being sent via a KU Band Satellite data link. Lieutenant Oscar Mack was also in the remote cockpit, sitting alongside Kirby. Madison was the "Sensor" officer and he was operating the ISS, or Integrated Sensor

Suite, as well as the GMTI, or Ground Moving Target Indicator. Mack could, if required, employ an array of weaponry, from hellfire missiles, to smart bombs, to the extremely rapid firing M61A2 Vulcan Cannon.

"Anything happening?" Rowe asked.

"Not a damn thing," Kirby replied. "All we've done for four hours is bore holes in the sky."

"What's the fuel situation?"

Kirby checked one of his instruments. "Hour sixteen of forty-two," he said. "You'll be in good shape."

Madison handed a cup of coffee to Rowe.

"Thanks, Hal."

"What's our armament mix, Oscar?" Madison asked the black sensor officer that he would be relieving.

"Eight hellfire missiles, two Vulcan cannons with three thousand rounds."

"We're monitoring Swift Strike again?" Rowe asked.

"Yes, sir."

"Damn," Madison said. "Nothing ever happens there. You know what I'd like to do with this. I'd like to fly it over Washington, and stick a hellfire missile right up Ohmshidi's ass."

"Whoa, that's pretty damn violent, isn't it, Hal?" Captain Kirby teased.

"Yeah, and to think that I have to sit beside this violent man for the next four hours," Major Rowe said.

"The next four hours, right," Kirby said. "Major Rowe, the ship is yours," Kirby said, getting up so

Rowe could take his place. "Soon as I fill out the flight log, I'm out of here."

"I've got it, Oscar," Madison said, slipping in to the seat Lieutenant Mack just left.

"Gentlemen, we leave it in your hands. Good hunting," Kirby said.

"Good hunting is right. I'm getting so bored sitting here doing nothing, if I see a good sized buck, I'm going to take him out," Madison said.

Five minutes later Kirby and Mack were gone leaving Rowe and Madison at the controls. Rowe slipped a CD into a player and they began listening to the music of Beethoven.

"That's nice," Madison said.

"Ha! I chose you because of your taste in music," Rowe said. "If I had to sit alongside MacMurtry and listen to his shit-kicking music for four hours, I'd go crazy."

"That's not the way to think about it, Major. You outrank MacMurtry, you wouldn't have to listen to his music, he'd have to listen to yours."

"Yeah," Rowe replied with a smile. "Yeah, that's right, isn't it?"

0608 hours, Firebase Swift Strike, Lancaster County, South Carolina

The first thing Captain J. C. Jones noticed when he awoke was that the generator wasn't running. Not only could he not hear the steady drone of the 500KW, he was also lying in a pool of sweat, because without the generator, there was no air conditioner.

Jones sat up on his bunk, then swung his legs over. He had been a Sergeant First Class before the United States Army collapsed. Now, in the South Carolina Defense Corps, he was a captain, and the site commander of Firebase Swift Strike.

"Dooley," Jones said. "Wasn't it your job to keep fuel in the generator last night?"

"That's right, it was, Captain, and I did it. Fact is, I refueled it at about four this morning. If it's stopped, it isn't because of a lack of fuel," Corporal Dooley said.

"Well, something is wrong with it," Jones said. He pulled on his trousers, then put on his boots. "I need to take a leak anyway, I'll take a look."

When Jones walked over to check on the generator he saw that the oil cap was off and that there was a great deal of dirt around the filter. In addition, the carburetor had been smashed. The generator had not just stopped, it had been sabotaged.

"What the hell?" he said aloud. He picked up the pieces of the carburetor and held them in his hand. "Who the hell would do something like this? And why would they do it?"

He glanced up into one of the nearest guard towers, intending to ask if the guard had seen anything.

The tower was empty.

At about the same time he saw that the tower was empty, he saw that, in addition to the generator being sabotaged, the uplink had been destroyed as well. He depended on the uplink for satellite communication. For all intent and purposes, they were cut off.

"What the hell is going on here?" Jones asked.

Looking toward the other guard towers, he saw that they were as empty as the first. He didn't have to ask the question a second time. He knew what was going on. The compound was being set up for an attack.

"Oh shit!" Jones shouted. "Get your weapons!" he shouted. "Head for the bunker!"

Even as he was giving the orders, he was dashing back to the hut to grab his own M-4. "Everybody, grab a weapon! Get into the bunker!" he shouted.

As the men started reaching for their clothes, Jones yelled at them. "You ain't goin' to a damn parade! You're goin' to war! Forget about getting dressed, just grab your piece and head for the bunker!"

At that moment there was a loud explosion in the motor pool as a mortar round took out one of their vehicles.

Firebase Swift Strike was on the South Carolina side of the North Carolina—South Carolina border, very near the tiny, and now all but deserted town of Betheny. North Carolina had not seceded, and was still a part of the America Islamic Republic of Enlightenment. The attack was coming from a large body of SPS men.

CHAPTER TWENTY-FIVE

UAV Remote Flight Control Facility, Fort Gordon

Major Rowe and Captain Madison were two hours into their four-hour tour of duty. It was considered counterproductive for any crew to be on such intense duty for longer than four hours. At 0800 Zulu, another crew would take over to continue the twenty-four hour mission of the Unmanned Aerial Vehicle.

"Hey, Hal, did you eat breakfast?" Major Rowe asked.

"At four o'clock in the morning? No, I'll eat when we get off."

"Where you goin' to eat?"

"I don't know, I hadn't thought about it that much. All I need is some bacon and eggs, maybe a biscuit or two," Madison answered. "What about you?"

"I'm going to the Good Egg," Rowe said. "I'm big on breakfast. It's my favorite meal, and they do know how to put on a breakfast. You want to come along?"

"Sure, why not?" Madison answered. Suddenly he leaned forward in his seat.

"Whoa, Major, check this out," Madison said, pointing to his sensor array.

"What do you have?"

"I'm not sure, but it looks like a lot of activity around Firebase Swift Strike."

"Better get their six on the horn, let them know what we are seeing here," Rowe said.

Madison punched in some numbers on the secure satellite phone, but got no answer.

"They aren't responding," he said after several tries.

Rowe shook his head. "This isn't looking good," he said.

"Think we should call QRT?" Madison asked.

"I'll call the Quick Response Team, but at this time on Sunday, all we'll get is the Officer of the Day, and like as not the OD will be some doofus lieutenant," Rowe said.

Everything Madison saw on his sensor array indicated that an attack on Swift Strike had begun.

"It's too late anyway. They're already hitting our guys!" Madison said.

"Damn," Rowe replied.

"Joe, I can take them out," Madison said. "Give me the word!"

"I—I don't know," Rowe answered. "I think we need to contact QRT on this one."

"Come on, Joe, those are the good guys down there in that compound," Madison said. "You know what happened at Camp Cassandra. That's why they asked for us."

"You know the rules of engagement as well as I do," Rowe said. "If this attack was within our borders we could act. But it's in South Carolina and we are supposed to get permission from the South Carolina Defense Corps."

"Do you think the SCDC wouldn't want us to act? We are officers, Joe. And we were officers in the pre-O time. We are trained to be able to make decisions when we have to."

"I'll call QRT and see what I can do," Rowe said, picking up the direct line.

"They better be quick," Madison said. "This is coming down now."

Firebase Swift Strike

Automatic weapons fire coming from the SPS attackers bounced off the rocky ground and cut through the thin walls of the compound huts. Jones, and the eleven others of his firebase team had taken shelter in the bunker, but they were greatly outnumbered, and outgunned by the attackers. They were also unable to contact the outside for help.

Bullets slammed into the sandbags and whizzed by overhead. In addition, RPG and mortar rounds were exploding all through the compound.

"Final defensive fire!" Jones shouted, and the defenders quit trying to pick out individual targets, but instead concentrated a withering fire in pre-selected zones that would prevent anyone from getting through. The concept of 'final defensive fire' had been developed during WWII to combat the "banzai" charges and it was brutally effective—but only so long as the ammunition held out. And at this rate of fire, that would not be much longer.

UAV Remote Flight Control, Fort Gordon

"They're attacking, Joe, they're attacking!" Madison shouted.

"Yeah, I see that."

"What do we do? Have we heard from QRT?"

"The QRT OD hasn't called back."

"What do we do?"

"To hell with the OD and to hell the rules of engagement," Major Rowe said. "Arm your weapons, Hal, I'm bringing it around."

"Yes, sir!" Madison answered happily.

Firebase Swift Strike

Neither the SPS attackers nor the South Carolinian defenders saw or heard the UAV overhead. The first indication anyone had that it was there was when the hellfire missiles started raining down on the attackers, slamming into them with deadly accuracy, taking out dozens with each blast. Then the South Carolinian defenders saw the ground being chewed up in front of them as the Vulcan cannon started firing, each round bursting into smaller, razor-sharp bits of shrapnel to rip through the flesh of the attackers.

Within two passes of the UAV, the attack had

been broken, and when Captain Jones moved his team, cautiously, out onto the battlefield, they saw legs, arms, heads, and the shredded torsos of scores of SPS fighters. Not one defender had been killed.

"What the hell happened?" one of the men said.

At that moment the UAV made another pass, this time making a wide turn.

"You've heard of manna from heaven?" Jones asked. "This was hell from heaven." Jones waved at the UAV.

"What are you waving at, Cap'n? There ain't nobody in any of the planes, is there?"

"That doesn't mean they can't see us," Jones replied.

UAV Remote Flight Control, Fort Gordon

"Ha," Madison said. "They're waving at us."

"I'll wave back," Rowe said, and he dipped the wings from side to side.

The phone rang and Rowe picked it up. "UAV ops, Major Rowe."

"Major Rowe, this is Lieutenant Townsend, Quick Response Team. I still haven't been able to get hold of Colonel Hicks, but as soon as I do I'll get back to you with . . ."

"Never mind, Lieutenant. We've already conducted the operation," Rowe said.

"Uh, yes sir," Townsend said.

"You give Colonel Hicks my regards now, you hear?"

"Yes, sir."

Rowe hung up the phone. "Quick reaction team? Quick, my hind clavicle."

Firebase Swift Strike

"I told you they'd see us!" Jones said happily and this time when he waved, all the others waved with him.

"Don't you feel a little dumb waving at a plane there ain't nobody in?" one of the men asked.

"They saved our lives," Dooley said. "I'll wave at it until my arm falls off.

Muslimabad

"What is going on?" Ohmshidi demanded angrily. "We have our people killed in Arkansas, and in South Carolina. You do know what can come from this, don't you? Something like this can spread, and the next thing you know others will be trying it. We need to do something, and we need to do it quickly."

"I have something in mind, Glorious Leader," Franken replied. "South Carolina has seceded and I . . ."

"No state has seceded!" Ohmshidi said angrily. "Secession is not legal. There are still fifty states in the American Islamic Republic of Enlightenment, and I will not hear of anyone saying that any state has seceded."

"You are absolutely right, Glorious Leader. What I meant to say is that there are some in South Carolina who have made the false and illegal claim that they have seceded. But, there are still many in South Carolina who are loyal to Moqaddas Sirata and I think there is where we can make a resolute demonstration that will be seen by anyone else who might have such treasonous ideas. I intend to conduct more military operations there."

"Yes. Do so."

Fort Morgan

"I strongly recommend these two guys as pilots for your Blackhawk," Jake said. "They were both Chief Warrant Officers, both of them received the DFC for their service in Iraq and in Afghanistan. Dan Lambdin and Bob "Clipper" Bivens. And for the Apache, Mike Lindell and Tom Hunsinger. I've served with all four of them, they are outstanding."

"Have you spoken to them?"

"Yes, and they are chomping at the bit, but I told them that you would have the final word."

"Listen, if you recommend them, that's good enough for me," Tom said. "Where are they now? I'd like to set up a training mission as soon as I can."

"They'll be here by midafternoon."

"Good. I plan to brief everyone tonight, and conduct the training operation just after midnight."

* * *

In 2006 as a sophomore running back for the Crimson Tide of Alabama, James Algood had made honorable mention all-American. Then, in the Cotton Bowl game against Texas Tech, Algood came out of the backfield to catch a pass that was thrown too high. Going up for it left him vulnerable, and he was hit hard by two Texas Tech linebackers, twisting his leg like a pretzel as they brought him down. Although he managed to hang on to the football, he felt an excruciating stab of pain when his knee went out.

Algood was carried off the field in a stretcher and taken immediately to ER, where surgeons worked hard to prevent the injury from rendering him permanently crippled.

"Algood, I can't tell you how sorry I am this happened to you," the coach said when he came to visit Algood a few days later. "You are one of the finest young men I have ever been around. And I'm not just talking football, I'm talking about your value as a human being."

Algood managed a chuckle. "Why do I think that sounds a little like a eulogy?"

The coach ran his hand through his hair and sighed. "I won't lie to you, son. I guess in a way it is."

Algood was silent for a long moment. "You're saying I won't play football anymore, aren't you?"

"That's what the doctors are telling me," the coach replied. "Unfortunately, that also means that your football scholarship is gone. But, if you want to stay in school, son, you let me know, because I promise you, I will find a way."

Algood thanked the coach and said he wanted to think about it. After the coach left, Algood cried into his pillow. As a young black man, it had seemed to him that there were only two paths open to him: a dead-end job working at the peanut oil mill, as had his father, or a life of crime, from petty to grand.

The first in his family to graduate from high school, Algood had come to the University of Alabama for one reason, and that was to get a ticket into the NFL. Now that ticket was snatched away from him in one career-ending play.

Algood completed that semester, then dropped out of school and joined the army. To his surprise and delight, the army had replaced football as his core and motivation. He went to Airborne training, Ranger training, and Special Forces training, and rose quickly through the ranks to become a Sergeant First Class. His proudest moment was standing at attention at a special awards ceremony at Fort Benning, where he was presented with the Distinguished Service Medal, a medal only one notch below the Medal of Honor.

Again, fate conspired against him when the United States Army collapsed. But he was being given a third chance, having joined the army of United Free America. And in this army, he was a captain, chosen to be second in command of an assault team organized to rescue Dr. Urban.

It was now 0230 and Algood and the others on the team were in a Blackhawk helicopter, its doors removed, beating through the dark toward a spot just north of Mobile, where they would conduct a training exercise. Tom Jack had chosen a barn just off Sewell Road because the approach to the barn, and the relative position of the barn, was very similar to the layout of the Tanner Cotton Oil Mill.

CHAPTER TWENTY-SIX

South Carolina

Fifteen two and one-half ton trucks, each truck carrying twenty men, and every third truck pulling a 155 howitzer came down Cashua Ferry Road. Just under two miles outside Darlington, they unlimbered the five field pieces and trained them toward the city of Darlington.

Before President Ohmshidi's incompetence and socialist programs brought about the collapse of the United States, the town of Darlington, South Carolina had been well known for the Darlington Motor Speedway. The races that once drew thousands of visitors to the town were no longer being held, and the track was now overgrown with weeds. Two young boys were at the track now, on bicycles.

"Go!" one of them yelled, then, making the sound of a roaring race car engine, or at least approximating the sound to the degree they could, they started riding their bicycles as fast as they could around the track.

Suddenly, no more than a hundred and fifty yards in front of them, there was a loud explosion, and heavy chunks of the track pavement were thrown up into the air. Both boys braked their bikes, skidding to a stop as there was a second explosion in what had been the press box.

"Darrell! What's happening?" the younger of the two boys asked.

They heard three more explosions, coming from the middle of town.

"I don't know!" Darrell admitted. "Come on, Leo, let's get out of here!"

The two boys headed back toward the entrance to the speedway, pedaling as fast as they could.

This time they heard a rushing sound and, looking up, saw something black hurtling through the sky above them, headed for the town. They watched it plummet to the earth, then erupt into another explosion.

"Someone is shooting cannons at us!" Darrell said.

There was another explosion in the road, right in front of them.

"Leo, stop! Stop! We've got to hide in the ditch!" Darrell shouted, and the two boys abandoned their bicycles then ran to the edge of the road and jumped down into the ditch just as another shell landed, and exploded in the road.

* * *

It had been almost fifty years since Dolan Kinder had heard the sound of an incoming artillery shell. Once when someone asked him what it sounded like, he described the sound as like a disconnected boxcar rolling down a railroad track. When he heard the sound from inside his small electric motor repair shop, he almost commented to a customer that it sounded just like incoming artillery. But before he could say the words, there was a loud explosion outside. That was followed almost immediately by the rushing sound of another incoming round.

"What is that?" the customer asked, alarmed.

"It's artillery!" Kinder said. "God help us . . . someone is shooting at us!"

"What?"

"Out back!" Kinder said. "There's a concrete stairwell going down to the basement of the jewelry store across the alley!"

There were two other explosions, one right on top of the other.

"What are you talking about?" the puzzled customer asked.

"Come with me, or stay here and get blown to kingdom come!" Kinder shouted, running toward the back door.

Still another explosion, right outside the front door, was all the customer needed to prod him. Dropping the electric drill he had brought to be repaired, he ran toward the back door, then followed Kinder outside.

"Down in there!" Kinder shouted, pointing across the alley from the back of his shop. What he pointed to was actually the outside entrance to a basement, with steps that went down about ten feet. The walls of the excavation were lined with concrete.

"Who is doing this?" the customer asked, even as there were two more explosions, one of the in the alley so close by that shrapnel whistled overhead and rattled against the side of the building, below which they were taking cover.

There were two more explosions somewhat farther away.

Out on the main streets of Darlington, away from where Dolan Kinder and his customer were taking shelter, there were burning cars and dozens of maimed and bloody bodies. Several of the buildings were burning.

The explosions finally stopped, but it did not grow quiet. There could still be heard cries of pain and calls for help. Adding to these cries, was the crackling sound of fire, now sweeping from building to building.

Two miles from town, Captain Yasir Wasim ordered the artillery to cease fire.

"Lieutenant Jabar, you stay here with the artillery," Wasim said. "We will go into town and mop up."

Wasim ordered all but the artillery crews to get back into the trucks, then, with him in the first truck, they drove into the burning town, getting there in less than three minutes. He parked the trucks just outside of town, then disembarked his soldiers. Dividing his men into ten groups of twenty, he sent them down the city streets.

"Shoot everyone you see," he said. "Men, women, children, and dogs."

"Everyone, Captain?" one of the men asked, not certain he had heard the order properly.

"Everyone," Wasim repeated. "We must teach these rebels a lesson. When they see what terrible retribution has been visited upon them, I think they will learn that any resistance against the forces of Moqaddas Sirata will be futile."

As Wasim started down Cashua Street, he saw a lot of activity at Public Square. The courthouse, which had not been directly struck by the bombardment, was the triage point and several of the wounded had been brought there. They were be given first aid by those who had not been wounded, though, at the moment there were no professional medical people present.

"Oh, thank God!" a woman said when she saw Wasim and his men approaching. "Here comes someone to help us."

Wasim pointed his automatic weapon at the woman and began firing. His opening rounds signaled the others to fire and for the next thirty seconds the sound of automatic weapons fire filled the streets of Darlington, not only from the group with Wasim, but from all the other SPS who had come into town and were now spreading out on the other streets. Within half an hour, all who had not been able to get to shelter were dead.

"My God, what has happened?" the customer who had taken shelter with Dolan Kinder asked. He started to climb up the concrete steps, but Kinder grabbed him by the waistband of his trousers and pulled him back.

"Don't go out there yet. You'll just get yourself killed," Kinder said.

"I've got to go out there, don't you understand? My wife and children are at home! I have to check on them!"

"Listen to me!" Kinder said sharply. "If your wife and children are already dead, there's nothing you can do about them. If they are alive, then they will need you to be alive as well, so getting yourself killed now would be about the most foolish thing you could do."

"Yeah," the customer said, coming back down the steps. "Yeah, I guess you're right."

Though it was hard to do, Kinder made himself wait for one full hour after he heard the last shot fired before he ventured out from his hiding place. As he walked through the streets of the town he had the feeling he was a witness to Armageddon. Three fourths of the downtown buildings were aflame, and the streets were blocked with burning vehicles and dead bodies. Some of the bodies, those that had been hit by an artillery shell, were mutilated and dismembered. Others lay as peacefully as if they were taking an afternoon nap.

Kinder felt his knees grow weak, and his head

begin to spin, and he had to hang on to a lamp post to keep from falling. He had seen many battle-fields in Vietnam where the dead had been ripped apart by explosions, but nothing he had ever seen anywhere could have prepared him for what he was seeing today.

He felt as if he should report it to someone, but who?

Columbia, South Carolina

"We can no longer go it alone," Governor Wallace told the head of the South Carolina Defense Corps. "We're going to have to have help from UFA."

"We are getting help from them," General Murphy said. "Their UAV over-flight saved Fire-base Swift Strike."

"That's not enough," Wallace said. "We need some boots on the ground."

"I agree, but I'm not sure that we have the right to ask them for any more assistance than they are already giving us. I mean, as long as we are trying to go it alone. Why would they even want to send us troops?"

"Perhaps we can make an arrangement whereby they provide us with advisors," Wallace suggested.

General Murphy laughed. "Why not? It seems to me that I read that's how we got into Vietnam."

"I believe you told me once that you know Jake Lantz."

"Yes, I know Jake."

"Then if you would, how about you being the liaison for me?" Wallace asked.

Murphy nodded. "All right, I'll do it."

Fort Morgan

"Deon, I've got a job for you if you want to do it," Jake said. "If not, I'll see if I can find someone else."

"I'll do it," Deon said.

"I haven't even told you what the job is."

"It doesn't matter. If you think the job needs doing, and you think I'm the one to do, I'll do it."

Jake chuckled. "Where the hell were men like you in the pre-O army?"

"We were around, Major. You just didn't always come to look for us."

"You may be right. You probably are right."

"What's the job?"

"We've got a request from General Murphy."

"Okay, you've got me there. Who is General Murphy?"

"Matthew Murphy. Last time I knew him was in Kabul. He was a Lieutenant Colonel then. Now he's Governor Wallace's top man in the South Carolina Defense Corps. It seems that, after the business up at Firebase Swift Strike, they've decided that it might be good to have a liaison from the UFA embedded with some of their troops."

"Ha, you mean like advisors in Afghanistan?"

"Yeah, well, hopefully, the guys from South

Carolina won't turn on you the way some of the Afghans turned on us," Jake said.

"We can't be sure of that though, can we, Major? Look at what happened at Camp Cassandra."

"Right, I guess I spoke without thinking, didn't I?"

"No problem," Deon said. "If you want me to go, I'll go."

"Good. I'll personally fly you over there tomorrow. That'll give you tonight to tell someone good-bye."

"I'm pregnant," Julie said that night, when Deon told her he was going to South Carolina the next day.

"Really?" Deon said as huge smile spread across his face. "You mean I'm going to be a papa?"

Julie laughed. "Well, that's what they usually call the male parent."

"Oh, Julie!" Deon said, grabbing her in a big embrace. "You've just made me the happiest man in the whole world! Oh, but I can't go to South Carolina, not and leave you behind like this."

"Nonsense, when we signed on to come down here with Major Lantz and Captain Dawes, we knew exactly what we were getting into. If Major Lantz thinks you should go, then go."

"But we need to get married," Deon said.

"Ha! You mean you are just getting around to asking me to marry you?"

"Well, no but . . ."

"Deon Pratt, are you saying you aren't asking me to marry you?"

"Yes, I am, but I'm not just now getting around to it. I mean, okay, yes, I am just now getting around to it, but I've been thinking about it for a long time."

"I accept," Julie said, giving Deon a kiss. "But, you go ahead, leave me back here to make all the plans so that, when you get back, we can have a real wedding, like Jake and Karen did, not something hurried."

"You're sure?"

"I'm positive," Julie said.

"I should have asked you to marry me six months ago," Deon said.

"Yes, you should have," Julie agreed with a smile.

CHAPTER TWENTY-SEVEN

Sikeston

At just after two-thirty in the morning the Blackhawk helicopter with Dan Lamdin and Bob "Clipper" Bivens at the controls put Tom Jack and his rescue team on the ground at a bend in the Wahite Ditch about 7 miles northwest of Sikeston. The Blackhawk was accompanied by a fully armed Apache gunship which orbited above as the troops off-loaded.

With Tom were his second-in-command, Captain Algood, and the team members he had selected; Kearny, Cooper, Lewis, Cates, Gilmore and Farrell.

The team was off-loaded in less than five seconds. As soon as they were clear, the helicopter took off again. For safety's sake the Blackhawk and the Apache would remain aloft and on station until they were needed.

By three a.m. the team was in position just outside the wall that surrounded the cotton oil mill converted to a prison. Tom had specifically chosen this night because there would be no moon. It was extremely dark, though the night-vision goggles Tom and his team were wearing enabled them to see everything quite clearly.

Willie had provided them with a layout of the prison to include where the guards would be and as Tom perused the area he saw two of them.

"Captain Algood, you take the one on the left," Tom said, quietly. "Kearny, you have the one on the right."

Algood and Kearny who, like the others, were wearing dark green anti-glare face paint, dropped their weapons and packs and armed only with knives crept forward.

Algood slipped quietly along the bank of the Wahite, using the sound of the rushing water to cover his approach. When he drew even with the corner of the wall, he moved up to the wall, then worked his way along the wall until he reached the other end. Looking around the corner he saw the guard walking toward him. Waiting until the guard passed him, Algood stepped up behind the SPS, clasped one hand across his mouth to keep him from calling out, then slashed his neck, cutting deep enough to sever not only the carotid artery, but also the windpipe, making it impossible for the guard to give an alarm.

With the guard dying behind him, Algood moved back to join the others. Kearny returned seconds later.

"All right, men, let's go in," Tom said.

Tom and his team moved quickly up to the wall.

Kearney had the rope ladder and he threw it up so that the hooks fell across the top, then he climbed up, looked around for second, and dropped down to the other side. The others followed close behind. Aided by their night-vision goggles, the men moved quickly through the night, crossing the open ground to the main building, which was almost entirely constructed of corrugated metal panels. Leaving the others outside, Tom and Algood went into the mill to locate and free Dr. Urban.

That's when they ran into their first difficulty.

"Damn, this cell door has a padlock," Algood said. "I thought it was supposed to just be barred shut from outside."

"Yeah, I thought so too," Tom said.

"Who are you? What do you want with me?" Dr. Urban called from the darkness of his cell.

"Dr. Urban, it's me, Tom Jack. Do you remember me?"

"Yes, I remember you. You were one of my patients once. What are you doing here?"

"We're here to get you out, but the damn door has padlocks on it, and we don't have a bolt cutter."

"Yes, they recently put on a padlock," Dr. Urban said.

"How are we going to get this cell door open without a key or a bolt cutter?" Algood asked.

"I don't know, I need to think about it."

* * *

Outside at that moment, one of the SPS guards, stumbled across the body of the guard Algood had killed, and he pulled a lever that flooded the compound ground with very bright lights.

Gilmore put his hand over his night goggles. "Son of a bitch!" he cried out. "I'm blinded! I can't see!"

"Lose the goggles!" Kearny shouted.

"Intruders! Intruders in the camp!" an SPS man called toward a low-lying barracks-type building. A handful of SPS men ran out from the barracks then, shooting in the direction of the Americans.

"Take cover behind the berm!" Kearny ordered, and even as he was giving the order, he stepped forward and started providing cover fire for his men as they scrambled to get into position. At least three of the SPS went down under Kearny's accurate fire, but several more came out, and as Kearny was the only visible target, they concentrated on him. Kearny was hit by several bullets and his blood shined red in the powerful lights as it sprayed from a dozen or more bullet strikes.

Kearny went down and seeing that, Cooper climbed out of the protected area and started toward him.

"Kearney!" Cooper shouted.

Suddenly the top of Cooper's head literally exploded and he went down, dead before he even hit the ground.

"Commander! Kearny and Cooper are down!"

Farrell called into the cotton oil mill. "What do we do!"

"Keep down, and keep shooting," Tom called back. "Stay right where you are until we get Dr. Urban out of here!"

"Tom, there is just one of me. Don't waste any more time or men on me! Get the rest of your men out of here now! If you don't you'll all be killed!" Dr. Urban said.

"We're not leaving you, Doc," Tom said. "Hey, Algood, isn't Lewis carrying some C-4?"

"Yes!" said.

"That's how we'll do it. Wait here, I'll be right back."

When Tom reached the top of the stairs, he was driven back by the bright light. Taking off his goggles, he threw them on the ground, blinked a few times and rubbed his eyes, then darted outside.

There was an intense gunfight going on between the SPS and the three remaining Americans. Tom dashed through the fire to the corner of the building then dived behind the berm where the Americans had taken up positions. Bullets kicked up the dirt all around him.

"Lewis, give me your C-4!" he shouted.

Lewis took a small bandolier from his shoulder and gave it to Tom. Tom ran back through the fire and reentered the mill prison. Because his eyes had been exposed to the bright light outside, he stood at the top of the steps for a moment, completely blind.

"Algood, I'm blind here!" Tom called. "Do you see my goggles?"

"Yeah."

"Hand them to me!"

Algood gave Tom his goggles, and putting them on, he was able to see again. Working quickly, he formed the C-4 around the padlocks.

"Okay, Doc, get away from the door!" Tom called. He set off the charge, destroying the lock. After that, he jerked the door open.

"Come on, Doc, let's go!" Tom shouted.

"I can't see!" Doctor Urban said.

"No sweat, grab hold of me and I'll lead you out," Tom said. "James, when you get to the top of the stairs, close your eyes and lose the goggles or the light outside will blind you."

"Right," Algood shouted.

When they reached the door, the three men ran through the fire until they reached the others. They were pinned down, but they were a strong enough defensive position that the SPS couldn't approach them.

Algood took the weapons from Kearny and Cooper, both of whom were dead, and gave one of them to Doctor Urban. "Make yourselves useful, Doc. Kill somebody," he said.

"I've never shot at anything but ducks and geese," Dr. Urban said.

"Good. They're bigger than ducks or geese, so you shouldn't have a problem."

"Farrell, give me the radio," Tom said.

Farrell handed the radio over to him.

"Boxcar, Top Tiger, this is Phoenix. We need you both, and we need you now!"

The helicopters were less than thirty seconds away and as they approached, the gunship called.

"Phoenix, this is Top Tiger. Where do you want the ordnance?"

Tom tossed a smoke grenade out into the opening. *"There's a building about one hundred meters north of the smoke. Waste it."*

The Apache started firing from several hundred meters away sending hellfire missiles into the barracks. The building went up with a tremendous explosion and as the SPS personnel started running, they were cut down, not only by machinegun fire coming from the Apache, but also from Tom and his men.

"Phoenix, this is Boxcar, get ready for pickup."

"Roger, drop the lines."

The helicopter came to a hover no more than ten feet above the ground. The door gunner of the helicopter was laying down covering fire as two lines were dropped down.

"Doc, you first!" Tom shouted. "Get hooked up!"

The lines had harnesses, which allowed the men to hook into them, then be winched up. The crew chief was handling the winch and as he drew each one up to the helicopter he would pull them on board, release them, then drop the line again.

"Gilmere, you take Kearny with you. Lewis, you take Cooper. We aren't leavin' them behind," Tom said.

The two men, with their load attached, were winched up as well, leaving only Tom and Algood on the ground.

Two more lines dropped and Tom and Algood

hooked themselves into the harnesses. Just as they started up, another group of SPS appeared, all of them armed with automatic weapons. They fired at the helicopter.

Clipper Bivens was holding the helicopter at a hover when he felt a sudden excruciating pain in his right foot. That caused him to jerk away from the anti-torque pedals, and the helicopter lurched and spun around.

"Take it, Dan, I'm hit!" Then, looking over at Lamdin, he saw blood and brain matter oozing from a hole in the side of his co-pilot's helmet. Lamdin's head was tilted forward.

Bivens grabbed the controls again and stabilized the helicopter. "Are these the last ones?" he shouted.

"Yes, sir!" the crew chief replied.

"I'm pulling pitch! Winch them up as I get us the hell out of here!"

The helicopter took off at maximum climb with Tom and Algood still dangling beneath. The crew chief and Lewis worked to bring them up. When they got them inside, Tom had not been hit, but Algood was bleeding from several wounds.

"Jesus, Cap'n!" Lewis shouted.

"Did the doc get aboard all right?" Algood asked.

"Yes, he did," Tom said.

"Good," Algood said.

Dr. Urban opened Algood's shirt and saw the wounds in his chest and abdomen. He looked up at Tom and, almost imperceptibly, shook his head.

The helicopter dipped its nose, and started south at maximum speed.

"Mr. Bivens, how are you doing, sir?" the crew chief asked.

"I'm losing a lot of blood," Bivens answered. "Maybe you'd better pull Mr. Lamdin out of his seat and sit up here, just in case."

"Whoa, hold it! You mean I might have to fly this thing?"

"You've got enough stick time, I think you can handle it."

"I wouldn't want to try and land the thing," Creech said.

"Just fly it until I get the bleeding stopped," Clipper said. "If I can do that, I'll be good to go."

"Right," Creech said. Creech signaled the door gunner and the two of them pulled Lamdin from his seat, then lay him on the Alclad floor alongside Kearny, Cooper, and Algood. When that was done, Creech crawled into the left seat. He put his hands on the cyclic and collective control sticks.

"Just keep us straight and level," Clipper said.

"Yes, sir."

"Take off your boot," Dr. Urban said. "Let me take a look at your foot."

With Creech at the controls, Clipper turned around in his seat and took off his boot. His sock was soaked red with blood. Gingerly taking off the sock, Dr. Urban saw an entry hole in one side of his foot and an exit wound in the other side.

"Here's a compression bandage, Doc," Tom said, pulling one from the helicopter first aid kit.

"Thanks," Dr. Urban said. He wrapped the

compression bandage around the wound and used it to stop the bleeding.

"How is Captain Algood doing?" Bivens asked as the doctor treated his wound.

"Not very good, I'm afraid," the doctor replied.

"All right, this'll hold me long enough to get us to Blytheville. Once we get there, maybe we can get him to a hospital."

"Get him to a hospital . . . ."

Algood was lying on the football field with the rest of his team gathered around him. Hospital? Was it so bad that he was going to have to go to the hospital?

"How bad is it, Algood?" his quarterback asked.

"The injured player on the field is number thirty-two, James Algood," the field announcer's voice said over the PA system.

"Come on, Algood, you can't be hurt. We need you, man, we need you."

"Shake it off, man, shake it off."

"What's the matter with you weaklings?" the sergeant in basic training yelled, spittle coming from his mouth as he shouted at the trainees. "It's called a confidence course, people, a confidence course. Is Private Algood the only recruit in the entire company with confidence?"

"Yes, James, I'll marry you," Carmen said. "Papa says I'm a fool for marrying a soldier, but I love you. I'd marry you if you were working in a car wash."

* * *

"Darlin', it's a boy."
"We'll name it Parker, after your father," Algood said.
"Daddy will be so proud!"

"Whoa, Dad, did you see that? I just made an eighty-yard touchdown!" Parker said.
"No fair, I wasn't ready," Algood said, laughing at his son's excitement as they played football on the X-box.

"Pop, what are you doing here? How'd you get here?" Algood said to his father.
"I've always been here, son. I've never left you."

"I'm afraid he is dead, Tom," Dr. Urban said, his hand resting on Algood's neck.

The helicopter, with four dead, beat its way through the dark night.

CHAPTER TWENTY-EIGHT

South Carolina

There were seven vehicles in the convoy. The lead vehicle was an up-armored Humvee, followed by two cargo trucks, then an armored personnel carrier, two more cargo trucks, and another up-armored Humvee to bring up the rear. Captain Bob Bostic, in the lead Humvee, was the convoy commander. He was in the right front seat, connected to all other vehicles in the convoy by radio. The convoy was made up of a group of former members of the US Army, determined now to free South Carolina from the Moqaddas Sirata. The group called themselves "Sons of Patriotism." Deon Pratt was also in the lead Humvee, though he was here as liaison only.

Two dozen or more goats scrambled across the road to get out of the way of the rapidly moving convoy.

"Hey, Cap'n, lookie there, what do you say I open up on those suckers? I could kill two or three of 'em and we could barbecue 'em for supper tonight," Rugen said.

Rugen was the gunner and he was standing up in the lead Humvee, with his head and shoulders sticking through the top.

"Negative," Bostic answered. "We aren't here to shoot goats."

"I do a damn good barbequed goat," Rugen said.

"Everyone keep a sharp lookout," Captain Bostic said to the rest of the convoy. "If we are going to be hit, this is most likely the place that it'll happen."

KARUMP BOOM!

"Holy shit!" Bostic said. "What was that?"

"Number five got hit!" someone shouted over the radio. "We're cut off!"

"Stop the vehicle!" Bostic yelled to the driver.

"Cap'n, we have to get out of the kill zone!" the driver called back.

"We're not leaving them. Stop the vehicle! Rugen, do you see anyone?"

"No, sir!"

"Shoot into the woods. Let 'em know we're here!" Bostic ordered.

The convoy came to a stop and the gunners on each of the vehicles started firing onto both sides of the road. Three RPGs came swooshing out of the trees, and three more vehicles were hit including the lead Humvee. Deon was literally blown from the vehicle, and when he looked back at it, he saw that it was completely engulfed in flames. He started toward it.

"No, Cap'n!" someone shouted, coming up from the next vehicle. "There's nothing you can do!"

"I'm not going to leave 'em there!" Deon said.

There was a secondary explosion in the Humvee and the shock wave knocked Deon down. When he got up he saw Bostic, Rugen, and the driver, obviously dead, their bodies blackened and burning.

By now the APC which had not been hit managed to pull around the burning vehicles as Deon and other soldiers piled into it. It backed out of the kill zone, all the while shooting into the direction from which the RPGs had come.

"Lieutenant, we have air cover on standby. Call them in! We need some air!" Deon shouted to Lieutenant Abner Garner. Garner was now the convoy commander.

"Yes, sir, I'll see what I can do," Garner said. He spoke into his radio. "Gunslinger, Gunslinger, this is Turtle, do you copy?"

"This is Gunslinger, over."

"Gunslinger, we need support. Can you home on me? Over?"

"Give me a five-second squelch," Gunslinger said.

"Squelch to follow."

Garner held the mike key down for five seconds, then released. Depressing again, he spoke into the mike. "Gunslinger, did you copy?"

"Roger that, Turtle. I see three burning vehicles."

"That's us. Your target is west of the road."

"Let me see what I can—ahh, I've got the bastards."

Shortly after that message the Apache attack helicopter came low and fast from the east. Deon heard the sound of the Vulcan gun, even above the slap of the rotors, then he saw several rockets zipping forward. Almost immediately thereafter explosions sent up fire and smoke from just beyond the tree line.

The Apache made a sharp 180 degree turn, then made a second pass with guns and rockets blazing.

"Turtle, this is Gunslinger. I think you can move in now."

"Thanks, Gunslinger, Turtle out."

The Apache passed low overhead, dipping from side to side as it did so.

"Medics, see to the wounded," Garner said. "Simmons, White, grab your squads and come with me. Let's check it out."

"I'm coming as well," Deon said.

Deon pulled his pistol and followed the others into the trees. There they saw six bodies, all wearing the forest green uniforms of the SPS.

"Damn," Garner said. "Just six of them did that to us?"

"That's what happens when you have position and surprise," Deon said.

"Yeah," Garner said. "Seems like I might have heard that once or twice in my young life."

"I can't believe we are actually doing this," Simmons said.

"Doing what?" Deon asked.

"Killing Americans."

Deon turned one of the bodies over with his foot, and stared down at him. The eyes were open, but glazed over with death.

"Once the sons of bitches put on one of these uniforms, they are no longer Americans," Deon said.

Fort Morgan

Shell Banks Cemetery is located on Fort Morgan Road, eight miles west of Highway 59, behind Shell Banks Baptist Church. Over the many years of its existence, going back to before the American Revolutionary War, Shell Banks Cemetery has been the final resting place for Indians, pirates, early Alabama settlers, and soldiers from the War of 1812, the Civil War, World War I, World War II, and the Vietnam War. The latest to be buried was John Deedle, and as Willie and Marcus came out to the cemetery . . . where Algood, Kearney, and Cooper were to be buried, they walked over John Deedle's grave.

"Who was John Deedle?" Barbara Carter asked. Barbara had come to the cemetery with Willie.

"You remember him, don't you, Becky?" Marcus asked his wife.

"Yes, I remember him," Becky said. "He was with all of you when you first came down."

"What happened to him?" Barbara asked.

"He was killed, less than three miles from here," Willie said.

"By SPS men?"

"No. By armed hooligans."

"Armed hooligans?"

"I don't know what else to call them. We were prepared and they weren't. They wanted what we had, and they wanted it badly enough to kill us for it. Or at least, to kill John."

Willie grew quiet then, as did the others, and while they were waiting for the funeral procession to arrive, they stood over John Deedle's grave in reflective silence. And though Will was silent, his mind was active, as he recalled the incident that had taken John Deedle's life. They were coming back from town when they encountered a roadblock, made up of abandoned refrigerators, and when they stopped, they came under fire. Bob Varney had come from the fort, flying the Huey helicopter they had used to escape Fort Rucker.

"If you can't get through, get out and move one or two aside," Bob said. "Do not get off the road, if you do you'll get stuck axle deep in the sand."

Starting the truck, John drove up to the barricades, then stopped. "We're going to have to go around," he said.

"No," Jake replied. "Bob lives down here, so I'm sure he knows what he is talking about. We're going to have to push a couple of the refrigerators out of the way."

John put the truck in neutral and he and Jake got out and started pushing refrigerators aside until they had opened a path big enough for the truck to get through.

"I think we can do it now," Jake said.

"Yeah, we've got it made in the shade," John said with a happy laugh.

Jake heard the solid thunk of the bullet hitting John. Blood and brain detritus erupted from the wound on the side of John's head and he fell toward Jake.

Jake caught him, and held him up.

"John! John!" he called.

John didn't reply, and as Jake made a closer examination of him, he realized that he was dead.[3]

"Here comes the funeral cortege," Becky said, and looking back toward the church Willie saw three hearses coming around the curve. There was a limousine following each hearse, and Willie felt a deep sense of sadness because he knew that in each of those limos were the families of the three men who had been killed.

"Let's go over there," Willie said and, as the train of cars following the limos stopped, and the doors opened to spill out the mourners, Willie and Barbara and Marcus and Becky went over toward the three graves that were already open.

There were twenty-six enlisted men and one officer dressed in the khaki uniforms that had been adopted by the army of United Free America. Seven were carrying rifles, and one was carrying a bugle.

Willie saw the wives and children, unable to hold back the tears, as they were led to a row of chairs adjacent to the open graves.

---

3. *Phoenix Rising*

The coffins were removed from the hearses, each being carried by six pall bearers, and brought to the gravesites. Each coffin was covered with two flags, the new flag of United Free America, as well as the Stars and Stripes of the United States of America.

Father Ken Coats stepped up to the three open graves.

"In sure and certain hope of the resurrection to eternal life though our Lord Jesus Christ, we commend to Almighty God our brothers James Algood, Andrew Kearny, and Paul Cooper, and we commit their bodies to the ground, earth to earth, ashes to ashes, dust to dust. The Lord bless them and keep them, the Lord make his face to shine upon them and be gracious to them, the Lord lift up his countenance upon them and give them peace. Amen"

With solemn precision, the flags were lifted, and held, tautly, above the coffins.

The officer in charge stepped to the head of the three graves as the seven-man firing squad stepped into place. The pall bearers raised their hands to render a salute as the firing squad lifted their rifles to their shoulders.

"Ready! Fire!"

The seven rifles fired as one.

"Ready! Fire!"

A second volley was fired.

"Ready! Fire!"

A third volley was fired.

"Order, arms!"

The bugler raised the instrument to his lips

then began playing *Taps*. This was the haunting melody that, ever since the American Civil War when General Daniel Butterfield rearranged the notes of *Tattoo* to make the melody slower and more stately, had put the troops to sleep at night, and for their final, everlasting sleep. It was a melody which would linger in the heart, long after the last note was silent.

When the last prolonged note faded away, the honor guard folded the flags into the tricorn, being careful with the Stars and Stripes that no red be seen.

General Jake Lantz presented both the US and the UFA flags to the windows.

"These flags are presented on behalf of a grateful people and the patriots who struggle to recover the United States, as a token of appreciation for your loved one's honorable service in this struggle."

"I wish you had left me in the prison," Dr. Urban said that afternoon. He was standing on the beach at the place known, geographically, as Mobile Point.

"Why do you say that, Doc?" Tom Jack asked.

"You lost three of your men in rescuing me. Three lives for one, and I'm much older than they were. That doesn't sound like a very good deal to me. And I feel responsible."

"I understand that the young woman you examined was killed by the Moqaddas Sirata. Do you feel responsible for that as well?"

"No. I was following the dictates of my honor, and the dedication of my profession."

"Let me ask you something. What makes you think that only the medical profession has honor and dedication?"

"No, no, I didn't mean it that way," Dr. Urban said.

"Look. I'm the one who selected the men for this mission. Yes, they all volunteered, but the final selection was mine. If anyone should feel responsible for those brave men getting killed, it should be me. And, while I do feel responsible, I am also tremendously proud of them. Whenever a man, or a woman, takes an oath of allegiance to the country they serve they are signing a blank check, payable with their life, if it comes to that.

"And disabuse yourself of the idea that this mission was just to rescue you. There was more to it than that. This was a mission to show the rest of the world that the real spirit of America isn't dead. James, Andy, and Paul gave their lives for that. I think you should honor them, rather than take on a sense of guilt."

Dr. Urban nodded. "Yeah," he said. "Yes, I will think of it like that."

"Are you going to be okay?" Tom asked.

"Yes, thank you. And, again, thank you for rescuing me."

Tom nodded. "I'm glad we had the opportunity. Oh, Sheri wanted me to invite you for dinner tonight."

"You tell her I'll be glad to come."

CHAPTER TWENTY-NINE

Onboard the John Paul Jones in the Gulf of Mexico

Captain Stan Virdin was standing on the bridge, looking through a pair of powerful binoculars at another ship that was about 6,000 yards away. They had been tracking the ship for some time now, and had established, from the outset, that it was a destroyer equipped with guns and missile tubes. The ship belonged to the navy of the American Islamic Republic of Enlightenment. Within the last fifteen minutes, the AIRE ship had decreased, by half, the distance between them. It was the closest any AIRE ship had come since they had started their patrol.

"Signalman, send a blinker message, tell the captain of that ship to come up on channel thirteen, 156.650 mhz."

"Aye, aye, sir."

The radioman responded, and a moment later all on the bridge could hear the call.

"Outlaw vessel, this is the AIRE destroyer *Ara Anwar al-Awlaki*, Captain Amara, commanding." Although the captain of the AIRE destroyer identified himself with a Muslim name, his accent showed, clearly, that he was an American.

Virdin picked up a microphone and looked at his signalman.

"Your mike is hot, sir," the signalman said.

"This is Captain Stan Virdin, commanding *John Paul Jones.* You are encroaching in UFA waters, and you are too close to the UFA drilling rigs. Back off."

"The American Islamic Republic of Enlightenment does not recognize the UFA. The drilling rigs are property of the AIRE. And you are illegally in possession of a ship that belongs to the American Islamic Republic of Enlightenment," Amara said.

"You're full of shit, Amara, or whatever the hell your real name is," Virdin said. "This ship belongs to the United States Navy, and until such time as the United States is reconstituted, it is under the protective care of United Free America."

"There is no such country as the United States of America, or United Free America. Withdraw and allow us free approach to the drilling rigs, or you will be fired upon."

"What did you say?" Virdin asked, snapping the question. "Amara, did you just threaten to fire on us?"

"Withdraw immediately," Amara replied.

Virdin looked at the radioman and made a

slashing motion across his throat, indicating that communication with the AIRE ship, *Ara Anwar al-Awlaki* should be broken off. The signalman did so, then nodded at the Captain.

"Send a FLASH precedence message to Firebase Freedom. 'From Captain Stan Virdin, commanding *John Paul Jones*. Have been ordered by AIRE Destroyer *Ara Anwar al-Awlaki* to withdraw from the drilling rig patrolling station or be fired upon. I do not intend to withdraw.'"

The radioman responded.

Firebase Freedom, Fort Morgan

"General, I just got a FLASH message," Willie said, stepping into Jake's office in the Headquarters Building.

"From Deon?" Jake asked.

"No, sir, from Captain Virdin."

"All right, let's hear it."

"'From Captain Stan Virdin, commanding *John Paul Jones*. Have been ordered by AIRE Destroyer *Ara Anwar al-Awlaki* to withdraw from the drilling rig patrolling station or be fired upon. I do not intend to withdraw.'"

Jake looked over at Tom.

"You know Virdin, Tom. What do you think he's asking?"

Tom chuckled. "If you notice, Jake, he wasn't asking, he was telling. He said he wasn't going to withdraw."

Jake smiled. "Willie?"

"Yes, sir?"

"Tell Captain Virdin to act at his own discretion."

"Yes, sir."

"As if he wouldn't," Tom said.

A moment later, Willie stuck his head back in. "It's too late, General," he said.

"Too late? Too late for what?" Jake asked, confused by the comment.

"It's too late to tell Captain Virdin to act at his own discretion." Willie smiled. "He said, and I quote, 'tell the general I've already sunk the son of a bitch.' End quote, sir."

Jake, Tom, and Willie laughed out loud.

"I'll say this for your friend Virdin. He's a cocky bastard, but it would appear that he has a right to be," Jake said.

Wardroom of the John Paul Jones

"Why didn't you tell me who the hell you were?" Virdin asked the skipper of the ship he had just sunk. "Amara? Tell me, Victor, where the hell did you come up with a name like Amara? Your name is Victor Anderson. Hell, I remember you when you were a midshipman at the Academy."

Amara, or Victor Anderson, was one of the eighty-seven men the *John Paul Jones* fished from the water after the *Ara Anwar al-Awlaki* was sunk. He was sitting in the wardroom now, drinking coffee.

"I got the name from the Internet," Anderson said. "I looked up Muslim surnames."

"Have you converted? Are you a Muslim now? And I don't mean just Muslims. Hell, I know there are good Muslims, I mean are you Moqaddas Sirata?"

Anderson looked around. "Not really," he said. "I guess if I had to say what I really am, it would be Baptist. At least, that's how I was raised, but truth to tell, I wasn't any better a Baptist than I've been a Muslim."

"Then what is all this? You commanding a ship, and not just any ship, the *Ara Anwar al-Awlaki*. That would be like naming a ship after Benedict Arnold.

"I'm a navy officer, Stan," Anderson said. "That's all I ever wanted to be, that's all I ever want to be. Hell, you know what it was like when everything collapsed, the navy, the army, the air force. There was nothing left. For more than a year I did nothing but pick shit with the chickens. Then, when I learned that all I would have to do to get back into the navy was change my name and pretend to convert, hell, I leaped at the chance."

"You could have done what I did," Stan said. "You could have joined with us."

Anderson shook his head. "I don't know," he said. "I have to admit that I did think about it, but I took an oath. I took the same oath you took. I, Victor Anderson, having been appointed an officer in the navy of the United States, do solemnly swear that I will support and defend the Constitution of the United States against all enemies, foreign or domestic, that I will bear true faith and allegiance to the same; that I take this obligation freely, without any mental reservations or purpose of evasion; and that I will well and faithfully discharge the duties of the office upon which I am about to enter; so help me God."

"And do you think you have done that?" Virdin asked.

"Well, yes. I mean, I'm not fighting against the United States."

"Where is the United States? The so called American Republic of Islamic Enlightenment isn't the United States."

"No, but it's what the US became."

"What about your oath to defend the Constitution. Do you think you are defending it?"

"I . . ." Anderson threw up his hands in frustration. "I'll tell you the truth, Stan, I don't know what the hell I'm doing anymore."

"Victor, I'm not going to hold it against you for sticking to your oath of commission. I think that basically your intention was honorable. But if you are willing to listen to me with an open mind over the next few days, I think I can convince you to join us."

"And if I don't join you will I, and my men, become hostages? Prisoners of war?"

"I doubt it. We aren't technically at war with AIRE, and as far as I know, we have no facilities for holding POWs, even if we were. I'm sure that when we get back, you and your men will be free to make up your mind as to whether to join us, or return to the AIRE. I have no intention of coercing you to become one of us. If you do, I want it to be of your own volition, and I will expect the same degree of fidelity toward United Free America as you have so nobly, but mistakenly, given to the AIRE. In the meantime, I seem to remember that you play a good game of chess. It's been a while since I've had a good, challenging game, and I'm looking forward to a few matches."

Anderson smiled. "You're on," he said. He held up his finger. "For the chess games. I'll need to think about your other offer."

"Good enough," Virdin said.

Mobile Point

As the *John Paul Jones* sailed past Mobile Point, Captain Virdin pointed out to Victor Anderson the masonry star fort at the mouth of Mobile Bay. Flying from the flagpole was the same banner that was, at the moment, fluttering from the truck of the destroyer.

"What you see there is the capital of United Free America," Virdin said. "Or, perhaps I should say that it is the temporary capital of a resurgent United States of America."

"Why don't you call it the United States?" Anderson asked.

"For the same reason this ship isn't flying the Stars and Stripes. We aren't the United States and won't be, until all fifty states are united as one nation, the nation you and I took our oath to serve."

"Do you think that is ever going to happen?" Anderson asked.

"If I didn't think so, Victor, I would not have aligned myself with this group of patriots."

"That's Fort Morgan?"

"Yes. Some scholars regard it as the finest example of military architecture in the New World. During the Civil War Admiral Farragut's famous line, Damn the torpedoes, full speed ahead, was delivered while he was under fire from the guns of the fort, and facing the torpedoes that blocked the entrance into Mobile Bay."

"And now we have another civil war, North against the South," Anderson said.

Virdin shook his head. "This isn't like the first civil war at all. We have men and women who have come from all over the country to join us. It might appear as if it is North against the South again, but that isn't true. In this case North and South is a geographic divide only, not cultural. Many of our citizens are new to the South, having come down here to find freedom."

"Do you think it's going to be a full-scale war?" Anderson asked.

"That I can't tell you," Virdin said. "I hope it doesn't turn into a full-scale war but I can tell you right now that if it does, we are ready for it."

"Captain Virdin, if you will take me in your new navy, I would be honored to serve."

"Where is your family, Victor? I wouldn't want you to put them in any danger."

"They are on my father's ranch in Wyoming," Anderson said. "To be honest, Stan, they are so remote that none of this has touched them. They will be safe there."

Virdin smiled, and extended his hand. "Welcome aboard, Captain."

"Captain?"

"You will be as soon as we can get you another ship and crew."

Columbia, South Carolina

It was early morning and Oscar Peters was walking his dog when he saw the three jet aircraft fly overhead, so low and going so fast that they flashed by a second before the sound hit him. Then, shortly after they disappeared, he heard a loud explosion and saw smoke billowing up. He gasped, thinking that one of the airplanes had crashed.

Then when he saw all three aircraft in a very steep climb he knew that one hadn't crashed, and he wondered what had caused the explosion. He didn't have to wonder long, because the three jets did a one hundred eighty degree turn then came back in a long shallow dive. He saw flashes of fire, then plumes of smoke trailing rockets that were fired from the aircraft.

There were more explosions from the center of the city and he knew, now, that the three aircraft were attacking! As the three pulled out of their shallow diving rocket run, he saw then the symbols on their wings . . . not stars, but the stylized O that had been first Ohmshidi's campaign symbol, and was now the national symbol for the

American Islamic Republic of Enlightenment. The city of Columbia was under an air attack from the AIRE air force.

The three jets made another one hundred and eighty degree turn, then started another attack run. Again Oscar saw flashes of light, and glowing tracer rounds streaming toward the ground. And, it looked as if they were shooting directly at him!

Grabbing his dog, Oscar dived beneath a hedgerow. Some of the bullets hit in the middle of the road, and it sent chunks of pavement flying. When the three aircraft finally left the city, nearly two dozen buildings were destroyed and a dozen more were burning. One of the destroyed buildings was the state capitol building.

Because it was so early in the morning, there were very few people in the capital so the casualties were light, but the building had collapsed in on itself, the columned front a shambles, the cupola, in fact the entire roof, missing.

"It would appear to me that we have no alternative," Governor Wallace told General Murphy later that morning as he and the general stood on the grounds of the destroyed statehouse. AIRE seems to have declared war on us, choosing us because we are isolated. We can't afford to be isolated any longer. When we send our nonvoting delegation to Mobile on the fifteenth of October, I am going to make a formal request that the state of South Carolina be accepted as a state in United Free America."

"Governor, I agree with you. But, as I'm sure you know, there are a lot of people in the state who don't want to join another alliance."

"Yes, and there are still a lot of people in the state who didn't want us to secede in the first place," Governor Wallace said. "But sometimes you have to do what is best for the whole."

"Maybe you could call a special session of the state legislature and get a vote of confidence. That way we could avoid a civil war within the state," General Murphy suggested.

"I would say that would be a good idea," Wallace said. He took in the smoldering pile of rubble with a wave of his hand. "But, where would we meet?"

"The Civic Center wasn't that badly damaged," General Murphy said.

It took a week to gather enough members of the legislature to have a quorum, but they showed up at the center. Nearly all had a story to tell of some atrocity committed by the Janissaries, or the SPS, or, increasingly, the AIRE military. There was a great deal of anger as they gathered, especially after seeing the destroyed state house.

Deon Pratt had returned to Columbia and was meeting with Governor Wallace and General Murphy before the legislature assembled. Governor Wallace had invited him to give a report on the observations he had made of the South Carolina Defense Corps.

"I think you have some fine officers and men,"

Deon said. "I saw them up close, and I admired the way they worked. But General, your army isn't big enough to stand off the AIRE all by yourself."

"Yes," Murphy replied. "Governor Wallace and I have come to the same conclusion. The task before us now is to convince the rest of the state."

Governor Wallace chuckled. "Fortunately, General, we don't have to convince the entire state. All we have to convince is the legislature."

"Do you think you can do that, Governor?" Deon asked.

"Captain Pratt, in the pre-O time, I was a pretty good politician. And I was known for the power of my oratory. I could get things done, and that was back when we still had Democrats and Republicans. There are no political parties now, there are just those of us who are left. We have but one issue that unites us all, and that is to survive. And yes, I'm reasonably certain I can get them to vote my way."

"We need to get the word out as soon as we can," General Murphy said. "If we are going to petition United Free America to let us join them, we need to have all our ducks in a row before the fifteenth of October."

When the joint session of the legislature opened three days later, the Speaker of the House introduced Governor Wallace. For the first several minutes of his address, he gave the legislators a rundown one what had happened in South Carolina over the last several weeks. The rundown wasn't necessary, there wasn't a man or a woman in the house who wasn't aware of the losses they had sustained against the SPS as well as the military of the AIRE.

"Now, I would like to ask Representative Billy Knowles to come up here, please.

Billy Knowles was a popular legislator who had been an All-American defensive lineman for the South Carolina Gamecocks. He was about 6 feet 7 inches tall, 275 pounds of muscle, and clearly the strongest man in the building at the moment.

Governor Wallace handed Knowles a rather stout, wooden dowel.

"Billy, if you would, I wonder if you would break this dowel for us," Wallace said.

Knowles smiled. "I don't know, it looks pretty stout." He held the dowel out in front of him, strained for no more than a second, and the dowel broke with a loud pop.

The others in the assembly laughed and applauded.

"Very good, Billy. And, as you said, that was a pretty stout dowel, but you were able to break it without much difficulty," Governor Wallace said.

Governor Wallace reached down under the podium, then brought out a bound bundle of dowels. He handed the bundle to Knowles.

"Now I wonder if you would break this for us." Wallace looked back out at the assembly. "Oh, and just for everyone's information, this is nine dowels," Governor Wallace said.

Knowles shook his head. "I can't break that, I'm not even going to try."

"Why not? There isn't one dowel in the bundle that is bigger than the one you just broke."

"But they're all together and . . ." Knowles started, then he stopped and flashed a broad smile. "Why do I get the idea that you have just used me to demonstrate a point here?"

Governor Wallace returned his smile. "Well, you are not only strong, you are also a smart man. And you are right, I have just used you to demonstrate a point." He addressed the assembly. "I have every confidence in General Murphy and the brave men and women of the South Carolina Defense Corps. But, General Murphy tells me that, like this single dowel, though we may be strong, we are not strong enough to withstand the might of all of the organization that calls itself the American Islamic Republic of Enlightenment."

Governor Wallace held up the bundle of dowels that Billy Knowles had been unable to break. "As I told you, there are nine dowels here. I didn't pick that number at random. There are now eight member states of United Free America. If we join them, there will be nine member states. We were asked to join, but we turned them down because of uncertainty among our own citizens. But I think now, since AIRE has singled us out for their military action, that we should revisit the idea of joining United Free America. In fact, I think we have no choice but to join them.

"We have been invited to send a nonvoting delegation to their national organization convention to be held in Mobile on the fifteenth of October. I propose that we not only send a delegation, but that we send that delegation armed with a petition from us that we become a member state. And since I can't introduce the question, I now ask that someone please make a motion to this effect."

"I make the motion that we petition United Free America to accept our request for membership," Billy Knowles said.

"I second the motion," the Speaker of the House said.

For the next several minutes there was a spirited discussion as to whether or not the motion should be adopted. The opposition was not against joining with United Free America. Nearly everyone present believed that would be a good thing. The opposition was from those few who thought that this would be best settled as a state wide referendum, rather than by legislative action.

Then, after a discussion of no more than half an hour, the motion was moved, and a vote taken. The motion carried without one dissenting vote.

CHAPTER THIRTY

Fort Morgan

"The jets that attacked Columbia came from Homestead Air Force Base," Jake said.

"Yes, that's the part of Florida than hasn't joined up," Bob said.

"It's not good having them down there, in a way it's as if they have us surrounded," Jake said.

"Why do I have the idea that you are about to make a suggestion?" Bob asked with a little chuckle.

"I don't know. Maybe because I do have a suggestion?"

"All right, let's hear it."

"It's simple, really. My suggestion is that we take the air base out."

"I don't know," Bob said. "So far our military activity has been limited to reaction. What you are asking now is that we become proactive, that we initiate the action."

"Yes. Bob, if we really are going to take our

position on the world stage, we can't just sit down here and wait for things to happen. We are going to have to be more assertive."

"I can see your point, but, I'm also a little concerned about spreading this out and causing collateral damage. It's one thing to make war against the SPS and the Janissaries, but I am convinced that ninety-nine point nine percent of the civilians are just what they have always been, Americans who want to get on with their lives. They have found themselves put into a position over which they have no control. I would hate to worsen that condition by putting them in danger from us."

"We can play laser tag with the warplanes at Homestead, and take them out with no danger at all to the civilians," Jake said.

"Laser tag? Oh, you mean pinpointing the targets with lasers. I've read about it, but it's not anything we had during the Vietnam War."

"Trust me, it will destroy the targets, and it will eliminate collateral damage."

"All right, Jake," Bob said. "I do trust you. Do whatever you have to do to put this in motion."

"I'll need Tom and Deon to volunteer again."

"I can understand why you would want to use them, they've certainly proven themselves. And I'm sure they will volunteer. I just hope you aren't going to the well too many times. Especially since Deon and Julie just got married."

"Yeah," Jake said. "All right, I'll leave Deon behind."

"How many men do you think you'll need?"

"Eight should do it," Jake replied. "That would

be Tom and whoever I get instead of Deon, and five more."

"That's only seven."

"I'll be the eighth man," Jake said.

Bob ran his hand through his hair.

"Wait a minute, hold it. What do you mean, you? Jake, there's no need for you to go."

"The hell there isn't," Jake replied. "I'm the one that came up with the idea."

"We've had advanced ground teams laser painting targets for years now," Bob said. "You didn't come up with the idea."

"I didn't come up with laser painting, no. But I came up with this particular op plan. Bob, I'm the best one to implement this and you know it."

"You're a general now, Jake, and not just any general. You are the top general in our entire army. And here you are, wanting to do the job of an O-3."

"Bob, is it that you don't want to send me because we have become close personal friends? You know damn well that can never let that be a consideration."

"That's not true, Jake, and you know it," Bob said, a little more sharply than he intended.

"I'm sorry, Bob," Jake said apologetically. "I was out of line with that comment. But please don't try and talk me out of this. I need to do this."

Bob looked at Jake for a moment, then he laughed. "I swear to God, Jake, if I thought there really was anything to reincarnation; I would swear you are George S. Patton."

"You want to see my ivory-handled pistol?" Jake teased.

Bob sighed. "All right, Jake, if you want to go, I won't talk you out of it."

Jake smiled broadly. "What makes you think you could talk me out of it?"

In the air over southern Florida

The floor of the C-17 had eighteen reinforced pallet positions which would enable it to carry over 170,000 pounds of cargo. It could accommodate one hundred and two fully equipped paratroopers, though now there were only eight. On the inside wall, just above Jake Lantz, the broken-letter words HYDRAULIC LINE SERVICE ACCESS were stenciled in black on a cadmium yellow patch. Through his buttocks, legs, and back, Jake could feel the power of the 41,000 pounds of thrust generated by each of the four Pratt and Whitney F117-PW-100 turbofan engines.

Jake had personally assembled the team and now, in the red night light of the cabin, he looked around at the others. The loadmaster was sitting on the canvas bench at the front of the airplane, connected to the pilot and co-pilot by a cord than ran from his headset to a receptacle on the forward bulkhead. Willie and Marcus had talked Jake into letting them come along, and right now Willie had his head back and his eyes closed, sleeping, or pretending to be asleep. Tom, Gilmore, Ferrell and Lewis were playing hearts.

Deon had insisted, with Julie's blessing, that he

be included with the assault team and he was just sitting there, staring straight ahead.

A short time ago the airplane had encountered some very rough air and Deon had thrown up.

Ferrell laughed. "Damn, Cap'n, I didn't know we were riding with a pussy."

The others laughed.

"Tell you what, Cap'n Pratt, I've got some bacon on me. It's raw and a couple of days old but still good. You want some? That might help," Ferrell said.

"Ferrell, if you don't shut up, I'm going to puke all over you," Deon said.

"You're okay, Cap'n, you're a good man," Ferrell said. "I can't think of anyone I'd rather be with, 'ceptin' maybe General Lantz. They tell me he used to gargle with glass, just so he could chew some ass."

Jake chuckled. "Ferrell, you are as full of crap as a Christmas goose."

The loadmaster leaned back to call out to Jake.

"General, the pilot says we'll be over the DZ in fifteen minutes."

Jake nodded, then looked toward his men. "Get ready," he said, though the order wasn't necessary as they had all heard the loadmaster's comments. They would be jumping, but rather than the conventional jump with a static line and chute, they would be making a HALO jump, meaning a high altitude egress, low altitude opening. The chute they would be using was the MC-4, a paraglide chute that would allow them maximum maneuverability once it was opened.

The loadmaster disconnected his headset, then walked to the back of the plane where he reconnected. Jake could see his lips moving, and knew he was talking to the pilot, but couldn't hear him above the noise of the airplane. Again, disconnecting, the loadmaster came back to Jake.

"Sir, we're going to depressurize the cabin now," he said.

"Helmets on, oxygen on!" Jake said to his team. Jake put his helmet on, then turned on the oxygen. The raw oxygen reminded him of the smell of air just before a rain. With the night goggles, everything took on a green tint.

There was a noticeable change in pressure inside the cabin as the crew chief bled off the pressurization. Because depressurization took away the cabin oxygen, the crew chief had also donned an oxygen mask.

"Stand up," Jake said. His words were transmitted by the helmet-embedded radio to the others, and his entire team stood.

"Check your equipment," Jake said, and each man checked the equipment of the man in front of him. Jake checked Tom's equipment, then he turned around so Tom could check his.

"Listen up. Captain Jack will be the first man out, I'll be the last man in the stick, and I don't want to be more than two seconds behind Jack, so when you get to the door, don't hang around."

The loadmaster opened the door and the noise level increased significantly. Also, because at this altitude the outside temperature was twenty-five

degrees below zero, even at this latitude, Jake felt
an immediate blast of cold.

The men looked at the lights beside the door.
Because of the night vision goggles, they couldn't
tell the difference in color, but they didn't need
to. They had made enough jumps that they knew
the positions of the standby and jump lamps.

The jump light came on and Tom was out the
door. In less than two seconds, Jake was out as
well. At first there was the familiar little drop in his
stomach but as his velocity stabilized he felt nothing more than a sense of freedom. He looked
around at the others and saw that all six were
falling under control. Then he looked down
where, far below, he could see the delineation of
sea and land as the surf broke against the beach.

"Sound off," he said into the radio.

"One okay." Tom replied.

"Two okay," Deon said.

Three to seven also replied. All jumpers were in
the air with radios and oxygen working.

They were out over the water, but the jump had
been perfectly timed so that, once they opened
their chutes, they would be able to glide to shore.
Looking back up Jake saw the airplane that had
brought them making a one-hundred-eighty
degree turn as it started back to Pensacola.

The eight men continued to streak down without a parachute. After a fall of two full minutes,
Jake deployed his chute. He felt the satisfying jerk
of the opening shock then started steering the
chute toward land. Hitting the beach, Patterson

took a couple of steps to stabilize himself. Looking around he saw that the others were down as well.

Moving quickly, the men got off the beach and ran into the cover of the trees. There, they gathered their equipment bags, then buried their chutes.

As they approached the air base through the darkness of night, and then the shadows of early morning, they could see the beacon light flashing white, white, green. They kept off the main road and followed a trail through the woods, finally breaking out on the far side of the base, well away from the control tower and administration buildings. There was only one runway to the airport, 05 and 23, which was 11,200 feet long. At least ten F-16s were parked alongside the runway, though none were in revetments.

"All right, you know what to do," Jake said. "Tom, you, Willie and Lewis take out the radar. Deon, you, Ferrell, and Cates take out the aircraft. Marcus, you come with me. We'll take out the SAM sights. Get to your objectives, get in position, set up your lasers, and wait."

Tom, Willie, and Lewis moved away from the others then set up their laser targeting equipment to await contact. As they waited, they lay in a ditch to minimize the chances of being seen. Both were wearing camouflage paint and an insect repellent to help with the swarm of mosquitoes that were hovering over a standing puddle of water.

CHAPTER THIRTY-ONE

"Phoenix, Lancer over."

The call came over the small radio they were carrying. Phoenix was Jake's call sign.

"Get ready," Deon said. "I think things are about to happen.

They heard Jake's response. *"This is Phoenix, go ahead."*

"Ready to tag?"

"Roger, ready to tag. One and two, tag now."

Deon painted all ten F-16s with his laser, then activated a transponder code.

"Lancer, do you have a reading?" Jake asked.

"I roger alpha one, delta one, kilo one," Lancer replied.

"That's affirmative."

"Keep your heads down," Lancer said.

"Get ready," Deon said to the others.

Suddenly four F-22 Raptor jets appeared, almost as if from nowhere. They passed over Deon's head, low and fast, the sound following them so loud that Deon could actually feel the shock wave. Rockets spewed forth from the wings of the four aircraft, then laced into the parked F-16s. As the four Raptors pulled up, all ten F-16s went up in huge balls of flame, and heavy, stomach shaking explosions rolled out across the field. At the same time the F-16s exploded, there could hear explosions in two other parts of the airfield.

There were a total of six Raptors that conducted the strike, four on the aircraft and the other two on the Sam and radar sites. Now the six jets reassembled into formation and pulled into an almost ninety degree climb, roaring up on twin pillars of fire from their two F-119-100 turbofan engines. Within seconds they were so high that all that could be seen of them were the little bright points of light that were their engines.

With the roar of the raptors gone the only sounds remaining were the sounds of the many fires the attack had started.

"Ha," Willie said. "I guess we waxed their ass pretty good."

"Yeah, I'd say we did," Tom replied.

At that very moment, Mike Lindell and Clipper Bivens were half an hour out over the water. Although Lindell was the command pilot, Clipper was flying.

"There's the signal," Clipper said, seeing a flash on his screen. "We're thirty minutes away."

Mike put his hands on the cyclic and collective. "Right, I've got it," he said.

On the ground Jake's team had already rendezvoused at the prearranged pickup point and they were now having their breakfast of MREs when they heard the popping sound of approaching rotor blades.

"Damn," Cates said. "I thought they were half an hour away yet. How'd they get here so quick? I'll wave them in." He started out into the small clearing.

"Wait a minute," Marcus said. "That's not a Blackhawk."

"How do you know?"

"I would recognize the sound of a Blackhawk in my sleep," Marcus said. "That's not a Blackhawk."

Cates laughed. "You're full of crap. I'm goin' to wave 'em in."

"Get back here, Cates, Marcus is right," Jake said, but his warning was too late. The helicopter suddenly popped up above the tree line and fired machine guns. Cates went down, then they saw the helicopter pass overhead, stand on the tip of its rotor blades, then come back, spitting fire from its guns.

"Son of a bitch! That's a Russian helicopter!" Jake said.

The helicopter was an MI-28 attack helicopter, bristling with a weapons array. It was also known also as a Hind.

They waited until the helicopter made its second pass, then Deon darted out into the clearing, intending to drag Cates out of the line of fire. He saw, right away, that it wasn't necessary. Cates was dead.

As the helicopter came back on a third pass, Deon ran hard back toward the tree line, even as the bullets were kicking up dirt on either side of him. He barely made it in time, diving over a bush, and rolling out of the way as the helicopter passed overhead.

"Are you hit?" Jake called.

"No, sir."

"There's no way our guys can pick us up with that son of a bitch here," Jake said. "We're going to have to bring it down."

"How are we going to do that, General? All we have are pistols," Lewis said.

Tom Jack smiled and held up his finger. "Not exactly," he said. Reaching into his equipment bag, he pulled out a short tube and rocket.

"Whoa! You brought along a Stinger?" Deon asked. "Damn, Tom, you're my man!"

"I can't get him from here, though," Tom said. "I'm going to have to get out in the clearing."

"Commander, that's not too smart," Lewis said.

"Lewis, are you calling a superior officer dumb?" Tom asked.

"What? Uh, no, sir," Lewis started, but when he saw Tom laughing, he added, "Just stupid, sir."

Tom chuckled, then stepped back out into the clearing as the helicopter was pivoting around for another pass. He stood there with his right arm behind his back, while his left arm was extended with pistol in hand.

"What the hell is he doing?" Marcus asked.

"It would be my guess that he is suckering them in," Deon said.

The helicopter flared to a stop, then hovered there for a moment, as if the pilots couldn't believe they were being challenged by one man with a pistol.

Suddenly Tom dropped the pistol, then brought the Stinger around, put it on his shoulder, and aimed.

Seeing that, the pilots realized they had been tricked. They dropped the nose, added power, and pulled collective as they tried to accelerate out of danger, but it was too late. Tom fired, and the missile flew forward, punching through the rotor blades and exploding in the engine compartment. The helicopter blew apart in midair, then crashed to the ground in flaming pieces.

"Phoenix, this is Hillclimber, do you read?"

Jake grabbed the SINCGARS (Single Channel Ground and Airborne Radio System) to respond. The radio used a transmission security key to generate a frequency hopping mode, preset by time of day supplied by a GPS receiver. This enabled them to talk in the clear, without fear of having their transmissions intercepted.

"We read, Hillclimber."

"Phoenix, pop smoke."

"We just did, Hillclimber."

"The only smoke we see is coming from what looks like a pretty big fire."

"Yeah, that would be us. But if you want, I'll be a little more conventional for you."

Jake pulled the pin, opened his hand to let the spoon pop free, then he tossed a smoke grenade to the side. Almost immediately it began gushing out smoke.

In the helicopter, Clipper was looking ahead toward the huge pillar of smoke when he saw a small, twisting rope of green smoke beginning to rise.

"Phoenix, we have green," Clipper said.

"Roger green, Hillclimber. Be advised, we have one KIA."

"Understand you have one KIA?"

"That's affirmative."

"There they are," Clipper said, pointing to a small opening ahead.

Lindell set up his approach, lowering pitch and decreasing power. As the rotor blades began to cavitate down through their own rotor wash, they started to pop loudly. Looking off to the left they saw the burning remains of a helicopter.

Lindell set them down, then waited as Jake and his team hurried toward them. Two of them were carrying a third man and the door gunner got out to help bring the body aboard.

"Everyone is in, Mr. Lindell," the crew chief said.

Lindell pulled pitch and the Blackhawk made a very steep climb out, then turned and started home.

Kuchenwerkstatt Gasthaus, Hamburg, Germany

"Have you eaten here before?" Aleksander Mironov asked.

"No, this is my first time," Bryan Gates said. He looked around the dining room and saw only two other tables occupied. "There aren't many here."

"It's always quiet during the day. They do most of their business at night. That's why Sorroto and Golovin chose this place to meet."

"Bitte?" the waiter said as he approached the table.

"You must let me order for you," Mironov said.

"All right."

"Gebratenen Lamm, Bratkartoffeln, Artischocken-herzen, und Ihre besten Wein, bitte," Mironov ordered.

"Sehr gut."

"I've never been that big on lamb," Bryan Gates said. "But if you say try it, I will."

"You won't be disappointed. The Kuchenwerk-statt is known for their lamb."

"How is my friend Nicolai Petrovich?"

"He is recovering well," Mironov said. "He wanted to do this himself, to have . . . what is it you Americans say? Closure?"

"Yes, closure."

"But I assured him that the job would be done."

"I thought when we got rid of the last . . . ship-ment, that there wouldn't be another," Bryan said.

"Nothing has been moved yet. That is why Golovin is here to meet with Sorroto. They are here to make the final arrangements.

"Yes," Bryan said.

Their meal was delivered, and for the next few minutes they ate with enjoyment.

"Are you sure about how you are going to do this?" Mironov asked.

"Yes. Why? Are you having second thoughts?"

"No, I'm not having second thoughts about doing it. Just about how you plan to do it."

"I'm the one taking the risk. All you have to do is drive the getaway motorcycle."

"But what you have planned, my friend. It is unheard of."

Bryan chuckled. "No, it isn't. Not at all. Haven't you ever seen the movie *The Godfather*?"

"No."

"When Michael Corleone kills Sollozo, he does it right in broad daylight, in the middle of Louis's Restaurant. The gunshots were so loud that it scared the shit out of everyone else."

"And that's what you are counting on?"

"Yes."

Mironov shook his head and chuckled. "Did you do things like this when we were enemies?"

"Here now, you don't want me to give away all my secrets, do you?"

"They are here," Mironov said.

Looking through the window, Bryan saw Sorroto and General Golovin coming up the walk together.

"Will Golovin recognize you?" Bryan asked.

"No, we have never met. But I have seen his picture many times."

"Yes, the same with me. I have never met Sorroto,

but I have seen the son of a bitch's picture, many times."

Mironov laughed. "*Da,* Golovin is also a *sookin sin.*"

"*Meine Rechnung bitte,*" Bryan said, asking the waiter for the check.

"*Ja.*"

"As soon as the waiter brings me the bill, you go start the motorcycle. From the moment it starts, count to ten, then race the engine to make as much noise as you can," Bryan said.

"*Da.*"

While they waited for the bill to be brought to the table, Bryan looked over at Sorroto and Golovin. They had chosen one of the small tables and were sitting directly across from each other. The approach to the *Herrentoilette* would take someone right by their table, so he could approach without arousing suspicion.

"Look, there is a fire exit just before you go into the men's room. I'll come out through that door."

"I'll be there, my friend," Mironov said.

At that moment the waiter brought the bill and as Bryan paid it, Mironav left the café. A moment later, Bryan heard the motorcycle start and began to count. Reaching into his pocket, he pulled out a snub-nosed thirty-eight revolver and held it unseen by his side. At the count of five he started toward the table where Sorroto and Golovin were engaged in conversation so intense that they either didn't see him approach, or paid no attention to him.

At the count of ten, the sound of the motorcycle became so loud that everyone in the café looked toward the window in obvious annoyance. Bryan stopped at Sorroto's table and raised the pistol. Sorroto barely had time to register surprise before Bryan pulled the trigger. Golovin looked on in total shock, first at the black hole in Sorroto's forehead, then toward Bryan. Bryan pulled the trigger a second time, again hitting his target right in the forehead.

For a moment the other diners thought they were hearing the motorcycle backfire, then a woman looked over and saw the two dead men at the table. She screamed, but by that time Bryan was climbing onto the back of the motorcycle.

Five miles away from the Kuchenwerkstatt Gasthaus they ditched the motorcycle and climbed into a rented Mercedes. Half an hour later Bryan was on an Air Lufthansa flight for Nassau.

CHAPTER THIRTY-TWO

From *Chronicle Magazine:*

Murdered, in Germany, Warren Sorroto, the wealthiest man in the world. Born Greygor Sorkosky in Hungary, in 1930, Sorroto was a wonderful philanthropist who gave away millions of dollars to help the American Islamic Republic of Enlightenment transition from the false religion of Christianity to the true faith of Moqaddas Sirata, a religion of obedience and perfection. Sorroto was a benefactor of our Glorious Leader, President for Life Mehdi Ohmshidi, may he be blessed by Allah, having assisted him in his initial run for president.

The murder happened in the Kuchenwerkstatt Gasthaus, a popular café in Hamburg, Germany. Witnesses say that that the killer approached the table where Sorroto and Dimitry Golovin, a Russian general, were taking their lunch. Without so much as a word spoken, he shot both of them.

It is reported that the killer had an accomplice who whisked him off on a motorcycle. The motorcycle, which had been reported stolen, was found abandoned a short distance from the café. There was no sign of the perpetrators.

It is now believed by the German police, as well as the Russian FAPSI, that it was General Golovin, and not Sorroto who was the primary target. There are rumors that some in Russia are trying to sell nuclear weapons on the black market, and they perceived General Golovin as an impediment to their plans.

Glorious Leader, President for Life Mehdi Ohmshidi, may he be blessed by Allah, expressed his sorrow over the loss of this great man.

Obey Ohmshidi.

Fort Morgan

Bryan Gates and Chris Carmack were walking on the beach, along the surf line. A sand crab scurried across the beach in front of them, and five seagulls, in a perfect V formation glided over them, their wings outstretched and unmoving.

"How was the weather in Hamburg?" Chris asked.

"Who else knows?" Bryan asked.

"As far as I know, just me," Chris replied. "I think that things like this are best kept off the books, even though at this point, there are no books. As long as neither Jake nor Bob know about it, their consciences will be clear."

"Conscience? Tell me, Chris, what exactly is a conscience?"

"It is something that tells you you did the right thing, even though it might seem wrong to others."

"The right thing would have been to kill that son of bitch before he ever had a chance to put that incompetent, socialist bastard in the White House," Bryan said.

"Did you really play Michael Corleone?"

"Yeah, I did. If Coppola had been there, he would have put me in that role instead of Al Pacino."

"Stick around, Bryan," Chris said. "We're starting a new nation here, and need good men."

"I have to stick around, Chris. I have no other place to go."

Mobile, October 15

Once again, representatives from nine states arrived in Mobile. This time they came as senators, two from each state, and as representatives, with the expressed purpose of declaring into existence the nation of United Free America. Until the new nation was organized, the number of representatives per state reflected the number of representatives each state had in the Congress of the United States.

There had been some discussion over the number of seats Florida should have, because in the pre-O days of the United States, Florida had 25 congressional districts. But only the north half of Florida was included in the alignment of states for United Free America, so, by mutual agreement Florida was given 12 seats. That gave the provisional Congress a construction of 88 House and 16 Senate seats. South Carolina, though it had made a formal application to join the UFA, was not yet included, and would not be included until their petition was voted on and ratified by the other eight states. South Carolina did send a delegation consisting of 6 representatives and 2 senators, but until such time as they were accepted into full union with the rest of the states of United Free America, the South Carolina senators and congressmen would be a nonvoting delegation.

It was quickly pointed out that Texas and Georgia, should they combine, could control the house. But no piece of legislation could pass without approval in both houses of Congress, and that gave some sense of balance to the proceedings.

Bob opened the session with an address to a joint meeting of the House and the Senate. After the initial welcome, he introduced Jake, to give a report on the military situation.

"Ladies and gentlemen of this, the organizing Congress of United Free America," Jake began, "I am pleased to report that the state of our military is exceptionally good. We have a well-organized military which by actual count is a defense force of 5,379 active duty members. The construct of our defense force is 3,207 in the ground service, 1,453 in our air service, and 719 in our sea service. Our sea service consists of two destroyers, one submarine, and one aircraft carrier. As yet neither our submarine nor our carrier has been deployed, but we expect to do so as soon as they are fully crewed. Eighty-five percent of our service men and women are veterans, twenty-six percent are officers.

"We have already been engaged in some significant military operations. One was the deployment of an armed, unmanned aerial vehicle, the MQ9 Reaper, which provided aerial support for an embattled firebase in South Carolina. The second was embedding one of our advisors with a combat convoy of the South Carolina Defense Core. That convoy came under fire, receiving rather significant casualties, but they were able to call in air support from their own resources. The third was the rescue from an AIRE prison of Dr. Taylor Urban. The fourth military engagement was the destruction of AIRE jet fighters at Homestead Air Force Base in South Florida. These were the same aircraft that attacked Columbia, South Carolina, inflicting heavy casualties on the innocent citizens of that city.

"In addition we have had some significant engagements at sea, interdicting would-be attacks on our offshore gas and oil rigs. In every case, I am proud to say that our military performed well."

A hand went up in the audience, and Jake called upon him.

The person Jake called upon, a large and

powerfully built man, stood and turned sideways so he could address both Jake and the others in the assembly.

"I am William Knowles, a part of the South Carolina delegation, and I would like to extend the thanks of the people of South Carolina for the military support we have received."

Another delegate raised his hand and, when called upon, stood. "Why are we helping South Carolina? They weren't here for the constitutional convention, and though I know they have applied to join us, they aren't a part of us yet. So why are we taking the chance of having one of our soldiers killed, fighting for South Carolina?"

"Because even though South Carolina hasn't joined us, they are an ally. And we have a long and storied history of providing military support . . . and sustaining casualties . . . in defense of our allies," Jake replied.

"Are we paying our soldiers?" another delegate asked. "And if so, how much are we paying them, and how are we doing that? What I'm asking is, where is the money coming from?"

"For the moment we are paying our soldiers an equivalent salary to what they were receiving at their respective ranks in the pre-O military. And we are paying them from our treasury," Jake said. "But part of what I hope we do here for these few days of meetings, will be to come up with a way that we can all participate in funding both our treasury, and our military."

"You're a general, I can see why you are interested," someone shouted, and the others laughed.

"Getting paid is nice," Jake said with a smile and a nod. "And finally, as I'm sure you can understand, though we have a good start in building our defense service, a military force consisting of only five thousand members isn't nearly large enough. We are going to have to start a very active recruitment program. My personal goal is to have one hundred thousand men under arms by the first of the New Year."

After the opening joint session, the senators and congressmen went to their respective chambers to work out the details of building a new nation. Since there were no political parties, there was no such office as a Senate Majority Leader, so a President Pro Tem was elected in the Senate, and a speaker of the house in the House of Representatives. Both positions were selected by voting at large.

Once the two houses selected their leaders, they were ready to get down to the business of organizing the new nation. The first person to request permission to speak in the Senate was a delegate from Texas.

"Mr. President?"

"The chair recognizes Senator Carter Davis from Texas."

Senator Davis stepped to the front and, since there were only 18 present, his talk was more of a conversation than elocution.

"This may sound a little far-fetched at first, but hear me out. Back home, when we had our state-wide meeting to select the senators and congressman, a question came up.

"I don't know how many of you are up on your history about Texas, but when Texas was first brought in to the United States, it was given the option of dividing itself into five states.

"For various and sundry reasons, Texas chose to remain a single state. But now the dynamics have changed. And the Texas delegation has been asked to petition this assembly for the right to enter into alliance with the new nation of United Free America, not as one, but as five states."

"Discussion from the floor?" the President Pro Tem said.

"Carter, wouldn't that give Texas almost absolute control of the Senate?" Senator Patterson from Louisiana asked. "You already have control of the House."

"That would increase the number of seats in the Senate from sixteen to twenty four. And even if every senator from the five Texas states would vote together, it would still be a minority. But I assure you, it would be a rare occasion for all ten senators from the five states to vote in a block. It is because of the varying philosophies throughout the state that we are asking for this move. There are some parts of the state, particularly our Mexican-American citizens, who have, in some cases, a family presence going back nearly four hundred years, who feel they aren't being represented."

As this discussion was going on in the Senate, the House was dealing with the same question.

CHAPTER THIRTY-THREE

Bob and Jake were discussing the Texas division bill over lunch.

"Senator Davis is right in his contention," Bob said. "Historically, Texas did have the option of entering the Union as five states."

"I wonder why they didn't."

"Well, when Texas first came in to the Union there were vast areas of the state that were almost totally unoccupied except by Comanche, and in the early days, Comanche and the Texans weren't exactly what you would call good neighbors. I think Texas decided to enter as one state as a matter of practicality."

"Yeah, but that's obviously not an issue today. What do you think about Davis's proposal?"

"I have no vote."

"No, but you have veto power."

Bob chuckled. "Yes, I do, don't I? What do you think?"

"It seems to me like it would give one state too

much power," Jake said. "That would give Texas ten votes in the Senate."

"Yes, but their total number of votes in the House wouldn't change," Bob pointed out. "And, breaking up the votes like that might make the House more balanced. As it is now, Texas only needs a couple of allies to control the vote. But this way, each individual state would be greatly modified. In fact, Georgia would become the most powerful state."

"Yeah," Jake said. "Hah, I hadn't thought about it that way."

When the House and Senate reconvened it was learned that, in anticipation of having their petition accepted, the eight additional senators were already present. There was no need for additional representatives, the current slate would merely be divided up among the four new states.

Though there was spirited debate, it passed by overwhelming majorities in both the House and the Senate. It was presented to Bob later that same day. As it was presented, the five new states were to be called; Texas One, Texas Two, Texas Three, Texas Four, and Texas Five.

Bob chuckled as he looked at the bill. "I must say you weren't all that creative in coming up with state names."

"It isn't without precedence," Davis said. "At least, sort of. There are North and South Carolina, North and South Dakota, Virginia and West Virginia, and now we have North Florida."

"I guess you have a point," Bob said. He looked at the bill that Senator Haris of Texas and Senator Billings of Alabama, the President Pro Tem of the Senate, as well as Speaker Baynard, Congressman from the 1st Congressional District of Georgia, and Congressman Buck Tinsley from the 5th Congressional District of Texas placed before him.

To approve the division of the current State of Texas, Be it enacted by the Senate and House of Representatives of United Free America in Congress assembled,

JOINT BILL 1. DIVISION OF THE STATE OF TEXAS

In accordance with the initial annexation of Texas to the United States, approved by Congress on 1 March, 1843, which included the following provision, to wit:

New States of convenient size not exceeding four in number, in addition to said State of Texas, and having sufficient population, may, hereafter, by the consent of said State, be formed out of the territory thereof, which shall be entitled to admission under the provisions of the Federal Constitution; and such states as may be formed out of the territory lying south of thirty-six degrees thirty minutes north latitude, commonly known as the Missouri Compromise Line, shall be admitted into the Union, with or without slavery, as the people of each State asking admission shall desire; and in such State or States as shall be formed out of said territory north of said Missouri Compromise Line, slavery, or involuntary servitude, (except for crime) shall be prohibited.

1. Be it hereby ratified that the above decree authorizing the subdivision of the State of Texas be enacted, with the provision authorizing involuntary servitude by election of the people of the state be excluded as an abhorrent anachronism.
2. That said division will be into a total of five States to be known as Texas One, Texas Two, Texas Three, Texas Four, and Texas Five.
3. That each State thus created be authorized two senators each, and that the total representatives of the states combined not exceed the thirty-two now authorized, the division of the representatives to be reached by mutual agreement among the new States herein created.
4. That the senators representing the four additional states of Texas be seated immediately and that the states of Texas One, Texas Two, Texas Three, Texas Four, and Texas Five, be immediately a participating part of the nation of United Free America.

Bob signed the bill with a flourish.

"Ladies and gentlemen, as the very first bill enacted by the new nation of United Free America, we have just added four new states," he said.

The announcement was applauded by all who had gathered to witness his signature on the bill.

On the following day, by unanimous vote,

South Carolina was brought in as well, and its senators and congressmen took their seats.

Their next act was to validate Robert Varney as President, his term to last for one year. Larry Wallace, current governor of South Carolina, resigned his gubernatorial office to accept the position of Vice President. A national election was set for the first Tuesday in November of the following year, twelve and a half months away.

Now, all that was left was the formal declaration of the new nation, and Bob Varney, at a joint session of Congress, called for the motion to be introduced.

"Mr. President, I move that this joint session of Congress enact the declaration of the new and fully independent nation of United Free America," Senator Davis of Texas One said.

"I second the motion," Congressman Billy Knowles of South Carolina said.

"It has been moved and seconded that this joint session of Congress declare into existence the independent nation of United Free America. All in favor, signify by saying aye."

"AYE!" The response was deafening.

"Opposed?"

There were no votes in opposition.

"Honorable ladies and gentlemen of this gathering, by the authority you have placed in me, I declare that United Free America exists!"

The assembly hall burst into loud and prolonged cheers.

* * *

That night the President of the new nation of United Free America gave a dinner for Jake and the original settlers of Fort Morgan, as well as for Tom and Sheri Jack, Deon and Julie Pratt, Chris Carmack and Kathy York, and George Gregoire.

Jake stood and raised his root beer.

"Has it dawned upon anyone that we are starting a nation with thirteen states?" he asked.

"Yeah," Bob said with a big smile. "I'd say that was a pretty good sign, wouldn't you?"

"To America," Jake said, holding out his glass.

"To America," the others said as one.

It was not necessary to specify whether "America" mean United Free America, or the United States of America.

Everyone knew that it meant both.